THE PERFECT STROKE

Lucas Brothers Book 1

JORDAN MARIE

The Perfect Stroke

by *USA* Today Best Selling Author
Jordan Marie

Cover Design by Robin Harper of Wicked By Design
Cover Model by Thomas DeLauer
Photographer by Michael Stokes
Editing by Daryl Banner

DEDICATION

To all the people who took a chance on me, read me, and encouraged me. I owe you the world.

XOXO
Jordan

Chapter One

C.C.

The trouble with being from a small town is that everyone knows everyone. I've lived here my whole life. It's not been good, but it's not been bad. We didn't have much—just me and Banger. Banger was my dad. Well, sort of. He's actually the old man that my womb donor shacked up with. She ran off with a traveling vacuum salesman when I was seven and it's just been me and Banger ever since. Yes, I know my life has been pretty cliché. I deal. Banger was a former POW. He's a big, growly, bearded mountain of a man who never made me feel unwanted. He didn't know much about having kids—never mind if that kid was a girl—but we muddled through.

By the time I was ten, I could change oil, rotate tires, and rebuild carburetors. By the time I was fifteen, I could rebuild an engine. I mastered transmissions at the age of sixteen. Banger said I was a natural, but the truth was that I just wanted to make him proud. He owned the only garage in town, and I wanted to make sure I helped him as much as I could.

He found out he had cancer on my seventeenth birthday. We got drunk together. Banger was many things, but he wasn't worried about legalities or society rules. It's probably one of the things I loved most about him. He passed away the summer I turned nineteen and I just kind of found myself taking over the garage. Now at the age of twenty-six, the people in Crossville, Kentucky know me pretty well. They've learned to trust my work, and Claude's garage stays busy. That's my name, by the way. Claudia Cooper. Banger always called me Claude and it just stuck. If it ever bothered me, I've learned to accept it now. I've found that with life, you just have to deal with what it gives you. Things could always be worse.

But back to why I'm in Lexington tonight. Lexington is probably the closest city to Crossville. It takes me almost three hours to drive here. I do it every so often, and I do it for one reason: If I don't escape Crossville from time to time, I'd probably end up being one of those nut cases on the six o'clock news who goes postal. Really, it's a public service I'm doing. People should be grateful.

"Ready for a refill, darlin'?"

I grin up at the bartender, who admittedly is the only reason I stayed at this bar. It's not my speed. I'm more into the biker bar about three streets over. One of my customers recommended this place because they have a live band on Saturday nights, so I said to hell with it. Ten minutes in, when the band started singing a Black-Eyed Peas song that I could barely remember, I knew I was in trouble. Then Mr. Tall—blue eyes, in faded jeans with holes, black t-shirt, and curly sandy-brown hair—smiled at me. He got me a drink and I've been here ever since. Sure, he got me a drink because he's the bartender, but he keeps looking at my boobs.

I think it's pretty clear what's going on here.

"Hit me," I tell him with an easy grin. Easy, because after a shot of Jack and then a glass of Jack and Coke on top of that, I'm pretty damn loose—so loose, that with this second drink, I'm pretty sure my ass will be finding a hotel to snooze the night away. Maybe I can convince the bartender to go with me. Again, do not judge me. The last time I had sex, I'm pretty sure, was two presidents ago. If you want to do the math, we're talking six years. Six years. Women can say what they want about vibrators, but they do not, under any circumstance, take the place of the real thing. And the bartender who keeps smiling at me definitely looks like he could be packing the real thing.

"Damn, babe. You're busy tonight," I hear a deep voice say in front of me. When I look up, another man who looks like he just stepped off the pages of the Sexiest Man Alive magazine is talking —unfortunately, to the bartender I've had my eye on. They share a quick but heated kiss. I cry a little bit inside, giving up my dream of me and the bartender tonight, and go back to my drink.

That saying about all the good ones being married or gay is so freaking true. It's probably why I am still single and my friend Raymond has a great guy at home.

"Can I buy you another, sweet lips?"

Sweet lips?

"I don't think so," I tell him, barely looking up. It doesn't matter what he looks like; being called sweet lips is enough to turn me off immediately.

"I'll have a scotch and get the lady whatever she's having."

"The lady is just fine. Persistent, aren't you?"

"Sometimes, it pays to be," he says, and finally his country twang and the aw-shucks-good-old-boy-vibe makes me look up. He's tall and broad, with brown, sandy hair shaved close, a five o'clock shadow—which is so dark I'd say it's closer to six—brown eyes, and a face that looks like a sculptor chiseled it from stone. A god, maybe. *He's that pretty*. Though he fires everything feminine up inside of me, his good looks are a turn-off. I've dated a perfect guy before. The only thing perfect was the reflection in the mirror. I don't need to go back down that road again—*ever.*

"I was just getting ready to leave," I tell him, and that's not completely a lie.

"Don't leave yet. You're the first thing I've seen that gives me a reason for being in this town. What's your name?"

"Well, it's definitely not *'sweet lips'*," I tell him, picking up the new drink the man of my dreams bartender—though gay and taken —puts down. The guy smiles at my comment and sits down beside me, then leans into me like we're long lost lovers. I try to ignore the way he smells, but find it's a little impossible. He wears a cologne that I've never smelled before. It must feed every pheromone I've got, because combined with his rugged male scent, it's making a woman like me drunk... and horny. *Dangerous.* He's definitely dangerous. I may want a good time, but this guy screams "player"—rich player. The bartender is much more my speed. It's not that I'm a snob. Just the opposite, really. I find that rich people are obnoxious as hell.

"I bet your lips are sweet though, darlin'."

Obnoxious—even if guys like him are cute when they're trying to get laid. I lean into him with a smile. I run my tongue over my lip, just for good measure.

"That's something you'll never find out," I whisper and take another sip of my drink.

He stops for a minute, like my reply shocked him, and then he gives me a deep grin that even makes his brown eyes twinkle. *Damn.*

"I always did like a challenge," he says, and I can feel excitement thrum through my system. I hear the alarm and danger bells going off... I just don't seem able to stop staring into his eyes.

Did I mention...damn?

Chapter Two

GRAY

She doesn't know who I am.

It's a strange feeling—although not at all unpleasant. Let's face it, I realize golf isn't the most exciting sport. The major draw here in the state of Kentucky is horse racing or college basketball, so odds were in favor of me not being recognized, but it surprises me just the same. Still, it's almost tourney time and golf has been monopolizing the news. It's not that I'm bragging or anything, but fuck, I've seen my face so often on the sports shows, I just assumed everyone else has. There can be no mistaking that this woman clearly doesn't know who I am. I haven't had a woman want me just for me and not my name or my bank account in longer than I can remember. There's just one problem. Sweet lips here, doesn't seem to want me. *Challenge placed and accepted.* I won't give up until I have her under me, screaming my name.

"I always did like a challenge," I tell her with a practiced grin. It's not really bragging when I admit that this grin has literally gotten me into the pants of hundreds of women, and some were even prettier than the beauty staring at me now.

She's a banging little redhead with green eyes who has legs that go for miles, curves that should be illegal, perfect tits, and an ass that I'm sure make men beg. Hell, I want to beg now. That aside, there's something about this particular woman that appeals to me in ways no other woman has for far too long. I could say it has to do with the fact that she doesn't know who I am. Perhaps it is, and the novelty will wear off—*after* I fuck her brains out.

"It wasn't a challenge," she says, taking a sip of her drink.

"It wasn't a yes," I tell her.

"Odd, I wasn't aware that was a yes or no question."

"Everything boils down to yes or no. *'I bet your lips are sweet',* definitely means I intend to find out. You letting me boils down to yes or no."

"So my answer here would be... no?" The way she tilts her head to the side and pulls her eyebrow up as if daring me sends a fire through my system. *Is it really because her reaction is such a change from the way women usually throw themselves at me?*

"I'd prefer if your answer was to bring your mouth to mine and let me taste your lips," I tell her, lowering my voice and angling my head so only she can hear me.

I watch her closely. I think I can see a slight shudder move through her. She's not completely unaffected by me. Is it a game for her? Playing hard to get to try and keep my interest? That's not out of the realm of possibility, though if true, it would disappoint me. Not that I truly give a damn. The endgame is just like it always is: *I'm getting between her legs.*

"You should at least get an A for effort."

"I'd rather show you what else I can earn an A in."

"There's a point where trying too hard comes into play," she points out, getting up.

Fuck. *I'm losing her?* Has this ever happened before? Hell, I don't think so, not even before I made it big.

"At least have a dance with me," I tell her, doing my best not to sound desperate. Shit, I feel a little desperate here and I still don't know what it is about her.

She looks me over and I hold still, letting her take her time. I make myself a promise that if she turns me down, I'm done chasing. She might have my interest, but I don't need to work this hard for it. When she inclines her head to indicate she's agreeing to the dance, I hold out my hand to her, standing. She puts her hand in mine. As I lead her onto the dance floor, I feel a zing of heat move from our joined hands and flood through my system. I almost wonder if I'm the only one who felt it until I hear her quick intake of breath and feel her hand jerk against mine. When she tries to pull away, I tighten my hold.

She's not getting away. Not yet.

Chapter Three

CC

I should probably have my head examined. I can't even fully blame it on not being with anyone in, like, forever. No, I think it might be pure madness that has me walking out to dance with this guy.

"Am I allowed to ask your name?" I ask to distract myself, because when he wraps his arms around me and pulls me into his body, that electric current runs through me again. I look up into his eyes and see something flash in them.

He hesitates, then finally answers, "Gray."

"Gray? Like the color?" I ask.

He gets a strange look on his face, before he grins again. "You don't like it? I happen to think it will sound beautiful when you're screaming it out tonight when I f—"

"I wouldn't finish that sentence if you want a chance in hell at getting lucky tonight, Gray."

"So you're admitting there's a chance?"

"It's getting slimmer."

"I can work with that," he says while I'm busy ignoring the way he smells. It's good. Not all cologne; there's something else, something deeply male that makes my insides quiver. Maybe I will go for it and end my long dry spell. It's just one night, right? It doesn't matter if he is too perfect. That doesn't mean I'm repeating history. I'd never have to see him again.

"You've gone quiet," he whispers against my ear as we're swaying to the music.

"I was listening to the music," I lie. "Is your name really Gray?"

"Is that so strange?"

"I don't think I've ever met one, so yeah. Though, my old man was named Banger, so..."

"You're shitting me? Banger?"

"I think that was his road name, but if he had a different one, he changed it years ago."

"I think I like him."

"He was a great man," I agree with a smile, feeling the familiar ache of sadness at the memory of what I lost.

"What happened?"

"Cancer," I whisper, hating that damn word.

"I'm sorry, sweetheart."

Everyone always says that, and I hate it just as much when this guy says it. It's fake. They might be sorry, but they don't truly understand. Very few do.

"So... the name?" I prompt him.

"My mother thought it would be cool to name her kids after colors."

"Colors?"

"Mmm-hmm. So, I'm Gray, short for Grayson."

"Well, hey, that's a good name. Much better than... Green?"

"That'd be my brother."

I pull away to look at him. "You're lying."

"Not even a little bit. I have five brothers and each one is named after a different color."

"That's not possible. There aren't six colors that would make..."

"Gray, Green, Black, Blue, White, and Cyan."

I figure my mouth drops open. I can't stop it as I digest the fact that five other men are out there with names like that. When I notice he's watching me, I smile at him and give a small pat on his shoulder, like I'm trying to make him feel better. "Well, hey, at least you got the better of the names."

"You won't hear me argue. Especially when it comes to Black and Blue. They're twins, by the way."

I snort in laughter and can't stop it. "Oh my God, you have to be making this up."

"Afraid not, so see, I'll need you to help me."

"Help you?"

"The way I have it figured, if you say my name enough in your beautiful southern drawl, I'll learn to love my name. Heck, it will make being called a member of the Crayon gang all worth it."

I laugh before I can stop myself. "Crayon gang? Ouch."

"It's okay. I had it better than my brothers."

"Name-wise again, you mean?"

"Well, that and the fact that my crayon is one of those thick, fat ones that—"

"Oh good lord..."

This time, he laughs. *It's a really good laugh.* It's a laugh that takes away any resistance—not that I had much to begin with.

"My name is CC," I tell him as I slide back into his hold.

"CC?"

"Yeah. In case, you know, you want to scream it out a lot tonight."

His grin widens. "I'll definitely make sure to do that. Often."

Goodbye dry spell... and good riddance.

Chapter Four

CC

"Did you enjoy your weekend off?" Jackson asks.

Jackson is my main man at the garage. The two of us do everything. We could use someone else working with us, but there never seems to be enough money to stretch. I pay Jackson really good though—probably double what anyone else would cost me. He's worth it, though. He's the best there is... next to me. Banger told me that, and it is something I always remember with pride. Banger always taught me that if you were going to do anything, you had to give a hundred and fifty percent. Him saying I was the best at something means I did something to make him proud. Jackson has a similar code to Banger, and that reason alone makes him worth the money.

I think back over my wicked weekend with Gray and can't stop the grin that blooms on my face nor the way my body heats up with the memory.

"I'd say that was a yes," Jackson says.

"Bite me," I tell him. Shit, I'm *still* grinning.

"I am hungry," Jackson says, "but you're way too salty for my tastes. Speaking of which, what are we doing for lunch?"

"Well, I need to drop the oil pan off that baby there," I tell him, pointing to the old Ford that's in bay number one.

"That means I'm going to be delivery boy today?" Jackson asks.

"Like every other day. You know you only do it so you can go flirt with Mary Ann at the diner."

"That woman can bake a mighty fine apple pie," he says, already walking towards the door.

I drop down on the creeper. "I doubt it's the pie you're interested in."

"Being around us men your whole life has destroyed you."

"Whatever. It's Monday, so make sure you bring me back the meatloaf platter."

"Got it. Be back shortly," he calls, but I can barely hear him over the loud roar of the air compressor and impact wrench in my hand.

Another day, another dollar.

Chapter Five

GRAY

"Will you give it a rest, Seth? I told you I'm here. I'll play nice. I'll even put up with Cammie."

"You need Riverton Metals on board for this tour, Gray—especially since Raver Athletics pulled out."

"They're idiots."

"No, they're a multimillion-dollar company that can't afford to have their name linked with a golf pro who is more famous for his hard drive into a tour official's daughter than driving the ball into the hole."

"Whatever. They'd be crazy to keep me out of the tour over that shit and you know it. My name brings in the fans."

"So do others. You're cutting your own throat here, Gray."

"Driving into Rachelle's hole was more fun."

"Her name was Michelle."

"Close enough." Honestly, I barely remember the girl. I was drunk as a skunk and the only brain working at the time was the one in my dick—a dick that got the workout of its dreams this past weekend, a dick that misses a certain redhead today. It was a damn good weekend, and if CC hadn't already been gone when I woke up Sunday morning, I would have tried my best to make it last for another couple of days. Cammie Riverton and her father could wait for all I care. I get that Seth is trying to help me out here, but I don't give a damn. I might need Riverton's name to get me back on the good side of the officials, but unlike other sports, as a member of the league, I'm an independent contractor. I decide what matches I want to do and where I will appear. I oversee myself. And that would be great, except being blackballed by the higher-ups means they push my entry into tournaments below everyone else, which in short results in filled-up courses and me out in the cold. So I'm trying to go with Seth's solution. What I really want to do is tell everyone to kiss my ass. I've never been good at towing the line; my mother could more than attest for that.

"My advice is to play nice and get this contract with Riverton and his support under your belt. Without it, you're not going to get half the publicity as the other pros on tour and you want that green jacket, even if you do try to deny it."

"Who gets that jacket has more to do with—"

"You and I both know that you can be the best player out there, but if you don't get the publicity, the powers that be will make it hard on you in every way they can."

I sigh. "Whatever. I said I'm doing it. I'm in this small Kentucky town now. I have no idea what time I'll get to Riverton's, though."

"Can't you just punch it in—?"

"Hell, some of these roads aren't even showing up on my GPS. I swear, Seth, earlier I came through a town called Pussy Holler."

"Sounds like you should live there."

"You got jokes. *Fuck!*"

"What's wrong?"

"Something's wrong with my car."

"Wrong? What happened? I told you to fly out there."

"I don't know. It just died. No warning or anything," I tell him, coasting to the side of the road. "The dash lights and things are on, but it won't hit a lick. Maybe a starter or something. I told you I'm not flying into a place where they only accept tinker-toy planes. That's not happening."

"I'm no mechanic, but since you already had it started and driving when it died, that doesn't sound like it," Seth says sarcastically.

"Fine, then. Alternator or something. I don't know," I grumble. I look out the windshield and can see a garage about twenty feet in front of me. That, at least, is a stroke of luck.

"You need me to locate a tow service?" Seth asks.

"No. I see a garage up the street here. Claude's Garage. If you don't hear from me in an hour, call the cops."

"Oh, will you stop? It's not like I sent you to the town where Deliverance was filmed."

"If I hear dueling banjos, just know I'm coming back to haunt your ass Seth."

"Yeah, yeah, check in in an hour and try to keep your pants zipped up. I know it will be hard for you."

"You said hard," I joke, breathing a little easier when I walk towards the garage. It looks normal. Hopefully I won't die at the hands of some Norman-Bates-wanna-be-grease-monkey.

"Fuck off," Seth says before disconnecting the call. I click off my phone, stow it in my pocket, and walk the rest of the way to the garage. Blue would have a freaking ball laughing at me right now. Suddenly all those times I made fun of him for taking mechanic classes instead of co-ed PE seems less amusing. Then I think of how grumpy Blue seems to be all the time and immediately nix the idea. Hell, if mom hadn't caught him with Sara Jane in the barn loft when we were kids, I'd think the man was still a virgin. I should have brought the Caddy, but honestly my Tahoe reminds me of home and I'd never admit it to my brothers or my meddlesome mother, but I miss Texas.

When no one comes out, I go through the open bay doors looking for Claude. The smell of oil and gas is strong. My nose curls in distaste. There's a reason I never paid attention to Blue. The interior is dimly lit. There are florescent lights humming above, the light is stark and shines mainly over the cars that are inside. An old truck is on one side, jacked up and on ramps. Coming out from under it are two oil-soaked legs in thick mechanic coveralls and steel-toed boots. Claude, I guess.

"Hello? I'm looking for the owner? Claude?"

Chapter Six

CC

I know that voice. I know the deep baritone that sends shivers down my back and tingles of need through my body. I've been thinking about that voice since Sunday morning when I left him lying in bed, sound asleep. I know that voice and that voice is here inside my garage. The shock of that causes the wrench I'm using to remove the plug from the pan to slip. The plug does indeed come out, but at an angle and before I'm ready. Oil spurts out onto my face and pours down my chin and neck. I quickly divert it to the draining pan, but the damage is done.

"Motherfucker," I gripe. It's not very ladylike, but cut me some slack. I was raised by a guy named Banger; most of my vocabulary isn't ladylike.

"Excuse me?" Gray asks.

I know it's him. I don't need to see his face. My problem is, I don't know why he's here. Surely he's not here to find me? How would he have done that? He doesn't even know my name. I mean, he called me CC, but I sure didn't tell him my name was Claude. And I know for a fact that I never once mentioned where I live. That's something I would never do, especially with a random hookup. Not that I've had those that often, or really much at all. If I did, my dry spell wouldn't have lasted so damned long. Still, I'm not stupid, and you never give out your personal info. Somewhere in my head, I hear Banger growl at me about sleeping with strangers. *Crap!*

"Shut up, Banger. You knew my bitch of a mom and you still slept with her. That didn't work out so well for you either, did it?" I whisper to the voice in my head. Yes, I realize that's a stupid thing to do, but I'm in a panic, and it seems better than having to talk to the man standing out there in my garage waiting for me to roll out from under this car. Shit!

"Listen, I need my car looked at. It quit out front and I have a meeting. Is Claude around?"

A meeting? His car quit here? Is he telling the truth? *Am I cursed?*

I push out from under the car with a sigh. I'm not one to hide, even if the urge is strong. I grab a clean shop rag out of the box to my right, hoping to at least get most of the oil off, then I get up. I'm still wiping up the mess that is me when I look at him. I don't think he recognizes me, at least not right away. Then again, I look completely different from the way I did this past weekend. There is nothing sexy about shop clothes, oil, and gas, or the skull cap I keep on my hair while at work. It's hot at times and some may think it's weird, but then I figure those people have never had to wash oil and gunk out of thick, curly hair, so it's just simpler.

"What's wrong with it?" I ask him, my voice sounding as miserable and uncomfortable as I'm feeling right now.

"I'm not sure. I was just driving down the road and it quit. It won't even crank. It's not the battery though, because the radio and lights come on."

He doesn't recognize me. I don't know whether to be relieved or upset. He's sexy as hell though, even if the mint green oxford is uncomfortably preppy and a far cry from the jeans and black t-shirt he wore over the weekend.

"I'll have a look. Where's it at?" I tell him, walking towards the door.

"No offense, but I'm in a hurry. Is the owner around? Maybe he could—"

"I am the owner," I tell him with a sigh, starting to regret my weekend with him even more.

"You're Claude?" he asks, and I ignore it. "It's just down the road there," he tells me, pointing up the street. I go to the tow truck, Gray following along behind me. "You're taking your truck? It's just right there," he says again.

I sigh. "If it won't start, I can't very well push it here, now can I?" I ask him with exaggerated impatience.

"Oh. Right." He climbs up into the passenger side of the tow truck just as I close the door. He looks around the old truck and I can literally see his nose curling in disgust. The old jewel ain't much, but it's not that bad. The seats are ripped and the black dash is now faded gray and cracked. The doors are squeaky and, there's dust and dirt everywhere. Still, it runs like a top. I take off towards the bronze-colored Tahoe and stop when I can park in front of it. I jump down and go to the Tahoe. I open the front door to it just as I hear Gray screech. *"What are you doing?"*

"Popping the hood," I answer, staring at him like he's crazy. I think he might be. Did he think I could tell what was wrong just from looking at it?

"But you're filthy!"

Oh, good Lord in Heaven, is this really the same guy who went down on me for a freaking hour? I reach in and pull the lever for the hood, slam the door shut a little stronger than necessary, then look at him, daring him to say anything. His mouth tightens up like he's dying to, but he restrains himself.

"Really," he goes on. "I think I can just call triple A, and..."

I ignore him. That seems to be the best option at this point and, since I chose it to begin with, I'm staying the course. His battery terminals are caked and I can tell from just looking at one that it's loose. I'm surprised he's been driving at all, though maybe he hit a bump or something and jarred it. I go back to the truck and grab a screwdriver, a wire brush, and a rag.

"What are you doing now?" he asks, sounding put-out.

"Cleaning your terminals. For someone who was worried I might get grease on his sweet leather interior, your battery posts are horrible. You got to clean under the hood sometimes too, Ace," I tell him. Once I have one of the posts clean, I tighten the connector to it and do the same to the other. The battery could be bad, but somehow I doubt it.

"It's not the battery. I told you the lights are on. Hell, even the radio still plays."

I ignore him. *Yet again.*

"Get inside and see if it will start," I tell him. He rolls his eyes at me and I briefly imagine stabbing him between those eyes with my screwdriver. The engine turns and tries to hit, but it doesn't have enough juice. I go back to the truck and get out the cables, pop my hood, and get ready to jump the engine. Just as I'm about to attach the ends to his battery, he grabs them out of my hand.

"Whoa, now. I don't think you should be doing that."

"Seriously?"

"Listen, I appreciate your help and all, but I told you my lights and things come on. If the battery was dead, that wouldn't happen. I'm pretty sure it's something more mechanical. I'll just call triple A and have them send a tow out, you can go back to drowning yourself in oil, and everything will be fine."

I sigh. "Listen. You're obviously not from here. So let me explain a few things. First of all, I'm the only tow service for at least sixty miles. Which means if you call roadside assistance, they're going to call me, and I'll have to come out anyway. Second of all, the nearest garage besides mine is at least two hundred miles away, which means your tow bill, while nice for my pocket, is not worth it. Plus, I have things I need to do today and I really don't feel like driving into the city. Third—and this might be the most important—I really would like to get you back on the road just to get rid of you," I tell him, taking the cables out of his hand. "Now, this is obviously not your area of expertise, but things work according to amps. That means, your radio or lights might work with just a little juice in your battery, but there might not be enough to, say, run your car at the same time, or even start it," I explain, attaching the cables. "It also means if there's not a good connection, the output of the battery might not be strong enough. Understand?"

"Listen, I just don't think you—"

"I liked you better when you didn't talk," I mutter, walking around and going to start his vehicle. When it fires right up, I slam the door—hard. He stands there looking at the car like it has Martians surrounding it and is getting ready to take him back to the mother ship. I proceed to take everything back to my truck while he stands there still looking at his car. When I slam his hood (*again too hard*), he turns around to look at me, his hand rubbing the back of his neck. He looks a little embarrassed, and that makes me feel marginally better. Now if he apologizes for being an ass, I might feel better about the weekend I spent with him. I've seen the signs and maybe it's because I've dealt with them over and over, but I really get tired of men who think I don't understand how to do my job just because I'm a woman.

"How much do I owe you?" he asks as he goes to his wallet, no apology in sight.

Okay, then. If that's how he's going to play it.

"Hundred bucks."

"You're kidding me! You weren't out here but for ten minutes! That's highway robbery. With prices like that, I'm surprised you get any business at all," he grumbles, handing me a hundred-dollar bill.

"Oh, what I did here was free." His mouth goes tight again. Strangely enough, this time I smile.

"If that's free, then why am I giving you money?"

"Because you were really that annoying. So I charged ten dollars for every minute I had to be around you. I probably should have charged more, but I'm feeling charitable." I jump up in my truck and leave Gray standing there with his mouth open.

Yeah, I liked him better when his head was buried between my legs.

Chapter Seven

GRAY

As I watch Claude drive back to her shop, I can't shake the feeling that I know her from somewhere. There's something about her voice ... and that face—well, what I could see of it that wasn't covered with oil. I have the strangest urge to follow her, but I can't because I have to meet with Riverton.

This is bullshit. I'm not Green after all. Being in the majors like he is, he has to deal with bullshit sponsors. Golf is completely different from baseball, and it's one thing I've always been thankful for. I'm also unbelievably fucking good at it. That's not ego, though I will admit to having that at times. It's just the truth. My sport is filled with middle-aged men; there's a reason they call me the young stud of the sport. I like that title. *I live up to that title.* I've become the face of the industry in just a few short years. I took a bunch of ribbing because I went into golf—most of it from my own brothers. But I silenced them all by bringing home the bank. Shit, I make more than Green and I don't have to tow the line like he does. That might be the very reason I'm resenting the fact that Seth has me out here playing nice with Riverton. I am not a yes man. I am who I am and I like being me. Kissing up to some man just so his company can smooth the way with the big-wigs in charge of the tour pisses me off. Everyone thinks money greases the wheels, that it's all about the money, but the truth is ... it's politics. In the big leagues, everyone has full pockets. They just want to show off who has the bigger dick. The people in charge of getting me exposure, ensuring my rank and position for the tournament, are major dicks.

As I pull up to the wrought iron gate with two giant R's detailed on it, I do my best to swallow the bile that comes up in my throat. Is this what swallowing your pride feels like? The urge to drive away is strong, but I beat that down too. I'll play nice. I'll send in the matches I'll appear at, and with Riverton behind me, I'll be welcomed with open arms. Then, fuck them all. Once I win that pretty trophy and jacket, I'm done. *D. O. N. E.* Then they'll be the ones crawling to me. I'll be the one in complete control.

I hit the button on the speaker and tell the voice who I am. The gates open. I pull up and look into my rearview mirror. As they slowly come to a close, I flinch. *One season*. That's it. I'll do this to become what I need to be. *The master of my own destiny*.

I drive towards the house and the strangest thing happens. I think about this past weekend with CC. That's where I wish I was right now. Back with her in that damn hotel room, listening to her laugh, feeling her legs wrap around me as I sink into her. But that's not what hits my gut and makes my hands constrict so tight around the steering wheel it could almost break.

It's the realization that the voice of Claude and CC are one and the same.

I'll be visiting a certain little mechanic again soon. *Very soon*.

Chapter Eight

CC

"We'll see you tomorrow," Jackson says, as if there are two of him. It always makes me grin. At times he sounds so much like Banger that it hurts.

"Later, old man," I tell him, getting that look from him I always get. There are only ten years difference between our ages, but Jackson seems so much older. Banger always said life can age you more than time, and Jackson seems to be a walking testament to that. We break apart at our vehicles. Once I start my car, Jackson takes off on his bike. Right before I put the car into drive, I realize I left my cellphone in the garage. With a groan—*because I really want to get home*—I switch the car off and go back the way I came. I have the phone retrieved and I'm locking the door when I hear his voice from behind.

"I think it's a crime to cover up hair that beautiful in that cap on your head."

Before I can even fully turn around, Gray's reaching up to pull it off. My hair tumbles over my shoulders and halfway down my back. As if by reflex, I use my hand to shake the curls out and comb it away from my face.

"I guess this means you know who I am now."

"I guess I do," he says, propping himself up on my door and caging me in.

"I guess I should give you a cookie or something," I mumble, finally getting the door to lock.

"I can think of something else I'd rather you give me."

"That's not happening," I assure him, stubbornly refusing to look his way.

"Why's that?"

"That ship has sailed."

"We could always take it back out to sea."

"The point of weekend hookups out of town is that they end at the weekend and they remain out of town," I tell him with a wince, trying to ignore how that makes me sound. "What are you doing here?"

"I had to come to town on business."

"This place isn't exactly industry row."

"No, but it does have its appeal, that's for sure." His finger wraps around a strand of my hair. I barely resist the urge to pull it away from him. I'm working really hard on ignoring the way his voice sends chills down my back. The man is like a drug! One that I definitely need to stop—cold turkey.

"Well, I hope you enjoyed your visit," I tell him, "but I need to get home. It's been a long day and Cat is waiting for me."

"You named your cat... Cat?"

"Cat could have been a person."

"Is she?"

"No."

"Then I'm right. Strange. I would have figured you for a dog person."

"Well, you don't really know me."

"You're definitely wrong there. I think I know a lot about you."

"Considering you didn't even know who I was earlier today, I think I can safely argue that you don't."

"If I remember correctly, proving you wrong is a lot of fun, so you can argue away."

"What're you—?"

"Remember? You said there was no way you could come again, and I told you that you could. All it took was sliding my tongue slowly against—"

"Okay, I think you should stop there. I've had a long day, and I'm sure you're anxious to get back on the road and go back to wherever—"

"Actually, it seems I'm going to be staying in Kentucky for a couple of weeks."

My heart stutters at his words, and a nervous tension gathers in my stomach. This news shouldn't affect me one way or another—but it does. I do my best to shake it off and not let it show.

"In that case, I'm sure I'll be seeing you around. Right now, however, I better get going."

"Right, home to your... cat," he says, and I don't correct him.

"Exactly. Take care, Gray."

"Maybe you could help me first."

"Listen," I start, but he holds his hands up as if to stop me.

"I need a hotel. I've driven around this place and I've yet to see one."

"That's because there isn't one."

"What??"

"Small town. There's no need for a motel around here."

"Where do people from out of town stay?"

"With family or friends...?"

"Are you offering?"

"Not at all."

"That's cold. You'd just send me out to sleep on a park bench?"

"I wouldn't do that if I was you."

"Are you afraid I'll be kidnapped for my sexy body and—?"

"Probed anally by little green men?"

"Umm..." I can't stop from smiling at the look on his face. I'm not sure why I like him, especially after today, but I can't deny that there's something about him. "Do you have many alien sightings around here?" he asks.

"Only on nights with the full moon, or the week after old man Jenkins sells some of his homemade preserves."

"Delightful..."

"Rest easy, Crayon-man. There's a bed and breakfast about three miles up that street," I tell him, pointing the way. It's on the right. Ask for Mrs. Casebolt. Now if you'll excuse me, I have a date with my bed."

"Maybe I could double date with you. I bet I could make it more interesting..."

"Cat already beat you to the punch. Nice try, though."

"We can let Cat have the couch."

"See you around, Gray," I tell him, walking to my car.

"You're just going to turn me out into the cold like this, after all of the nice things I did for you this weekend?"

"They were nice," I tell him, looking over the top of my vehicle.

"I definitely thought so," he says, looking like he's got me right where he wants me.

"But not so great that I'd kick Cat out of bed."

"You—"

"Later, Crayon. Watch out for Mrs. Casebolt."

"What do you mean?" he calls out loudly, as I get in my car and slam the door.

I start my car up and put it in reverse. I back up until my passenger window is even with him, then I roll it down. "She's got grabby hands. Then again, you might like that," I tell him and roll up my window before he can reply. I look in my rearview mirror once I get on the road and see him standing there. I can't make out his face, but I still smile.

Chapter Nine

GRAY

I've been in Kentucky for three days, *only three days*, and I'm going insane. Mrs. Casebolt does indeed have grabby hands. My poor ass has been pinched more than a fat baby's cheeks. Shit, I probably have bruises. Riverton has been dicking me around making appointments that he mysteriously doesn't show for, but his single, annoying daughter does. Cammie isn't bad-looking, don't get me wrong, but she's a bitch. Even while she's trying to hide it and make herself appear to be the answer to every dream I've ever had, she's a bitch. It's this innate piece of her that shines through even with her smile. She's also on the market for a husband, and that right there is why my dick will never get around Camilla Riverton. I will never tie myself to a woman. My brother Green did that, and it had horrible repercussions. We all thought his woman was a keeper, and we were all wrong... *horribly wrong*. Even if that wasn't true, however, Cammie would be the last woman I'd ever look at.

After three days of dodging Mrs. Casebolt's grabby-hands, three days of being cat-fished by Riverton, and three days of ignoring Cammie's very large hints, I'm about to go insane. Not to mention the fact that it's also been three days since I've seen CC. That is unacceptable. Riverton is out of town today and if I'm going to survive my next meeting with him, I'm going to need a good distraction.

Which is why I find myself pulling up to Claude's garage. It's not sitting great with me that I'm on the edge of chasing a woman. I've never done that in my life, but desperate times call for desperate measures. I tell myself that if I were back home in my own element where beautiful women are a dime a dozen, I wouldn't chase CC—I wouldn't even think about it. *Bullshit.* I'm lying out of my ass. This morning alone, the waitress at the local diner gave me all the appropriate signals and she was definitely pretty, but her hair wasn't bronze auburn with streaks of gold, her smile didn't quite make her eyes sparkle, and her curves were lacking.

So here I am...

"Can I help you?" A man asks, coming out of the bay door of the garage. He's big and broad... and definitely not CC.

"I'm looking for CC."

"Who are you?"

"I'm a friend of hers. Gray Lucas," I tell him, reaching out my hand.

He wipes oil off his hands with a rag and stares at my outstretched hand, but doesn't bother to shake it. "CC's never mentioned you."

"Do you know all her friends?" I ask him, starting to wonder exactly what kind of relationship they have.

"Pretty much."

"Well, we've just met recently. So maybe that's why."

"Recently?"

"This past weekend."

He looks me over, and then the strangest thing happens. He gets a big smile on his face. "Now I get it," he says.

"Jackson, have you seen my torque wr—*What are you doing here?*" CC asks when she comes outside. She's dressed in the coveralls she wore last time I was here and, sadly, her hair is all covered up again, but even so, she looks hot. Hell, she looks sexier like this than Cammie does in those short skirts and clinging blouses she's been wearing around me. My dick stretches against my jeans, hardening and lengthening all at once, wishing it was closer to the woman in front of me. The one who is currently shooting daggers at me. Damn, even pissed off she looks hot.

"Well hello to you too, beautiful."

"What are you doing here?"

"Is this dude the reason for that wicked smile you had Monday?" the man asks.

"Piss off, Jackson."

He laughs in response. "I'll take that as a yes. Hell, it must have been good for the fucker to follow you all the way to Crossville."

"It wasn't," CC says at the same time I add my, "It was." This exchange makes the man laugh even louder. I might grow to like him. He's starting to remind me of my asshole brothers. *Grow to like him?* Nah, I won't be around that long. But I can appreciate that he won't be competition to get one more taste of the woman in front of me.

"Maybe you need a reminder," I tell her with a grin.

"Maybe you need a reality check," she returns.

"Maybe I do. Actually, I was hoping you would go to lunch with me."

"Why would I do that?"

"She'd love to," Jackson says, and yeah, I might like him.

"*What?* I would not. Jackson, stay out of this."

"Listen, Claude. It's lunchtime, and Mary Ann is off today, so it's your turn. If the dude is desperate enough to track you down, then the least you can do is have lunch with him."

Okay, maybe I don't like him. I'm not desperate. My dick could possibly be. *Still...*

"C'mon, CC. You only live once. I promise not to bite, unless of course you ask me to," I goad her.

"That won't happen."

"It might. Remember Saturday when you wanted me to bite you on the—"

"Stop!" she screams, looking at Jackson.

He laughs, shaking his head and walking back inside the garage. "Bring me a burger box, when you get done playing," he says before he disappears.

Once he's gone, CC stands looking at me with her hands on her hips. "What exactly do you think you're doing?"

"Asking a beautiful woman to lunch?"

"Gray..."

"CC, we had a great weekend together. I want to spend more time with you. Nothing heavy, and it doesn't have to go any farther than lunch if you don't want it to, but besides the sex... which by the way, was off the charts..."

"It was, but—"

"*Besides* the sex," I interrupt her, "I just had a good time with you. You're funny, cute and just fun to be around in general. So will you please go to lunch with me?"

"You said *'please'*."

"That, I did."

"I bet that's something you don't say to women very often."

"Only to my sisters or my mother."

"Oh my God, you have sisters too?"

"Have lunch with me and I'll tell you all about them."

"If I agree, it's only because I'm curious."

"I'll take what I can get."

"Okay, fine. Give me a couple minutes to get ready."

"I'll be right here waiting," I tell her, feeling something click into place.

Shit, maybe I am desperate.

Chapter Ten

CC

"You clean up good, Cooper," he observes as he sits across from me. We're at the local diner and I have the summer salad special in front of me, but I'm having trouble eating. I find myself staring at Gray instead, wondering exactly how this happened.

"I didn't clean up. I just took my coveralls off."

"And let your hair out of its prison."

"My hair wasn't in a prison," I tell him, self-consciously pushing my fingers through it.

"It's a crime to keep that hair covered up, sweetheart."

"Listen, Gray..."

"It's beautiful, like the color of a flame that shines in the moonlight. It reminds me of bonfires we have back home."

I want to ridicule his words for being way too poetic, but instead they make the butterflies in my stomach jump around. The words should sound totally fake, like a man trying to get in a girl's pants a little too hard. Instead, he makes them sound sincere, as if he truly believes it. Suddenly, the thick, curly monstrosity of hair on my head and my freckles don't feel like a sore spot to me anymore, and that's crazy. I can almost feel myself blush at the way he's staring at me. *Damn.* I clear my throat, needing to pull this conversation back to even ground.

"Weren't you supposed to tell me about your sisters?"

Something moves through his face and he watches me for a minute before leaning back against the cushioned seat in our booth. "What about them?"

"Were they named after colors, too?"

"Flowers."

"Flowers?"

"Yep. If you ask me, they got the better card in the draw."

"Well, not necessarily. You'd be awful silly with the name Iris."

"Point made. In any event, I have three sisters. All younger, all designed to drive each of us brothers batty, and all named after flowers."

"Well, driving brothers batty is what sisters are supposed to do."

"Do you do that to your brother?"

"I don't have any, but if I did, I'm sure I'd make that my goal."

"What about sisters? Or..."

"No one, just me."

"I'm sorry, sweetheart."

His apology is sincere, and the grave look on his face is testament to that, but it makes me feel uncomfortable. He doesn't know me. Why would he be sorry? I shift in my chair, not sure how to react to this man. "It is what it is. So what're your sister's names? Daisy, Rose, and Iris?"

"Spoken like a woman who clearly doesn't know my mother," he says with a laugh.

"Okay, I'm almost afraid to ask... but what are they?"

"Petal, Maggie, and Mary. Mary being the youngest—eighteen."

"Well, Petal is a little strange, but still it's kind of pretty, I like it. Those aren't bad names. I don't even see flowers in them, though I guess Mary..."

"Short for Marigold."

"Umm... okay, not horrid. And Maggie?"

"Magnolia."

"Yikes. Okay, that one might be a little..."

"Named after the tree under which she was conceived at a free love rally."

"Oh my."

"Exactly."

"Your mom must be quite the character."

"She is. Are you going to ask about Petal?"

"I figured that one was self-explanatory."

"Lotus Petal Lucas."

"Umm..."

"There you go, that's the look."

"What look?"

"The look my brothers and sisters see every time someone asks our names."

"So, I take it if you ever have kids, there will be no names after flowers or..."

"I doubt I'll ever have kids, but Green did."

"You don't want kids?"

"I don't want the wife that comes with them."

"A wife doesn't have to come with them exactly, not these days. My mom didn't exactly stick around."

"They're still there somewhere, ready to cause trouble. Not worth it. Besides, my life isn't one that would make having a kid easy."

"Why do you say that?"

"I'm on the road a lot."

"You're a salesman?"

He gets a strange look on his face. "Something like that. Anyway, I don't really want to settle down, and kids definitely make you do that."

"Yeah, I guess so. I'm not sure what my life would have been like without Banger and this small town, so I can see that."

"You're happy here?"

"For the most part. I don't have any complaints. And Claude might be horrible, but at least it's not named after a tree I was conceived under. Then again, knowing my mother, she probably doesn't know the tree nor the man who was there."

"Banger wasn't your real father?"

"He was, in every way that mattered," I tell him, daring him to argue.

"Good you had him."

That's the understatement of the year, so all I can do is nod in agreement. "What's your mom's name?"

"Ida Sue, though she once had the courts change it to Lily."

I laugh. "She wanted to be named after a flower too?"

"Her full legal name is now Peace Lily, so that would be a yes."

"I bet your grandparents are interesting."

"I never got to meet them, but I hear they were. They definitely raised a proud, independent, strong woman and, despite her naming abilities, mom is a hell of a woman. Though, I do think she might have cried the day Black graduated the police academy."

"She doesn't like having a cop in the family?"

"She's learning to accept it. It became easier when his twin Blue decided to go into ranching full-time. She said it evened out the karma, whatever that means."

"You have a crazy family."

"That I do," he agrees, taking a bite of his food.

"I think you're very lucky. It's obvious you care about them."

"I am and I do, though sometimes I want to kill them too. I'm feeling very lucky, especially since you agreed to come to lunch with me. I'm having a good time."

"I am, too," I admit, surprised. I don't know what I expected from him, but I can't lie. This has been the best lunch date I can ever remember.

"I'm glad. It will make it easier."

"Make what easier?"

"Getting you to agree to have dinner with me tonight."

I smile despite myself. Taking a bite of my salad, shaking my head in disbelief. "We'll see," I tell him, but inside I know that if he asks, I'll be agreeing.

"I'll take that," he says. "And just to sweeten the pot, if you agree, I'll tell you all about how my mother and father met."

"As long as you leave out their romps under the Magnolia trees."

"Oh, no worries, nobody ever needs to hear that story. Even though it's one of Mom's favorites."

"Now I'm scared again."

"You should be," he quips with a wink before he waves for the waitress's attention to get us some refills. As I watch the way Rachel looks at Gray and he seemingly doesn't even notice, instead looking right at me, I can feel something inside of me giggle happily.

Damn. I think I'm falling under the spell of a traveling salesman. Maybe I'm more like my mother than I ever suspected.

Chapter Eleven

GRAY

"Fuck, you look good," I tell her.

The words slipping out of my mouth before I can stop them. Not that I would, but that seems to be a problem with this girl. She's unlike the playthings I'm used to. By all rights, I should have forgotten her, but the memory of our weekend is just getting stronger and stronger with each minute I spend close to her. Lunch today was fun and one of the best times I've ever had—*with anyone*. She entertains me, makes me laugh, and I actually like spending time with her. So much that today I found myself actually ignoring my rock-hard dick and concentrating on getting her to talk more.

I'm at her house picking her up for dinner. After our lunch date, I practically had to beg for her address—another first for me. Once I got it, I left and went back to schmooze with Riverton some more. While I'm enjoying the game I'm playing with CC, the same cannot be said with Riverton. He's set a meeting up tomorrow afternoon. If that doesn't work out, I don't care what Seth says, *I'm done*. I'll find another sponsor. They might not have as much pull with the higher-ups at the tournament, but surely there is someone else who will get me the leverage I need with the committee. *Someone who doesn't have Cammie for a daughter.* That's all that is important. I'm not about to get jerked around, unless it's by CC. She can jerk me all she wants. Visions of her hand moving up and down on my cock spring to mind. Just like that, my semi-erection blooms into a full blown concrete crushing stiffy. *This woman is killing me*. If I don't get in her pants again soon, I'm liable to start drooling and talking gibberish. I'm not far from that now, especially when she's standing in front of me wearing that auburn and gold hair down so that it curls loosely on her head, framing her face. She's wearing a dark green silk dress that dips down enough to highlight her cleavage, short yet just enough to cover her thighs, but only after it curves and hugs the cheeks of her ass. She looked good this past weekend, but standing here right now, I can't remember another woman before her. This is my first clue that I might be in trouble. My second is when she laughs, those thick beautiful lips curve up into a smile. They shimmer in the pale light with her lip gloss—pale pink in color. I imagine the color in a perfect ring around my shaft. Jesus, I can feel pre-cum gathering on my dick. If I don't get inside this woman soon, I'm going to blow.

"You don't look so bad yourself," she says. It takes a minute for the blood flow to leave my dick and rush back to my brain, allowing me to remember what we were talking about.

"Are you ready to go, sweetheart?" I've used that endearment a million times, with a million different women. Suddenly, it sounds fake and wrong. CC isn't like them. She deserves something special —something different. *And there's yet another clue that I might be in over my head with this woman.*

"I guess..."

"You don't sound too sure."

"I'm still not convinced this is a smart thing to do."

"You think too much. I don't remember this side of you when we were in Lexington."

"It didn't matter then."

"Explain," I tell her, helping her put on her jacket before leading her out the door and waiting for her to lock it.

"It was one wild night out of time. No consequences, no repercussions, and no worries. You're in my hometown now. The place I've fought to make a name for myself that I could be proud of. A name *Banger* would be proud of. It has taken me years to live down my mother's past. The last thing I want is for people to think I'm anything like her."

"This sounds like a deep conversation. You can tell me more about over steaks and wine."

"I don't think that's on the menu at Rosie's, and that's the only restaurant in town."

"True, but we're not going to Crossville. We're going to Addington," I tell her, and I can feel the muscles in her back tighten at my words. "Is something wrong with Addington?"

"It's just not my normal kind of town. I'm more at home in Rosie's diner, so unless you're going to take me to Mickey D's, I'm not sure I'm—"

"Stop worrying. First of all, the way you're dressed is way too fine for fast food. Secondly, as much fun as I had at Rosie's Diner with you earlier today, I want a good thick steak. I'm assured that the place to find that around here is Addington."

"Listen, Gray..."

"Look at it this way: In Addington, no one will know you, and it will be like we continue our weekend with no worries."

"It's not that far away."

"Does it really matter? It's dinner, and if anything else happens, we're both adults and it will be behind closed doors."

"You're right. I'm just being silly," she says, with a shrug. This side of her surprises me. I'm definitely intrigued. I'm going to have to learn more about her mother. She's mentioned a little about her, and I know the story isn't pretty, but it seems to have left enough scars on CC that it alters who she is, and for some reason that makes me mad. CC shouldn't have to worry about how people look at her, or what she does—*for any reason*. I live in a small town in Texas, and with mom's history, I know a little bit about the damage small-minded people can do. Still, it pisses me off that CC ever had to experience any of it.

We're mostly silent on the way to the country club. Riverton couldn't believe I was actually staying in Crossville. Though I assured him I was fine here, he insisted he add me as his guest at the country club in Addington, stating that it was the only place around to get a decent meal. After calling and making sure he had added me on the roster, I made dinner reservations for me and CC. I wanted to give her a great night out and a good meal seems like step one. As hard as Riverton has been pushing his single daughter down my throat, I doubt me taking another woman out was what he had in mind when he added me to the guest list. *Too damn bad.*

"Wait. Why are we here? You can't be a member, and this place is..."

"Members only, yeah I know. I've got a friend on the board here. He offered the use of the place while I'm in Kentucky," I tell her as I close her car door.

"A friend? Listen, Gray..."

"Relax, sweetheart, it's all okay. I promise," I tell her, putting my finger under her chin and tilting her head back to look at me. I read something in her eyes that I can't put a name to, but CC shakes it off and gives me a small smile, allowing me to lead her toward the club. Still, there's a tension in her that I've not felt before and I don't like it. I'm about two steps away from suggesting we go somewhere else, even if it is fast food, but decide against it. I'm sure she'll loosen up once dinner is served. She owns a garage and both times I've been there, there hasn't been a lot of customers. I'm sure she just feels out of place. Things will lighten up when she gets some good food, maybe dessert, and then the goal is to spend the rest of the night loosening her up in ways I've dreamed about ever since I woke up alone in that hotel in Lexington.

Chapter Twelve

CC

I know that Gray thought he was being sweet bringing me here. He doesn't know my history and, though we might have spent one mind-blowing weekend together, he doesn't know anything about me. It's just one night, and no one will expect me to be here. I'll just grin and bear it. The sooner we get food and get out of here, the better. There's no point in causing a scene. To do so would mean me explaining way too much to Gray about my past, which would be stupid. He's a one-night stand. Okay, two nights. And he's only here for a limited time. I can't let myself forget that. *I am not my mother*. I am not the woman who goes from man to man because I can. I am not the girl with wanderlust in her eyes, never happy if she's not on the road, off to the next best thing. I have roots here. I have a job—a business. I have goals, even if I can't remember what those goals are anymore. There's a reason I made them. I am not... *her*.

Mental pep talk done, we sit at the table and get our menus. As I look through the different entrees, I find myself missing the meals offered at Rosie's diner. It's not that I don't like a nice night out. I've had a couple when I've been to the city with friends, but honestly, the diner is more my speed.

"I guess David was right."

"David?"

"I'm here on his guest list. He said this was the best place to eat in three counties around here. I have to say, the menu definitely looks great."

"It does," I tell him, wondering if he can tell that I'm lying. I'm busy trying to figure out why it makes me sad that Gray seems so at home here. The man who talks about his brothers and sisters reminds me of a country boy. This Gray seems one step away from...

Something uneasy shifts in my stomach. He's wearing a suit. He's different. Even his attitude seems different. It's a cold reminder that though I might have slept with him, I don't really know anything about him.

"What are you thinking?" he asks, and though I know he's asking about what I want to eat, my first thought is, I'm thinking I should have never agreed to go out with you. I don't say that. It's there though...*on the tip of my tongue*.

"You order for us," I tell him, literally unable to care less what he orders and just wanting it over and done at this point.

"You sure?"

"Surprise me." I don't even pay attention as he orders.

"Why am I getting the feeling this isn't going well?" he asks.

My head jerks up so I can look at him. "I'm not really a country club kind of girl."

"What kind of girl are you?"

I study his face, trying to figure out if he's truly interested, or just trying to get into my pants. I can't decide. I take a breath and decide to just put it out there.

"I'm just guessing, Gray, but I'd say that a mechanic hasn't set foot in the doors of this place, unless it was the back entrance to get to the garage area so they can work on club cars or something."

"Why does it matter? You're here now. You're here with me and I want you here, that's all that matters."

His response annoys me. I'm not sure why I thought he would understand, but I did. "You're right."

He sighs, as if he can hear the doubt in my voice. He stands up, reaching for my hand. "Come on."

"What? Why?"

"We're going to get out of here. If you're not comfortable, then we'll go somewhere where you are."

"Gray! Is that you?" The high-pitched voice, squealing until it rakes across my nerve endings, cries out. I know that voice. I abhor that voice. The fact that the voice is calling out Gray's name only makes me detest it more.

I look up at Gray and see a look of distaste cross his face. I feel a little better. I would almost smile if the bane of my entire childhood, Cammie Riverton wasn't standing there looking at Gray like a moon-eyed dog in heat. What the hell?

"Cammie," Gray says, and I think maybe I mistook his look, because his voice sure does seem awful warm now—welcoming, even.

"What a great surprise seeing you here! I thought you said you had another business meeting today."

"I did, I was..."

"*Oh my God!* Claudia Cooper, is that you?"

I grind my teeth together, wishing I had the superpower to turn invisible. "That'd be me. How are you, Cammie?"

"What on earth are you doing here with Gray? How could you two possibly know each other?" she asks. Her voice is so snide and her eyes shoot imaginary bullets at me. I probably shouldn't do it, but as always when Cammie is involved, I find I can't stop my mouth from reacting.

"I gave him a head job and he's taking me to dinner as a thank you."

"You what?" Cammie asks, her head reeling back as if I slapped her. I probably spoke much too loudly for this place too because it's deathly quiet now, and I can see all of the eyes on me. I'm in too deep to back down now.

"I said I gave him a head job and he's buying me dinner to show me his appreciation." I hear Gray cough and when I look over at him, he's smiling proudly and giving me a look I can't quite decipher.

"Dear Lord! I can't believe you," Cammie whispers. "Gray! I don't think my father will want to do business with a man who..."

"She means my car broke down and she fixed it."

"She does?" Cammie asks, confused.

"Yes. A part of the engine is referred to as heads. Sometimes they blow a gasket," he explains, but he's looking right at me. I do my best to give him an innocent look. I know I fail. I don't give a damn. I just want out of here.

Why is Gray doing business with Cammie's father? A better question might be: *why do I even care?*

Chapter Thirteen

GRAY

"Goodness, I should have known that's what it was. Really, Claude was always so coarse, it shouldn't surprise me that she hasn't changed," Cammie answers, as if CC isn't even in the room. I see CC's face tighten and her eyes narrow. I am tempted to see just how this exchange will go down because I think I might get an honest look at CC—and that is very enticing indeed—but Seth would probably kill me. I wasn't sure I liked Cammie before this, and now I'm positive. The little minx currently trying to figure out how to leave, however, is someone I definitely like. After this, I believe she does in fact owe me a head job.

"I like the way CC is upfront. Kind of like, what you see is what you get. It's much better than trying to figure out who a person is when they pretend to be someone else entirely," I tell Cammie.

I see CC sit up at my barb just as it flies over the top of Cammie's head. Cammie might be pretty in a clean, polished, Ivy League kind of way, but she's obviously not the sharpest tool in the shed. Maybe her parents kept her too sheltered. If that's the case, they didn't do her any favors.

"I suppose," Cammie agrees reluctantly. "But really, Claude, you should be more aware of your surroundings. I mean, you are sitting at my father's table. Your behavior reflects on him."

"Well, we wouldn't want that, would we?" CC asks loudly, and I'm thinking this could get ugly real fast. "Tell me, Cammie, how is dear old Dad? Still feeding your trust fund monthly?"

"I think you should leave now. Gray, you're new to the area, but I think you can clearly see that CC and her kind of people don't exactly mix well here."

"I was just telling him that very thing before you got here," CC says, standing up. "And if there's one thing that I'm thankful for Cammie, it's that I don't *mix* well here. Gray, it's been real. Don't bother getting up, I'm sure Cammie here would be more than willing to take my place."

Before she can finish her sentence, I'm up with her. I wrap my hand around her wrist and pull her towards me. "Cammie, if you'll excuse me, I'll be seeing CC home."

"Of course you will. It's the gentlemanly thing to do. It's a shame I couldn't have warned you sooner. We're still on for lunch tomorrow right?"

I feel CC jerk away from me, and it's annoying. I barely know the woman and I can feel myself getting embarrassed all because I have a business luncheon with Cammie and her father. What the ever-loving fuck? My brothers would be laughing their asses off at me right now.

"Wouldn't miss it. I'll see you then."

"Definitely," she chimes. "CC, I do hope you find a way to get your anger under control," she calls out. Either Cammie's smarter than I gave her credit for, or she's just a bitch.

"Cunt," CC growls under her breath.

I feel myself grin a little. I always did like my women with a little bite. The little tigress in my hands right now definitely bites—and boy, does she have claws. I manage to get her back to my vehicle and I forcibly, *over her objections*, buckle her into the seat. Truthfully, I'm afraid if I don't buckle her in, she'll take off running.

"Well, that was interesting," I tell her, leaning against the opened passenger door and taking a breath as soon as the seatbelt buckles. Damn, why do I feel like I just wrestled a mountain lion? *Why am I wondering what my mother would think of CC?* "Care to tell me what that was all about?"

"Not especially," CC all but grunts, looking very put-out with me.

"I think I'm owed an explanation, don't you?"

"Cammie Riverton is a cunt-a-saurus," she says with a smile.

"And you don't think you need to explain that further?"

"Nope." She shrugs, picking at imaginary lint on her dress.

"You could have ruined my chances of sealing the deal with Riverton Metals."

"He's a slime ball. You're better off," she grumbles. "So... see? I did you a favor."

"He might be, for all I know. I don't really give a fuck. I need his backing for my tournament. His name and wallet are instrumental in achieving my dream."

"Tournament? I thought you were a salesman?"

"No. You assumed I was a salesman. I just never bothered to correct you."

"What do you do then?" she asks.

Shit! This wasn't exactly the conversation I wanted to have tonight. I sigh, seeing no way around it. I rub my forehead in aggravation. *Will she know who I am?* Will it change how she is with me? I don't know why, but I don't want that to happen... which is weird. I usually play the whole I'm-A-Golf-Pro-Fuck-Me card right away. CC is different. I've said it before and I have a feeling I'll be saying it again for as long as I'm around her.

"I play golf," I tell her, nervously waiting to see what her reaction will be.

"Golf?"

"Yeah," I say, wincing at her disbelief.

"Like... weird-hats-crazy-pants-ugly-shirts, *golf*?"

"I don't wear clothes like that, but yeah."

"But you don't look like you're eighty!"

"What? I'm not. What are you—?"

"Oh my God! I had sex with a grandpa! How old are you? I mean, I knew you were older, but Jesus!"

"I am not old! What are you going on about? I'm thirty-five, for God's sake. You know, not only old men play golf."

"I know."

"Well, there you go."

"I've been miniature-golfing before. Little kids eat that up, but seriously, dude. We're talking regular golf here, right? Where you hit those little balls with sticks and try to knock them in a hole?"

"It's a little more complicated than that. And there was once a twelve-year-old who played in a tournament, I'll have you know."

"Golf," she says again, reproachfully.

"What is your problem now?"

"Well, I mean, if I was gonna have a one-night stand with an athlete, I'd much rather it was football or basketball... something. I mean, at least then I could brag a little. I can't here."

"Why the fuck can't you?" I ask her, getting annoyed and forgetting the fact that I don't really want a woman to fuck me just so she can brag.

"The first thing they would ask me is if you smelled like muscle rub!"

"What? Jesus!"

"I mean, I never noticed you smelling like that stuff, but now that I think about it, you did have to—"

Before she can finish her rant, I lean down and pull her towards me. The seatbelt holds her in place, but I bend to get to her. My lips crash against hers, stopping her tirade and ending it with a muffled *umph* of a noise that vibrates against my lips. My tongue pushes in and I groan at the familiar taste of her mouth—sweet, hot, sugar and spice. It's a flavor I've never had before. *CC*, and instinctively I know I will never find it anywhere else. It's all her and I have a feeling it could be more addicting than any drug. Her tongue boldly wraps around mine. That's another thing that's all

CC. *She is not shy*. She knows what she wants and she goes after it completely—body and soul. As her tongue tangles with mine and fights for dominance, my dick hardens, pushing against my slacks. God, she's something else. I thought I had somehow imagined just how great her kisses were. I now instantly know I was wrong. They are that great. Her fingers bite into my shoulders as my hands push under her dress. Her hot skin greets my touch—*hot enough to brand a man*. I pull away for a breath and she whimpers, her mouth following me. I groan, giving in, and dive back into her mouth to drink again, before slowly breaking away.

When the kiss is over, our foreheads remain connected. Her hands remain on my shoulders and I sure as hell will not take my hands off of her unless she makes me. She takes a very shaky breath, swallows, and then slowly pulls away from me. She looks at me, her green eyes almost glowing.

"You kiss pretty good for an old man," she says, and I don't know what I expected, but it wasn't that. I laugh before I can stop myself. Shit, this woman constantly surprises me.

I might be in over my head.

Chapter Fourteen

CC

"You okay, C?" Jackson asks, when I drop my damn wrench again.

"Yeah, I'm fine," I mutter, lying out of my ass. I'm not fine. I'm very far from fine. My mind is where it has been for the last three days ever since Gray dropped me off at my house after our date—a date which started off horrible, got worse, never did result in food, and ended with a kiss that has haunted me ever since. It doesn't matter. It can't matter, and for several reasons. The biggest of those being that Grayson Lucas is some kind of golf god. I googled him after our date and what I learned was enough to blow my mind... and turn my stomach. He's famous, he's rich, and worse...he's a big time player. His exploits with women have been plastered on every tabloid coming and going. Just last month, his biggest sponsor booted him because there was a video uploaded of Gray online. *A sex video.* A video of him and two other women—one of those being the daughter of a very well-known golf sponsor. Gossip on the net was that he was shuffling to find a new sponsor, one that would get him back in the good graces of the upcoming tour promoters and committee. That would be why he is here and why he's dealing with David Riverton. All that together spells disaster with a capital D, and reveals a million reasons why I have to stay away from Gray.

Which is why when my cellphone *(a number I gave him after he kissed me again on our horrible date)* rings for the fifth time today, I ignore it.

"That lover boy again?" Jackson asks, and I ignore him, finally getting the last bolt on the radiator assembly we're installing tightened. "He seemed like a nice guy, C. He made you smile. Cut him some slack."

"You know anything about golf, Jackson?"

"Golf?"

"Yeah. You know, little white balls being whacked with a club..."

"I try not to watch anything that involves balls being whacked, C."

"Well, it seems Gray is, like, a mega golf star."

"Mega?"

"Sponsors, tours, trophies, lots of money."

"*No shit?*"

"No shit."

"Damn. What's he doing in Kentucky? We're not exactly the golf capital of the world."

"Courting David Riverton as a new sponsor."

"Fuck."

"That about sums it up."

"Still, woman, just because he's working with that fucker doesn't mean you have to write him off."

"He's got money..."

"So?"

"By 'money' I mean he's loaded. Hell, if he didn't need Riverton to smooth over his black marks with the tour people, he probably could be his own sponsor."

"Black marks?"

"Sex tape of him with two other women, one being the daughter of one of the major tour sponsors."

"Jesus."

"He's bad news, Jackson. So, can we just forget it? In a few days he'll go back to wherever they have golf games and it will be over."

"I'm sorry, C. Seems you've inherited your old man's ability at picking partners."

"Yeah, it appears that way," I tell him with a sigh.

We work for a couple more hours getting caught up, for the most part. The phone has finally stopped ringing and I'm doing my best not to feel sad about that. *I can't be*. There's no room for Gray in my life, even if he wasn't a player.

"Want some lunch from the diner?" Jackson asks, and I'm not really in the mood, but I say yes anyway.

"Sure. Chicken salad."

"Ugh, rabbit food. I expect better of you, Claude," Jackson says, using my name because he knows it irritates me. In response, I flip him off. He's laughing as he slams the door behind him. I busy myself picking up tools and trying to clear my head when the object of my thoughts makes an appearance.

"Your phone not working, sweet lips?"

My head jerks up at Gray's voice. He's wearing a worn Metallica t-shirt and jeans and he looks like anything but a golfer, which pisses me off. His hair is ruffled with these soft curls on top of his head that are starting to hang loosely because his close cut is growing out. Somehow, it looks even better on him now—another thing to piss me off.

"I hated that nickname back at the bar. It made me write you off immediately. I should have listened to my gut," I tell him.

"Sweet lips? But it fits you, because woman, your lips are the sweetest I've ever tasted."

"I guess I should be flattered because from what I've read, that covers a lot of territory."

"Aww. You've googled me. I guess I'm the one who should be flattered."

"Whatever," I mutter, going back to picking up tools and ignoring him. It works pretty good until he comes up behind me and wraps his arm around me, pulling me back into him and not letting me move. I try to jerk away, but he still doesn't let me go.

"What do you think you're doing?"

"Asking you if your phone is working," he whispers against my shoulder. I can feel the heat of his breath on my neck and it radiates, even against my coveralls, but it's not enough. I suddenly wish I didn't have them on. I wish I didn't have *anything* on. I wish it was just the two of us, skin against skin...

"You need to let me go. You'll get filthy," I tell him, stressing the word he used when I worked on his vehicle.

"But CC, I love getting filthy with you."

The words piss me off because it sounds like a line. Then I realize who I'm dealing with and admit that everything out of his mouth is probably a line. We had a one-night stand and that was all it was and that's over. Just because we had a good lunch date... *an awesome lunch date*...just because he made me smile, and just because he makes me laugh and his kisses melt the clothes off my body, none of that means anything. *It's just a game*. It's meaningless and I might be tempted to bite for however long it lasts until he leaves, but I will not become one of his play toys. *I am not my mother.*

I bring my elbow back and deliver a blow to his gut. It's weak and nowhere near what I'm capable of, but it's enough so that he gets the point and lets me go.

"My phone works just fine."

"Then why aren't you answering it?"

"*Gee*. Maybe because I don't want to talk to you?"

"Bullshit."

"Whatever."

"You wanted to talk to me enough to give me your damn number."

"That was before."

"Before what?"

"Before I..."

"Before you saw shit on the internet about me."

"Maybe. Is it true?"

"What if it is? What does it matter? It happened before I met you. Hell, we've only really had one date. Why is your nose out of joint about it?" he asks, sounding agitated.

"Maybe I just don't want to see my picture on the internet as another notch in Grayson Lucas's bed post."

"I'm fine with that."

"So, if you don't mind—Wait. What did you say?"

"I don't particularly want you to be plastered in tabloids either. I don't enjoy that shit."

"For a man who doesn't enjoy it, there sure are plenty of them."

"And most of them are put up there by the women in question."

"What? Why?"

"Because believe it or not, some women live for being seen as one of Gray Lucas's exploits."

"Gross."

"Thanks."

"Well, you know what I mean."

"I do. Which is why I want to go out with you. Well, one of the reasons. I want to get to know you more, CC. Is that so bad? You're unlike anyone I've ever met and, more importantly, I actually like you."

"And it has nothing to do with sex."

"It has everything to do with it."

"Which is exactly why my answer is no."

He growls and moves back towards me, pushing me up against the concrete wall and holding my hands against it so I can't push him away. My eyes are captured by his and I swallow at the look of intensity on his face.

"Gray..."

"Can you deny that you don't remember the weekend we shared and want more of it? That the kiss we shared a few days ago doesn't haunt you? That you don't wake up in the middle of the night wishing I was there so you could wrap your legs around me and pull me deep inside of you...?"

"Damn it, Gray, it was just—"

"Because I do, CC. I do, and it's driving me crazy. I've never done that before in my life and you, goddamn it, you are haunting me all the time. I want to be with you again. It has everything to do with sex and..."

"I'm not going to be like those two women you did that video with. Go find sex with whoever—"

He pushes his finger against my lips. My eyes go wide, but I hush because his face is intense and there's something there that... *I like.*

"It has everything to do with sex because I want that again... with you. I'd be lying if I said I didn't. But it's more than that. You might be the first woman I've liked outside of sex. You're funny, you're intelligent, you keep me on my toes, and you don't try to flatter me just to get what you want."

"That's because you're an asshole."

He laughs, and somehow that's an even better look than the intense one he wore a few minutes ago.

"That's exactly what I mean, CC. You don't give a fuck about who I am. I want that. I want you, all of you, even your mouth which is delectable and annoying at the same time."

"Wow, that's some sweet talking you're doing there, *Grayson.*"

"So what do you say, sweet lips? You willing to go out with me?"

"If I see a camera within a mile of me, I'll geld you."

"Ouch. That's a bit drastic, don't you think?"

"I'm serious."

"Point made. So you going to go out with me tonight?"

"No."

"CC..."

"I have something planned already, but... I will go out with you another night if you call."

"If I call, will you answer?"

"I guess you'll have to try it and see."

"You're going to keep making me work for it, aren't you, Claudia Cooper?"

"How do you know my name?"

"Well, Cammie mentioned it, but I knew before that. Claudia 'Claude' Cooper, born January third..."

I hold up my hand to stop him. I don't care how old you are, a woman never wants her age given out to the man she's slept with, at least not this early on—not that I'm planning on anything with Gray being long term...

"Okay, that's enough," I tell him, trying to stop my brain from dreaming. Although, I'm thinking it's more like my libido.

"You aren't the only one who knows how to do research on the web. I'm calling you tonight, Cooper. You better answer," he says, turning away.

I choose not to answer now. Instead I watch him walk away, wondering what I'm getting myself into.

Chapter Fifteen

GRAY

Me:

Are you naked?

My text is simple and straight to the point. It has been two days since I saw CC at the garage. We talked on the phone last night and, as much as I'd love to tonight, I'm out with Riverton and his annoying as hell daughter. The thought of CC in bed naked makes my dick feel like a bottle rocket set to blow. Damn, I have to get ahold of this girl soon. I'm starting to think I might have imagined how great it was between us. I'm not sure reality can live up to the dreams I've been having of her.

CC:

And if I am?

I read her text, feeling a thrill run through my body. My hand practically shakes as pictures of CC naked on silk sheets flashes through my mind.

. . .

Me:

I need you to not move for about thirty minutes.

CC:

Why thirty minutes?

Me:

That's how long it will take me to get there.

CC:

Go back to your business dinner.

You're interrupting my alone time with Bob.

Me:

Bob?

I feel a stab of jealousy that I try to ignore.

CC:

Battery operated boyfriend.

Me:

Don't you dare! Your orgasms are mine.

CC:

Sorry. I'm afraid the phone signal is going out.

"Grayson? Did you hear me?" Cammie asks, and I reluctantly put my phone down.

"I'm sorry. My manager wanted my opinion on some contracts he got in today." My eyes automatically go to the wall across from me and the large clock that proclaims I've only been here for an hour. How long do I have to stay before I can make an excuse to leave? If I don't get out of here soon, I may go crazy. "What was it you were saying?"

"I was asking if you'd like to go out with father and I sailing."

"Sailing?" I'm pretty sure Kentucky is nowhere near the ocean.

"A hobby of mine. I have a couple of sailboats docked in the Kentucky Lake. I'm going to take them out this coming Sunday and stretch the sails. Hell of a way to relax," Riverton says, and I nod. The last thing I want to do is go sailing with Riverton and his daughter. I can hear Seth in my head demanding I agree, however.

"Sounds fun. I'd love to join in," I lie through my teeth.

"How grand! I can hardly wait. Sailing is one of my favorite pastimes. Isn't it marvelous how much we have in common, Grayson?" Cammie asks.

"Amazing," I tell her, hoping the sarcastic intent is somehow hidden enough it goes over her and Riverton's heads.

"I think I'm going to leave you two kids alone and find my bed. I'm not as young as I used to be," Riverton says, standing up. He reaches his hand out to me, but I'm feeling my stomach drop to the bottom. The last thing I want to be, is alone with Cammie. I shake his hand, clearing my throat.

"I was hoping we could discuss the upcoming tour, sir."

"I'm much too tired for business tonight, son. We'll talk about it this weekend and then we'll take the boat out."

"Sounds good," I tell him, inside calling him an asshole. It's not that I'm wanting to leave Kentucky. With CC here, I'm finding the last thing I want to do right now is leave. It's just I don't like being jerked around, and I'm pretty sure that's exactly what Riverton is doing. I'm not sure why he would want someone like me for his daughter. Fuck, if I was a father, I'd be the last man I'd want for her.

"You want to retire out into the garden?" Cammie asks.

I have to restrain myself from groaning. *Retire?*

"Actually, I should be going. I have a conference call early in the morning."

"Oh, no! Grayson, don't leave."

"Again, I'm sorry, but I..."

"Well, I demand you spend a few minutes out in the garden with me. Why, we barely got any time alone with daddy here monopolizing all your time."

"Well, there are things we needed to discuss. He *is* the reason I'm here, after all."

"Just think. If not for that, we would have never met. It's funny sometimes, how fate works," she says, taking my hand and pulling me out the French doors. Hell, she's talking about fate. Everything in me is screaming that I need to run away fast and hard.

She leads me to a bench outside that is surrounded by perfectly sculpted hedges, rose bushes, and other flowers. It's pretty, I suppose. Her hand is wrapped so fucking tight around mine, I'm pretty sure that the blood supply is cut off.

"I can't tell you how much fun I had tonight, Grayson. I just love being around you. You know how you meet someone and something just clicks and you instantly feel comfortable around that person?"

I listen to her words and an image of CC comes to mind instantly. I smile before I can stop myself. "I know exactly what you're talking about," I tell her without thinking.

"I knew it!" she squeals, and then before I can think over what we've talked about, her lips are on mine and her tongue is plunging into my mouth. *Her taste is wrong*. The feel of her in my arms is wrong. I don't push her away, but I do nothing to deepen the kiss. She pulls away with a satisfied look on her face and I have a bad feeling that this is going to mean trouble.

Shit.

Chapter Sixteen

CC

"Have I told you that you sure clean up good, Cooper?" Gray asks when I open the door.

He's standing there dressed in jeans and a t-shirt holding a bottle of wine and some flowers, and he's wearing a grin. It's been four days since our conversation at the garage. He hasn't missed calling or texting, and I'm starting to look forward to hearing from him. All of that spells trouble, but I'm ignoring the signs. I'm charging ahead because for the first time in my life, I see something in front of me that I want to keep. I know I can't. That's just the way life is, and there's no way someone like Grayson Lucas, golf star extraordinaire, will want me for anything long term. Still, for as long as this lasts, I'm going to take what's there and worry about tomorrow, *tomorrow*.

"Cooper? What happened to sweet lips?" I ask him, opening the door wider so he can come inside. He shrugs away my question as I close the door behind him. I turn around to walk back towards the kitchen when he wraps his arms around me. He holds me close, the flowers and wine bracing against my back.

"I've missed you."

I realize I'm dealing with a player, and those words are probably just another line designed to get my pants off of me, but the thing is... it's a very good line. Plus, I really want him to get my pants off.

"Scruffy is a good look for you," I tell him, moving my hand along the five o'clock shadow on his face. Any look is good on him. I don't think you can make him look bad—at least, physically.

"Can I have my kiss now?" he asks. Last night during our phone conversation, I told him he could have a kiss if he could remember what I was wearing the night we met. I really didn't think he could, but he nailed it, all the way down to the sea foam green, lacy silk panties and bra I wore. I reach up to give him a peck on his cheek.

"There."

"Um... no. That is not the kiss we discussed."

"It's not?" I ask as innocently as I can pull it off.

"Definitely not. There was no tongue action in that."

"I don't remember tongue action being discussed," I tell him with a grin, breaking away. I take the wine and flowers from him and lead him into the kitchen.

I have a small house. It was Banger's and the only true home I've ever known. It's an open concept with the living room and kitchen as one large space. It's too small for a dining area, so there's a breakfast bar. It's two small bedrooms and a bath. I'm sure it is nothing like what Gray is used to, but I don't sense him checking it out and finding it lacking, so I relax a little.

"Tongue action was implicitly implied."

"Say that ten times really fast."

"Why, Cooper, are you trying to get me to show off how well my tongue works?"

"I think I can remember," I tell him, shaking my head. "I hope burgers and fries are okay. Honestly, it was a long day at the garage and I was too beat to worry about dinner."

"Burgers and fries are my favorite," he says, and though he's probably lying, I relax that much more.

"Thank you for the flowers and the wine. You didn't have to," I tell him, running tap water into a vase and then placing the flowers in it. I half-arrange them, smiling because I can't remember the last time a man brought me flowers... *If ever.*

"I did it with an ulterior motive," he says, and I jump because he's right behind me. He wraps his arms around my waist, pulling me back into him. His face slides against mine, the stubble on his face scratching softly against my neck.

"What would that be?" I ask, my voice breathless.

"You. I want you," he says, his lips following the pulse point in my neck.

"Gray..." I protest, but even I know it sounds weak.

"God, I've been thinking of nothing but you for days," he groans, his hands moving under my shirt, sliding slowly up my stomach, teasing my warm skin until he cups my breasts. I want to give in. All week I said I was going to, but now...

"Gray, I don't think we should do this," I tell him, forcing myself to pull away. Once his hands leave me, I feel strangely deprived. God, I'm a bigger mess than even I knew.

"What's going on, Cooper?"

"It's just... I don't think I'm ready to just jump into bed with you."

"It doesn't have to be a bed. The floor, the wall—hell, the kitchen counter works for me."

"That's not what I mean and you know it."

"I don't see the problem. We've already slept together. Did you forget?"

"No. That was different."

"I don't see how. Besides, you can't deny that we've been talking all week, and I think it was pretty clear from our conversations where this was headed. So why the sudden hot and cold, Cooper?"

His words make me feel like I'm on trial, which sucks. He wants full honesty? Fine.

"It was different before because there was nothing but one night of sex."

"Two," he corrects me.

"Whatever. The point was it was a space out of time where I let go of my better judgment and just took something I wanted."

"Me."

"Yes, you."

"So go ahead and take me now. I'm okay with being used, sweetheart."

"That's just it. I know you now. I know *way* too much about you now."

"Wait, let me get this straight. Before, you could fuck me because you didn't know me. Now, you can't because we know each other?"

"It's not that simple, Gray. I mean..."

"You realize you have this shit backwards, right? Most women insist on knowing a man before they spread their legs for him."

Heat rises in my face and I want to slap him for trying to make me feel embarrassed over making the decision to have a one-night stand. *Sanctimonious asshole.*

"That's the problem, Grayson Lucas. Entirely too many women have known you. I just don't want to be one of the long list of numbers."

His face goes hard and he looks at me so intently, I want to take a step back. "What the fuck was this week about if you were never planning on sleeping with me? Because I got to tell you, I'm a little old for the whole come-over-and-watch-movies-and-hold-hands phase."

"Were you ever in that phase?" I ask before I can stop myself.

"Answer the question, Cooper."

"I do want you. I just... I guess I just need time. You have a long history, Gray. I don't think I trust that I'm not just..."

"What if you are? How will you know? Or how will I, if we don't see what's between us? Jesus, Cooper, you overthink shit way too much."

"You have a sex tape on the internet, Gray," I remind him, my stomach curling in distaste.

"Again, it was before I met you, and I knew nothing about the making of it. My lawyers had it taken down."

"It's still there."

"You know the drill, Cooper. Once it's on the internet, it's always there. If you show me the site, I'll report it. It's all I can do."

"Gray..."

"CC," he starts, using my nickname. Strangely enough, I already miss him calling me Cooper. "I like you. I'm pretty sure you like me, but I'm not going to fight your fears every time we get together just to..."

"I'm not afraid," I lie, because I'm kind of terrified.

"Your doubts, then."

"What is this, Gray?" I ask him, needing it defined. I want to know what he's thinking, where he sees this going. I want to have no surprises.

"What do you mean?"

"I don't do great in relationships. I don't know how to..." How do I explain to him that I don't trust people? How do I tell him that I've never had a real relationship? He really would think I'm a freak if I told him exactly how much I feel out of my depth right now.

"Why do we have to label anything? One day at a time, Cooper," he says, his face going soft as he walks towards me. "Let's just see what happens."

"What are you doing?" I ask him unnecessarily when he comes up to me and cups the side of my face, pulling my lips to his.

"Kissing you and then, with any luck, kissing you some more."

"Until..."

"Until we're not kissing and we're doing so much more."

"Aren't you hungry? I have the food ready to fix, and..." I'm rattling on nervously, but he stops me with just a faint touch of our lips.

"I'm hungry, but not for food."

"Gray..."

"Are you with me?"

I look into his eyes, finding them so deep and intense. *Am I?* Why am I so nervous? I've withstood bigger storms in my life than Gray, right? If this all blows up, then it will be my shame alone and I'll just go on. If it doesn't, then could what started off as a one-night stand become something... more?

"I'm with you," I whisper, making my decision and throwing caution out the door. Banger would either kill me or be proud.

"Thank fuck," he groans, putting his hands under my ass and pulling me up his body. I wrap my legs around his waist and hold onto his shoulders.

"What are you doing?"

"Waiting for you to tell me which way is your bedroom, and if you don't hurry, then I'm going to fuck you against the wall because that's how much I need you right now."

"First door on your left down the hall," I tell him, grinning.

I guess food will have to wait.

Chapter Seventeen

GRAY

My patience is almost at an end and I don't want to scare her by acting like a Neanderthal, but there's no way I can stop it. I'm usually smooth with women, but CC is unlike any woman I've ever known. Hell, her effect on me is completely brand new. She lights a fire inside my blood and whenever she's near, I can feel it burning.

I devour her lips as we make it to the door of her room. I kick open her door and it slams against the inside wall, bounces back enough that I have to push against it again as we cross the threshold. The bed is just about five feet in front of me, but that's five feet too much. I turn and push her against the wall. For a second I gain my sanity enough to worry I've hurt her, but she's busy pulling my shirt up my body. I alternate bracing her body with one hand and letting the wall support her while I get the damn thing off, grinning as she throws the shirt to the floor.

"So much better," she breathes. "God, I love your body."

"It's all the swinging and driving balls into holes," I tell her.

She lightly runs her nails on the middle of my chest, playing with the fine line of hair I have there, then stops to look up at me. She's laughing, her eyes shining, her lips in a full smile that pull apart as the laughter bursts out.

"Maybe I'm starting to gain a new appreciation for golf."

"Hold tight baby and I'll make sure you do."

Her hands move up my body slowly and link behind my neck. "I'm holding," she whispers right before she brings her lips back to mine. I capture them, sucking on them, moaning at the burst of flavor that hits my tongue—strawberries from her lip gloss, and a sweetness in flavor that reminds me of sugar and candy. It's a taste I associate solely with CC now, a taste that has become my one addiction.

A taste I have to get more of.

Her tongue wraps around mine, mating with it and feeling so perfect that I groan. Never. Never has a woman got to me the way that CC continually does. That means something, I'm sure, but right now, I don't have the energy or the spare brain cells to think about it.

"We need you out of these damned clothes," I mutter when we break away and I finally drag air back into my lungs. She grins at me, her hands going to unbutton her pants.

"Let me down," she breathes. My fingers tighten into her ass, automatically fighting the command. I don't want her out of my arms. Where CC is concerned, I find I react very much like a caveman. "Gray," she whimpers, her hips thrusting against me. Need is heavy in her voice. "I want to feel my skin against yours" she says, and her words somehow seep through the fog in my brain. The same brain that is insisting I take her, but is too lust-filled to work out the logistics.

I gather her one last time against my body, angling and tilting her so that her pussy is aligned perfectly with my dick and then I grind into her. Even through our clothes, I know she can feel how hard and ready I am. I want her to know exactly what she's doing to me. Her hands have moved and I can feel her nails bite into my back as she struggles to remain tightly pressed against me—not wanting to let go—*just like me*. Finally, she takes control and pushes away from me and I'm forced to set her on the floor. My hands feel empty and I'm tempted to keep one hand on her as she undresses, except I need my own clothes out of the way. I immediately go to work unbuttoning my pants and shoving them down my body. I kick them somewhere, not really giving a fuck. I'm just thankful I had the foresight to take off my shoes when I first got here.

When I look back up, CC has already undressed except for her bra and panties: little pieces of dark blue silk that cling to her body and highlight her creamy white skin perfectly. I didn't take the time to admire her body the first time we were together. That night was a haze of lust and the buzz of alcohol. *This is different.* The lust is still here, but I'm stone cold sober and the truth is: I've never seen a more beautiful woman. Everything about her is perfect from the way her hips curve out into an hourglass figure to the perfect rise of her breasts. Her breasts move with every hard breath she takes and overfill her silky bra. Breasts that are perfect and mine to play with.

I drop to my knees in front of her without a second thought. I've had a lifetime of making women get on their knees to please me. This is just another thing that sets CC apart.

"Gray?" she whispers.

Her hands go to my shoulders. They feel small against the muscles there—*small but perfect.* My arms go around her, pulling her into me, and I kiss her stomach. Warm, soft skin brushes against my lips and I taste her delicate, sugary sweetness with a kick of something that hits my system and grabs hold of me like nothing before—and, I fear, nothing after. *Pure CC.*

"Shh..." I quiet her, letting my lips trail down the small area to the rim of her panties and breathe in the scent of her desire. Slowly, I push her panties down, revealing her pussy to me. I kiss down one hip and then the other. Greedy woman that CC is, her fingers curl into my hair and she does her best to pull me tight against her. I resist, but only because I plan on showing her who exactly is in charge. I push her underwear down, letting them pool at her ankles. "Step out of them, sweetheart," I encourage her, moving my hands along the backs of her legs. Once she does, I push my head between her legs. She widens her stance for me, but growls in frustration when I don't immediately give her what she wants. Instead, I find myself kissing along the side of her knee, tasting the skin there. The taste is much the same as her sweet lips with just a hint of salty flavor mixed in. I run my tongue along her thigh, moving closer to the center of her—the part where we both want my mouth. I know she feels the same because of the way she's trying to ride the side of my head, thrusting that sweet pussy towards me. She's hot and full of desire. I'm going to make sure I give her exactly what she wants... *except it'll be at my pace.*

I capture a small bite of her thigh between my lips, sucking on it. I make a mark there. I can tell by the small pop when I release suction, and I love the look of her darkened red skin almost as much as the hiss of breath she releases above me. I move my tongue over the skin, licking it, and rewarding it for taking my mark.

"Gray... son..."

CC uses my full name, stopping halfway to moan so it comes out broken in half and something about that grabs hold of me. It makes me feel powerful that I'm doing this to her. It's my touch, my lips, *me* who is making her let go of her control. Since I've been in Kentucky, one thing is clear to me CC rarely lets down her guard or gives up control, yet she does both of those things with me. *Both*.

I nibble up her thigh, pulling just enough to let her know I'm there and what I'm doing. It's not designed for anything other than teasing. My hands clench against the backs of her thighs as I bite a little harder, pulling the skin out this time before letting go completely and kissing away the sting.

"Gray, please," she whispers.

Her voice is hoarse and threaded with passion. I growl, giving in to the pleading in her voice and my own desire to taste her.

I shift so that I'm facing her. I look up and those green eyes are liquid pools, shining so bright they might be the most beautiful thing I've ever seen. I keep my eyes locked on her even as I bring my hands up her legs and use each thumb to pull apart the lips of her juicy little cunt. The liquid proof of her hunger has the swollen lips of her pussy coated slick and wet. I flatten my tongue to lick it up, all the while watching her. Her taste literally explodes in my mouth. I'd forgotten it. It's haunted me, and yet there's no way I could have recalled just how good it is. It's sweet, tangy, earthy... *CC.*

The small taste does nothing but spur me on. I slide my tongue inside, still holding it flat and licking from the bottom all the way to the swollen nub that pulsates at the top. CC's head goes back and she moans. Her legs quake, but smart woman that she is, she uses the wall to hold herself up. I lash my tongue against her clit, feeling more of her juices drip onto my tongue, and I greedily suck it all in. CC is moaning now, looking down and trying to watch everything I'm doing. Her own hands go to her breasts as she teases her nipples, helping to build her own pleasure. If there's one thing about CC that I love the most, it's the fact that she's not shy. She takes what she wants and she doesn't back away from showing me what she enjoys. But then, I know what she likes.

With that thought in mind, I push her slightly so she knows to put more weight on the wall. I brace my hand on one of her thighs, then lift her other leg and hike it over my shoulder. That move brings her pussy impossibly close. Her cream, her scent... it's smothering me as she's basically sitting on my face now. She's so hungry for more, she's thrusting down on my face, crying out because the way I have her now has opened her up and left her vulnerable to my every lick, *my every touch.*

"Shit..." she whispers above me. I smile, pushing up on her body and moving my face down. I stiffen my tongue so I can push it inside of her, licking the walls I'm going to be thrusting into and widening with my cock. My dick is hard enough to pound nails. I can't remember being so ready to explode. I can feel pre-cum slithering down the side of my shaft and balls. I need to finish her off like this and get inside of her before this is over.

I reluctantly take my tongue out of her sweet little hole, I'm enjoying toying with. CC whines in dislike too, and that makes me smile. To reward her, I take two of my fingers and run them through her juices, not stopping until I can manipulate her clit with them.

"You like that, sweetheart?" I ask her, letting my warm breath tease her pussy even more.

"God, yes... You have a magic tongue, Gray."

"Is that so?" I ask her, grinning as I use my fingers to push against her clit. It immediately plumps up against my fingers, pulsing hard. She's close to coming.

"Oh, hell. Do that again," she demands, trying to grind down even harder on my face. I pinch her clit this time, pulling on it just to add to the sensations. CC's hands pull my hair so tight, if I don't get her off soon, I may have a few bald spots. Time to stop messing around. I let my fingers glide back down her pussy, coming together just as I reach her entrance. I dance them around the opening, watching as her breath comes in ragged bursts.

"I'm going to make you come, CC. And then when I'm done, I'm going to fuck you so hard you won't be able to walk," I warn her. I think she might be beyond talking rationally because she's thrusting down on me, her body trembling.

"Gray, please," she pleads. The words are weak and hunger for more pulsates in every syllable. What man could resist?

I thrust two fingers inside of her, going as deep as I can go. At the same time, my tongue goes back to licking on her clit. CC cries out above me, her sweet cream bathing my face as she pushes down on me, and rides. I give her what she wants, letting her control the way her clit moves against my tongue. Her thighs tighten up against my face. She rides me hard and fast trying to get her orgasm. I thrust my fingers in and out of her, pulling them apart and stretching her walls as she sucks them deeper into her depths. *Heaven.* So wet and hot... *tight.* I can barely keep my wits about me as I think of getting my dick inside of her. I pull her harder against me, eating that sweet cunt as much as I can. Just as I angle my fingers to scrape against her walls, I suck her clit in my mouth and hold it while thrusting into her over and over—pounding her pussy with my hand. It doesn't take a minute before she's crying out her release and coming all over my fingers and face, her entire body shaking. I keep up my actions until she's ridden the orgasm as far as she can and she's brokenly saying my name over and over. *My name*. I feel a sense of pride in that. Finally, I kiss against her clit and the inside of her thighs, while slowing my strokes with my hand to a very leisurely pace. This allows her to come back down to earth, but not completely settle.

"Damn," she says. "I thought our weekend would be hard to top, but..."

I pull away to look at her. Her eyes are glazed, but she's looking down at me and smiling.

I bring my hand down, hating the fact that I'm leaving her body, even knowing I'll soon be sunk inside of it. I stroke my cock a few times. My hand and fingers are covered in CC's cum. I allow the liquid to slide over my cock, painting it in the woman I'm going to fuck into oblivion soon. I squeeze the head tight, trying to beat back my own fucking climax. That's not going to happen until I at least get back inside of her for a few minutes.

"Ready for round two?" she asks, even though she's still breathless.

Did I mention she's perfect?

"More than ready. Time for you to move that cute ass of yours to the bed."

"I thought you wanted to take me against the wall?" She grins, moving away from me and all but hopping backwards on the bed. Her hands go behind her and she wraps each one around one of the wood bed posts on the headboard. She slowly spreads her legs, daring me to come aboard.

"I will. Right now, I plan on sinking balls-deep inside of you."

She lets go with one of her hands to reach across to her nightstand drawer. She blindly feels around and then comes out with two condoms, tossing them at me.

"Safety first?" I grin, grabbing one and tearing it open with my teeth.

"I'm a safety girl," she agrees, her eyes following me as I slide the latex over my dick.

"I like that about you," I tell her, positioning my cock at her entrance.

"You do?" she asks, bringing her eyes back to me.

"It's one of the many things I like about you, Cooper," I tell her, and before she can give me some smartass reply, I push inside of her, bracing myself over her body and not stopping until I'm balls-deep and my cock is pushed in so fucking far she's completely filled.

"Fuck," she huffs as a giant breath leaves her body.

"You okay?" I ask, needing to make sure before I continue.

"Just being reminded how those internet sites weren't exaggerating when they were talking about your nine iron."

I've always hated that garbage, even if I did enjoy the ladies who helped give me the reputation as the golf stud packing nine inches of steel.

"Nine? I must demand a reprint. It's more like twelve," I joke, starting to move inside of her.

"Now who's embellishing?"

"You think so?"

"I was guessing around ten," she says, starting to adjust to the rhythm I'm setting.

"Silly woman. I will make it my mission to prove you wrong," I groan.

After that, neither of us can talk because she's squeezing my cock inside of her and my balls are so tight, I know my orgasm is close and there's no fucking way I'm going to come unless she does again. So I set my mind to that. Right now, that's all that matters.

Later, I'll think about how it's possible that CC manages to give me the best sex I've ever had and still make me laugh at the same time. *Much later.*

Chapter Eighteen

CC

"Tell me again why we have to get up from here?" I whine, curling under the covers. It's been two days... two glorious days since I let Gray back in my bed. Two days in which we've been boinking like rabbits. My body is sore in the most delicious places. I'm fast becoming addicted to having him around, which is probably bad. It's also why I'm whining about not wanting to get out of bed.

"Because you are having lunch with your friend today and I have that meeting with Riverton."

"That name isn't allowed in my bed," I grumble, running my hand from the top of his chest down his stomach, loving the heated skin and soft masculine feel of him. *All man*. That's who Grayson Lucas is, and what a man. I feel every feminine thing in me stretch and purr just looking at that smile on his beautiful face.

"Will you tell me the history between you and... the ones who shall not be named?" He grins. I want to keep the happy in the room, but I swear, one thought of Cammie and her father nearly sucks it all out. It's not Gray's fault. He has no idea the can of worms that are the Rivertons. *I wish I didn't.*

"That's a long, horrid story, one that would ruin my good after-sex mood."

"Humor me," he says, pulling me into his warm body. I drape

my leg over him, his heated body feels as if it's branding my leg. His fingers sift through my curls, and my eyes close. *This*. Just like this, being here with Gray, is as close as I've ever come to perfect. I don't want to move. I don't want to talk. All I want is to lie here and soak up this feeling and hold it close so that I can remember it years from now.

"Believe it or not, there was once a time when Cammie and I were good friends."

"Yeah, I'm not buying that. You two are way too different."

"Well, it was the second grade," I correct, and he laughs.

"Now that makes sense."

"Yeah we were friends up until the fifth grade."

"What happened in the fifth grade?" Gray asks, sounding distracted.

I look up and can see him from my peripheral vision playing with my hair, combing through it and then bending down. A second later, I feel a light kiss on the top of my head. I close my eyes and savor that feeling. I'm going to be honest. Banger was an amazing man, but he wasn't very demonstrative. I can't remember getting kisses or hugs growing up. Heaven knows my mother wasn't one to do that. Banger... well, I always knew he loved me. That was never a question, but he wasn't really the hugging or kissing type. The closest he came was hugging me and slapping me on the back when I rebuilt my first engine. It purred like a kitten when he tried it out. He half hugged me and half gave me an approving slap and told me he was proud of me. I felt like I hung the moon. So, Gray doing this now feels... strange and good. Very good. *Too good.*

"You with me?" he prompts me when I get lost in my thoughts.

"Cammie's mother learned of our friendship."

"And?"

"And that was it. Her daughter couldn't fraternize with someone below their standing in the neighborhood."

"What a bitch. I'm suddenly glad that's one Riverton I haven't met."

"Yeah, Cammie's parents divorced a while back. Davina moved to Paris with some shipping tycoon. She didn't want Cammie."

"Shit, that's rough."

"Yeah. Some mothers shouldn't have kids," I agree, but I'm thinking completely about my own mother.

"I'm sorry," he says, and I shrug off his concern, feeling my face heat. I don't want anyone to feel sorry for me. I especially don't want them to know how much my mother's actions hurt me.

"Anyway, once Cammie realized she shouldn't be seen with someone who was beneath her, that pretty much ended our friendship."

"That's it? I could have sworn there was more animosity than that between the two of you."

"Well, add in high school, us liking some of the same boys, years of resentment and a few other spices, and you have a recipe for disaster."

"Women are just too fucking complicated."

"This is why I prefer to hang around men."

"Well, that's one thing I can be glad of," he says, flipping me over until he has me pinned on the mattress and he's leaning over me. "Being a man, I can tell you, Cooper, that I'm glad you prefer hanging around me too," he whispers, bending down and placing a small kiss on my chin and then slowly moving along the main bone in my jawline. He's cupping my face with his hands, his thumb brushing against my skin, and he's holding me so gently I could get lost in the feelings he awakens inside of me.

"Well, I aim to please."

"Show me," he says, sucking gently on my neck and nibbling there. I'm trying to concentrate on what he's saying, but the desire he's stoking inside of me makes it impossible.

"Show you what?" I gasp just as his hand moves between my legs.

"How much do you want to please me?"

"We'll be late," I tell him, but not really giving a damn. I'm sure he can tell that by the way I spread my legs to allow him easier access.

"I don't really give a fuck," he says as his fingers slide into my pussy.

"In that case," I gasp as he thrusts his fingers hard and deep inside my walls.

"Yeah?"

"Fuck me, Gray. Oh god, fuck me and don't stop."

"I got you," he whispers against my lips, driving his fingers in again just as his tongue thrusts into my mouth. "I got you," he says again, when we break apart for a moment. *He does too*. He has me. I'm addicted to this man. It's never happened before, but it's too late to stop it now. I let myself get lost in the sensations he's creating in my body and try to ignore the fear—at least for now.

Chapter Nineteen

CC

"You're late," Miranda grumbles as I walk through the diner to the back booth—the same booth Miranda claims every freaking time we eat here. She demands we sit at the back of the room, and she always faces the doors. She's got more than a few issues. She's also the one friend besides Jackson that I allow in my life, so I put up with her quirks. God knows I have more than enough of my own.

"I had sex," I tell her, smiling sweetly and grabbing a menu. "Have you already ordered? I'm starving."

"Wait... you had sex? You're smiling and you're starving? Who are you and what have you done with my best friend? You know the one. The one who is always grouchy, says men aren't worth the trouble, and who eats like a horse but usually not until the afternoon so she can wake up?"

"Hmmm... Yes, I had sex, and it was awesome sex, so of course I'm smiling. It's almost noon, so I'm awake enough and I'm starving because having sex on the regular is exhausting. I need food to keep up my stamina."

"I've entered some kind of alternate universe, haven't I? That's the only explanation. Oh, and I think I hate you in this universe, too."

"Why's that?"

"Because the beauty of our relationship is that we both bitch and quarrel about men and go long periods without sex. We whine about how lacking our vibrators are and eat chocolate. It's our thing."

"What can I get you girls?" the waitress asks, interrupting us. Miranda orders tuna salad and an iced tea. Usually I would order the same, but today I really am hungry.

"I'll have the turkey club, no mayo, and an order of fries, and a tea to drink too, please?"

The waitress leaves, and I catch Miranda staring at me with her mouth open. My best friend since sixth grade, Miranda Kerr is everything I'm not. She's tiny, small-breasted, and so pretty it hurts. She's got dark black hair and shining blue eyes that look almost lavender in color. She wears glasses in the newest, trendiest frames and has plump to-die-for lips smothered in dark red lipstick. We don't match at all—the grease monkey tomboy and the book nerd, girly-girl—but somehow we click on every front. I trust her with my life. She's as loyal as they come.

"I think I could hate you," she huffs.

"You can't. You love me. Besides, you have Kurt, right?"

"Wrong. I kicked him to the curb."

"What? Why? I thought you two were getting along great?"

"I thought we were, too, and then I discovered he was getting along just as well with a girl in Harvest Corners," she says, naming a small town two counties over.

"That asshole."

"Amen to that."

"Why didn't you call me?"

"You were gone to Lexington for the weekend. I didn't want to bother you, and I've been so busy with training that I hadn't been able to check in with you until now. Though, it sounds like I should have. So tell me all about your new boy toy! And leave nothing out."

"There's not a lot to tell. I met him in Lexington, and we—"

"You're kidding me? You are on friendship probation! You should have told me that you met someone!"

"Well, at the time I didn't think it'd be anything past the weekend..."

"The weekend?"

I feel the blush hit my face before I can stop it, and I shrug. "Yeah, well..."

"How have we lost touch this much?"

"You've been busy, Mir. I have, too. It happens."

"Yeah, well, we need to put the kibosh on that right now."

"Hey, it's not completely my fault. Kurt didn't exactly give you spare time to—"

"You're right. Let's not talk about that douchebag anymore. That's over and done. *D. O. N. E.*"

"Douche canoe is more like it."

"Girl, you ain't lying."

"So tell me more about Mr. Curl-My-Toes-For-The-Weekend and how it's still going on! Was it that good?"

"Umm, it was better than good."

"Better? You're saying on a scale of one to ten, he's a...?"

"Off the charts."

"*Holy fluck*," she whispers the fake curse word in awe.

"I know," I agree, and in my whole life, it's probably as close as I've come to sounding like a giddy teen discussing prom.

"You told him where you lived?" she asks, and again I feel the telltale heat spread on my face. What is up with that? I'm not a blusher! Then again, I'm not the kind of woman who discusses boys at a crowded diner either.

"Well, no. That was by accident?"

"Accident? He's not a stalker, is he? Did he follow you and find you? Oh my God, C! You have to be careful. This is the kind of shit they make TV movies about!"

"He didn't follow me home. At least, not on purpose. His car broke down while he was in town for business. He had no idea that I was here."

"I don't know, C. That sounds kind of fishy to me."

"Well, it's not. He had no idea it was me. In fact, he was kind of a jerk until he figured it out."

"A jerk?"

"He's kind of..." I sigh. I don't really want to talk about this part even though I know that I need to, at least with Mir. Besides, if there's one thing that worries me the most about Gray—other than the fact that he's not going to be around for a very long time—it's that he has money. He has lots of money. He deals with people who have money. He deals with people I can't stand. He deals with people who would rather see me dead than draw another breath.

Okay. So there's lots of things that worry me about Gray. They all stem around his money, though.

"Earth to C! Hello, can you hear me?" Mir asks, waving her hand in my face like an idiot.

"Stop that." I knock her hand out of the way. "He has money, Mir."

"So? That's good, honey. Geez, you had me thinking that he had herpes or something."

"You don't get it. He's here on business."

"C, I hate to break it to you, but not everyone in the world holds down a job that keeps them in one place. This is good. That means he can come visit you when he's on the road, and..."

"He's here on business to meet with David Riverton."

"Flucking hell."

"Yeah."

"Does he know what a butt-munch the man is?"

"Probably not, but then again, Gray has money. I imagine good old Dave is much nicer to him than he has ever been to me."

"That wouldn't be hard to do. I'm sorry, C."

"It can't be helped."

"I'm proud of you."

"For what?"

"Well, this guy works with Riverton, and yet you're not kicking him to the curb. You get major props, lady. He's either special to you or he's got one hell of a..."

Even before she finishes the sentence, I know what she's going to say. I squirm in my chair because I might have sounded giddy, but I don't do this female sharing thing easily—even with Mir.

"Oh. My. God," she says. I'm looking down at my shoes, and even though I know I'm in trouble, I'm still surprised when she continues. "Claudia Cooper! You got a hold of the holy grail."

I look up, side-eyeing everyone around us to see if they are paying attention to Mir. Thankfully, they don't seem to be. "Mir!" I grumble.

"You did, didn't you? You hooker!"

"What are you talking about?" I ask, almost afraid of what she'll say next.

"The three-peater."

"The what?" I ask, having no idea what she's talking about. Though he usually does give me three orgasms before he's done—that I'm not going to discuss with her at the diner.

"Here ya' go, ladies," the waitress says, thankfully interrupting our conversation. We spend the next few minutes arranging our food, and just when I think we've finished this whole conversation, Mir starts back up.

"A three-peater. That means he has brains," she says, holding a finger up. I nod because Gray is extremely smart and witty, it's one of the things I really like about him. "He has money, or at least a steady job so you don't have to keep his ass up," she continues, holding a second finger up. I don't respond because I figure she knows that. "And finally, he has at least seven inches when you take a ride on the man train."

"You did not just say that," I gasp, knowing I'm blushing from head to toe now. I look all around us, just knowing everyone has heard what she said.

"I did, and from your reaction, I can tell the answer is affirmative. So how much are we talking here?"

"Will you stop? Honestly, Miranda, I am not answering that at all. No way."

"So more than seven?"

"Oh my God! Who are you and what have you done with my quiet, kindergarten school teaching friend?"

"Answer the question and I'll let it drop."

"I will not."

"Fine, I'll just ask him when I see you two out together."

"You would not!"

"Try me. Now are you going to give the deets or what?"

"I have no idea!"

"Bullshit!"

"It's true! I haven't exactly taken the time to measure it."

"Measure what?"

I look up at the question to see Mir's sister Valerie standing at our table. Christ! That's all I need. Crosstown has three methods of communication: telephone, telegraph, and tell Valerie. Seriously, when you need something spread around town, all you have to do is let Valerie know and it's all over this town and two counties over by nightfall.

"C has gotten ahold of the mythical bigfoot."

"Jesus," I mutter.

"Mythical bigfoot?"

"Her new boy toy is big."

"Ohhhh... Do tell! Give me all the juicy details, and I do mean juicy," Valerie says, pushing Mir over and sitting down with us.

"There are no details! I keep telling Mir! I haven't measured it! I have no idea."

It's a bold faced lie. I mean, I haven't measured his dick. I did read the tabloids though and the general consensus from all the women in his harem is that Gray, golf's new young stud, is packing a very thick nine iron between his legs. I think they might be doing him a disservice. After experiencing him inside of me, it definitely has to be more than that.

"You flucking hooker! You're holding back from us," Mir says. Jesus! I hate that she knows me so well.

"Shit. If I tell you, will this conversation please drop?"

"Totally," Mir says.

"Absolutely," Valerie joins in, and for some strange reason, I don't trust either of them.

"I mean it, and Val, if this gets out, I will tell Elmer at Pro-Hardware you have a thing for him," I warn her. Elmer is a fifty-year-old, never-been-married-before bachelor who goes cruising parking lots looking for women. Not just any women, however. No, Elmer wants women that are at least twenty years younger than him. Never mind that he's got a beer belly, thinning hair that he combs over, and none of his own teeth. No, the real problem is that the man is as stingy as they come. He probably has more money in his checking account than even Grayson. But the reason it's there is because he is a skin-flint. According to a very good source (Valerie), the man has only used one pack of light bulbs in two years. The reason for that is, he gets out one light bulb and uses it in whatever room he's in. When he leaves that room, he unscrews it from the lamp and moves it into the next room with him. Rumor has it—again from Valerie—he also takes the time to separate every roll of two-ply toilet paper so he gets twice the use out of it.

"That's just mean, C."

"Promise."

"Fine, I promise. I don't see what the problem is. If I had a man with a big dick, I'd be shouting that shit near and far. Hell, I'd be so loud in the bedroom that the whole county would know it anyway," Valerie says, and I flip her off.

"Spill," they say together, and I take a breath. Did I mention this oversharing and girl-time isn't easy for me? Yet another reason why other than Miranda and, obviously sometimes by default, Valerie, I don't have girlfriends. You wouldn't catch Jackson asking me about the size of Gray's dick.

"I honestly haven't measured it. Though the tabloids say he is nine inches."

"Sweet mother of... Wait. Hold the *flucking* presses and call Maury to find the baby daddy. Did you say tabloids?"

"Yeah."

"C, you said he had money, but you didn't say he was famous. Just who the hell are you dating?"

"Damn it! If you're dating my man, I'm going to hate you for life!"

"Trust me when I tell you, Valerie, that I'm not dating the lead singer from that band."

"His name is Adam and he's mine. His wife is the only thing in my way, but that won't last much longer. She doesn't understand him like I do."

My eyes go over to Mir, who's pointing a finger at her head and spinning it in a circle to indicate that her sister's whack-a-do. That's a sentiment I wholeheartedly agree with.

"It's Grayson Lucas," I tell them, and they look at each other in question. It's good to know I'm not the only one who doesn't follow golf. "He plays golf," I add.

Valerie is the first one to look him up on her phone. *"Oh. My. God,"* she whispers to her screen.

"Sweet Jesus," Mir adds, yanking her phone over to look at it.

"Does he have a brother?" they both say together and I laugh—a real laugh, because just like that, I'm good. I feel really good. They aren't saying Gray is out of my league. They aren't telling me I'm crazy for seeing him. Just the opposite, and so I laugh and then proceed to tell them about his colorful (pun intended) family.

This might just work out after all.

Chapter Twenty

GRAY

"What do you mean we're taking the boat out?" I grumble, trying to keep my game face on, but really just wanting to get the hell out of here. I feel like I'm in level three of hell. Three levels, because there are three major things fucking with my plans for the day. One, I'm on Riverton's sea cruiser, which is most definitely not a sailboat. Secondly, Cammie has been flirting and pawing at me for the last hour, and finally, Riverton is M.I.A. "Your father's not even here yet."

"I told you, daddy said he may be held up at the office and for us not to wait for him," she says almost giddily. Hell, I'm a man, and I'm the first to admit men are usually clueless, but even I can see the calculation in Cammie's eyes.

"Honestly, Cammie, I have plans for this evening. We can just reschedule this and do it some other time."

"What? *Why?*" she whines, her face scrunched up and sounding like a small child. "I'm here and, Gray, I am the CEO for daddy's marketing. It's really me you should talk to about this anyway."

"You are? Then why has your father been..."

"Daddy was just being generous with his time, Gray. He likes you, but I'm the one who usually makes all of the decisions about corporate sponsoring. I had the cook prepare us a nice lunch. How about we take the boat out? There's a nice island in the middle of the lake. We can drop anchor close to it and enjoy lunch and talk business?"

Warning bells are going off in my head. Cammie's got me in her sights and that is reason enough for me to turn her down. On the other hand, it appears I'm never going to get to talk to Riverton one-on-one about any of this. If Cammie is really the one in charge here, it would be smart to deal with her, get it over with, and put this entire trip behind me.

"I have dinner plans tonight I can't be late for," I warn her. I promised CC I'd take her out to make up for the other night and I have every intention on keeping that promise.

"I can always call the club and..."

"It's not the club. I have dinner plans with CC tonight."

"CC?" she asks, sounding confused. "Are you dating Claudia?" The tone of her voice gets on my nerves as well as the scandalized look on her face.

"We've gone out a few times, yes. Is there a problem?"

"Well, no. I mean, who you see is your business, I guess. I just thought that you and I had a connection."

"Listen, Cammie. You're a very nice person," I lie through my teeth, "and I have the upmost respect for you, but I'm afraid I have one rule when it comes to business. I don't date people I work with—*ever*."

"But..."

"I just find it bad practice to mix business and pleasure," I tell her, cutting her off. "I'm sure you understand."

"Well, not really. I mean, we're both adults, we have similar interests and..."

"It's just a personal rule," I tell her again, stopping her before she can keep going. I need to shut this down and get it under control. She studies me for a minute, then something passes over her face and I feel another warning bell go off, but a second later the look is gone and I have to wonder if I imagined it.

"Fine, then. We'll be business partners," she says, holding out her hand. I take it and I can't help but feel that this seems way too easy.

"Business partners," I agree.

"And friends. We can be friends, right? One can't have too many of those."

"I completely agree," I tell her with a smile, starting to feel very relieved that all of this is out in the open. It's the best thing really, to be upfront with each other.

"Great. Now that we have that out of the way, why don't we skip taking the boat out and instead have a business luncheon at the club. We can discuss what our sponsorship exactly entails?"

"Entails? You would sponsor me for the golf tournaments I make. Your name would go on my gear..."

"It's much more involved than that, surely you understand," Cammie says, then links her arm into mine as we begin walking towards the docks.

"I mean, I know there's more business to be decided and, of course, a contract, but..."

"It's not just that, Grayson. If Riverton Metals is going to sponsor you, then you are in essence going to be the face of our company."

"Of course."

"That means social engagements..."

"What type of social engagements? I mean, I do have the tour, and..."

"Dinners, parties, autograph sessions while out on tour. And there will be..."

"I'm a golfer, Cammie. Not a rock star."

"In some circles, I'm sure you can agree that is the same thing," she says, and before I know what's happening, she's led us to her father's limo. Who has a limo just waiting in the parking lot for whenever you need them? *Cammie and David Riverton, I suppose.* The driver comes around and opens the door and Cammie slides in. "Are you coming, Grayson?" she asks, waiting.

I stare at her for a minute. I have this horrible feeling I'm selling my soul to the devil. I hear Seth's voice in my head demanding I go through with this meeting. I take a deep breath and agree before I can talk myself out of it.

As I'm closed in the car with Cammie, I just know I'm going to live to regret this.

Chapter Twenty-One

CC

"I can't believe you're asking me to do this, Gray," I growl, feeling completely out of my depth.

"It's one business dinner. It won't be that bad," he says, kissing the back of my neck.

"It's one business dinner at that damn country club with Camilla, her father and a bunch of other..."

"Sweet lips, I told you. Cammie said she'd be on her best behavior. I talked with her about you. It's going to be fine. I promise."

"That's just it. I don't want you to talk with her about me. I can fight my own battles, Grayson Lucas. I've been doing it way before you came in the picture."

"Point made. I just really want you with me tonight. Is that so hard to understand?" he asks, pulling away to button his cufflinks. *His cufflinks*. How did I get here? This is not who I am. My eyes travel down his body and then I remember why: *sex*. Heart-stopping, take-your-breath-away sex. I thought it might cool off after a few days. It's been two weeks, and if anything, it just keeps getting better. I don't know how that's possible or how to explain it. The simple truth is that I'm addicted to Grayson Lucas—so much so that he's practically living here. He still keeps his room, but he's definitely here ninety percent of the time. I might have even given him a key the other day when he said he was going to cook dinner for me and have it waiting when I got home from the garage—a dinner that happened to be amazing, and the fact that dessert was him eating me after...that just made it even better. He still has the key. I don't know a woman alive who would judge me. There are some things a woman can't resist and Gray does indeed have a magic tongue. That said, I'm not sure even a magic tongue is enough to make me go through with this damn dinner.

"I have another question. How did you know what size to buy this damn dress?" I ask him through the mirror. It's a red dress that's all silk and hugs my body like a glove. It shows way too much of my breasts, though at least the valley it exposes is covered by a small scrap of lace that stretches across the front. The dress ends just above the knee and it's so tight that walking normal, (*and not like a damn duck*) isn't exactly easy. Then comes the heels. I am not a small woman in any sense, but I'm a firm believer that a woman who stands five-foot-ten shouldn't wear four-inch heels. Okay, well, let me amend that: *I* shouldn't wear four-inch heels. I'm not graceful like most women. Instead, I feel like freaking Godzilla standing over everyone else and teetering on the edge of a cliff because my balance sucks. The only saving grace is that Gray is so tall that he's still taller than me, even in these damn shoes. I turn around to look at him and my stomach is so queasy, I feel like there's a war going on inside of it.

"Sweetheart, a man knows the measurements of a body he worships. It was easy."

"I don't think we should talk about how easy it is for you to figure out a woman's measurements," I tell him, more than slightly annoyed and ignoring his sweet talk.

"Fair enough."

"Besides that, where did you find a place that sold dresses like this around here?"

Gray breaks eye contact and looks down at his tie and then turns away heading to where his shoes are. "It wasn't that hard," he says, and his voice sounds... different. I see those red flags—the ones I seem to see a lot when Gray is around.

"Gray?"

"It's a little shop in Addington," he says and shrugs. "What does it matter? It worked and you look gorgeous. You're going to be the most beautiful woman there. That's what is important."

"I guess so," I tell him, still not convinced. I can't help feeling like Gray's keeping something from me.

"Are you ready, sweet lips?" Grayson asks once he has his shoes on. He looks amazing, and as much as I don't want to go to this damn dinner, I do want to be around Gray. Besides, as much as I might want to deny it, Gray and I are dating. Hell, we're practically living together. There's a perverse side of me that wants to see what life with a pro-golfer is truly like. I realize I'm looking for reasons to push him away even as I want to keep him close. There's a need inside of me to prove that we're just too different to ever make this work. Jackson is right when he tells me I'm a complicated woman. I sigh and take a deep breath for courage.

"As ready as I'll ever be."

"That's my woman," he says, and he has no way of knowing how his words set off butterflies in my system and how they warm me. I want to be his woman, even though I'm trying to find reasons to keep him away. *See?* Complicated.

He wraps his arms around me and hugs me close. He kisses the side of my neck and I can feel his tongue coming out to lick along my pulse point.

"Thank you for doing this for me, Cooper. I know you'd rather be shot at than go to this thing. It means a lot," he whispers, and a little more of resistance fades. This is why I agreed to go to the damn dinner. *Gray's sweetness.*

"Let's just get it over with," I sigh grudgingly.

He laughs and leads me to the door. "It won't be that bad, sweet lips. It'll be over before you know it. We'll make an appearance and leave as early as we can get away with," he says, closing the door behind us. The sound of it echoes and feels as if it is signaling my doom.

"It will be that bad. I'll have to be in the same room with Cammie Riverton and her father."

"Cammie promised she'd be on her best behavior. She knows you're important to me. It will be okay, you'll see."

"You told her I'm important to you?"

"Of course," he says, acting like those words don't mean anything... like they didn't just shake up my whole world. I sit in the car as he closes my door and I can only think one thing: *I'm important to Gray Lucas.*

Chapter Twenty-Two

GRAY

"Why are all the women wearing white?" CC growls when we reach the large conference room where the dinner is being held. I get a bad feeling in my stomach as I look around. All the men are in black suits just like me, but that's not the problem. Like CC said, all of the women are wearing white. The only one not is CC who is wearing the polar opposite: *red*. Fuck. She freezes in her tracks, which is okay because I've come to a stop too trying to figure out exactly what is going on. "Gray!" CC hisses and I wince. This could get ugly. I need to try and pave things over as best I can.

"Umm, I'm not real sure," I tell her. Wow, that was really smooth.

"You're not sure?" she asks, outraged. I'm not sure how a woman can whisper and screech at the same time, but CC has that ability down.

"Well, no. I mean, I wasn't told there was a theme or anything..."

"I'm leaving! I knew it was a mistake to let you talk me into this," she growls, turning away.

"Listen, we're already here, so why don't we just make an appearance and then we can leave? It seems silly to not at least—"

"*Silly?* Did you see anyone else wearing red, Gray?"

"Umm, well..."

"The servers!"

"Well, technically they're wearing black and red," I say and then wince. I know what she's saying. You'd have to be stupid not to. Why did I have to pick out red for CC to wear?

"Why am I wearing red? Did you do this to me on purpose, Gray?" CC asks, echoing my thoughts—well, *some* of them. I turn to look at her, shocked that she would even have that thought in her head.

"Of course not! I like you in red. It reminded me of your hair—which I love. I almost went with the green, but..."

"But why?" CC asks, and I can tell from her face that she's not going to forgive me anytime soon.

"Well, the saleslady said that the green dress was last year's, and when I told her it was a special night out... I'm sorry Cooper, I fucked up," I tell her, truly feeling bad. "Come on. We'll go and I'll just call Riverton and explain that something came up."

She looks up at me, her face heated almost to the red of her dress, but at least she doesn't look like she wants to kill me now. That's an improvement. I cup the side of her face, wanting her to believe me.

"Gray, I—"

"Grayson! What are you doing standing over here in the corner like you're hiding?" Cammie's high-pitched voice calls out from behind us. I see CC eyes close and a look of disappointment—or something, I'm at too much of a loss to describe right now—comes over her face. I feel like lead settles in my gut because this feels like my fault.

I turn around, intent on hiding CC behind me. I let my body completely block her.

"Cammie, I'm sorry, I'm afraid that something came up and—"

"It's my fault. My dress snagged on a piece of trim that was loose by the door," CC says, moving to stand beside me. I immediately wrap my arm around her, anchoring her to me. I steal a glance at her. She looks calm, cool, and collected—not like she's just been sucker punched by her stupid boyfriend.

Boyfriend? Is that what I am?

"Claude, my how... colorful you are tonight."

"Thank you. I'm afraid Gray and I missed the memo about the dress code...?"

"What? Oh, the color! Yes, it's our annual black and white ball."

"You didn't tell me that when you invited me," I tell her, wondering if this had been her plan all along. Women are spiteful creatures. Is this all because I've shot Cammie's advances down?

"I didn't? I'm sure I did. Perhaps you didn't hear me? You know how men are Claude, you mention a formal dance they tune us out."

"I know exactly what happened," CC says, and though she's smiling, I can see the anger in her eyes. I really need to get her away from Cammie before this whole thing blows up.

"Oh well. It doesn't really matter. You look lovely and you fit in just fine, Claude. It's good you got here when you did, Grayson."

"It is?" I ask, just anxious to put some distance between CC and Cammie.

"Yes! Father was asking where you were. He and Adams would like to see what a big time golf pro thinks of our greens," she explains, wrapping her hand in mine and all but pushing CC out of the way. I look around her to try and see CC, but Cammie starts talking again. "You don't care if I borrow your man for a little bit, do you, CC?"

"Actually, Cammie, if you don't mind, I'd like to—" I start to argue pulling away from her.

"No, not at all," CC says so sweetly, and it surprises me so much that I stop. She doesn't?

"You don't?" I ask before I can stop myself.

"Of course not. It's all business. Right, Cammie?"

"Of course. Grayson, Claude runs her own company—such as it is. I'm sure she knows how this is done. She realizes she'd just be in your way."

"She wouldn't—" I start again.

"I'll be here waiting when you get back, Gray," CC says, and she looks perfectly happy. I can't tell if I'm falling into a trap or if she's sincere. I'm still trying to figure it out when Cammie pulls me into the other room.

"Grayson! I was just wondering where you were," Riverton says as we reach his side.

"I'm running a little late," I tell him, looking over my shoulder to see if I can get a look at CC. I can't find her anywhere. *Did she leave?* Shit. I have to get out of here...

"It's fine. Adams and I were just wondering how you like our greens. How about we take you for a quick tour?"

"Well, sir," I start, but he cuts me off.

"Adams here is interested in working with you to create a line of clubs."

"Clubs?"

"Exactly that, Lucas. And I'd like you to be the face of them."

"Well, sir, I don't know if I'd want my ugly mug on anything," I joke, still trying to look around behind me for CC. I catch a glimpse of her smiling in the corner and talking to someone, which allows me to breathe a little easier. Maybe I'm overreacting after all.

Chapter Twenty-Three

CC

"You're the last person I ever expected to see here, CC!"

I look up at Jason and can't help but smile. He doesn't mean anything by it; he knows me and he knows everything that's gone down between me, Cammie, and her father. He's a hundred percent right. This is the last place I would choose to be. I've known Jason my whole life. His parents have money, and he does by default, I guess, but he doesn't lord it over people. He's as nice and easygoing as they come. In fact, I'm kind of surprised he's here himself.

"No offense, but I didn't really think I'd find you here either."

"Yeah, it's not my favorite thing, but my parents are out of town and mom is one of the ones that started this horse and pony show."

"Ah. Family blackmail?"

"Exactly," he laughs.

"What are you doing here? Not that I'm not glad to see you, but... well, you're not exactly dressed for the black and white gala."

I look down at my dress with a wry smile.

"Yeah, I'm a little..."

"Colorful?" Jason supplies helpfully and I laugh.

"Pretty much," I sigh. "My boyfriend picked out the dress. I'm afraid he didn't know about the whole black and white thing," I tell him, and I'm pretty sure that's the case after hearing Cammie talk. I'd lay odds that she's somehow responsible.

"Oh, wow. I didn't know you were dating someone. Who's the lucky guy?"

That's when it hits me. I referred to Gray as my boyfriend. My boyfriend. How did that happen? My heart speeds up and, for a moment, I think I might hyperventilate. *My boyfriend*!? Oh, God. What have I done?

"You okay, CC?" Jason asks because—well, heck, I don't know. Maybe he can read the panic on my face. If anything is true in this moment, it's the fact that I am in major panic mode.

"Umm... yeah, I think I just need to catch my breath. My dress may be a little tight. Excuse me a minute, Jason." I don't wait for him to answer, heading out of the room because the air in here feels as if it is suffocating me. I head towards the restrooms and see a small side entrance that says "Employees Only". I head there. I don't really know why except I know that's the one place I won't see Cammie Riverton and I don't want her to see me when I'm in the middle of a meltdown. I don't want to give her that satisfaction.

Once I get inside, I drag air into my lungs. It shouldn't come as such a huge shock that I have feelings for Gray—that I care for him. I mean, I am sleeping with him. Somehow, however, it is. I have a boyfriend. I have a rich, famous boyfriend. *What the fuck am I doing?* I look out the window and try and get control of myself. That was probably the worst thing I could do, however, because Gray is standing there... but he's alone. *Alone with Cammie*. Something inside of me twists in pain as I see her reach up to brush something off of his face. Gray's back is to me so I can't see what he's doing, but seeing them like this is enough. I can't handle it. I need to leave. I need to get back to my world. I've just been kidding myself.

My hand moves up to the wall to brace myself because suddenly I'm feeling dizzy. This is just too much. It's all too much.

Cold hits my hand and I look up to see the lid of a control panel. I open it to discover that it's the controls for the outdoor sprinkler system. I look back at Cammie and Gray and, without taking time to second guess myself, I hit the switch to on. Then, I turn the flow all the way up to maximum output.

"Take that," I whisper, then walk back outside, making sure not to be spotted. Maybe I'll get lucky and it will drown Cammie.

Chapter Twenty-Four

GRAY

"I was wondering, David, when the contracts would be ready. Seth would like my attorney to go over them before the first tour stop next month."

"You see that, Adams? Our man here is always thinking business. He's nothing like what the tabloids have painted him to be."

"I wondered," Adams said as they discuss me. It's on my mind to walk away. No amount of money is worth this shit. I'll just pay my own way and say to hell with the committee. If I win enough of the damn grunt tours they somehow corral me into then they can't keep me out of the big ones. "There were rumors..."

"Bullshit rumors. Grayson here has been all business and upfront with me since he got here," Riverton says, and I'm taken aback. I even feel a little guilty for not liking the man. Maybe I had him pegged all wrong.

"Thank you, sir. I really appreciate that."

"Just stating the facts, boy." *Boy?* Really? It's been a long fucking time since I've been called a boy. I wouldn't care if it is a long fucking time before it's ever said again.

"Adams here knows that a man has to sow his oats once in a while," he says, and while I really don't wish to have my sex life reviewed by these idiots, I clamp my jaw tight and let them go on.

Whatever. As long as I nail down the contracts and get the fuck out of here, I'm happy. I just need to get back to Cooper. I'm just about to tell him that when he claps me hard on the back. "Hell, boy. In my day, I had my own wild days. A man needs that."

"Daddy," Cammie says, and it's the first time I see true emotions on her face. Is it hurt? Anger? Maybe a mixture of the two.

"That's all in the past, princess. All in the past. Anyway, Adams and I are going to leave you young kids alone to get better acquainted. They're dating, Adams. You know I wouldn't let someone harmful into my family, not after the shit we endured."

Whoa! *What the fuck?*

"David, I think you have the wrong impression..."

"Daddy, please do. There are things Gray and I need to discuss," Cammie jumps in, screeching over me. She reaches up and kisses her dad's cheek. Before I can catch my breath, they're gone. I'm left with Cammie.

"What the fuck is going on here, Cammie? Why does your father think the two of us are dating?"

"Because we are."

"The fuck we are."

"Really, Grayson, hanging around with that mechanic is having a bad effect on you. We don't use those words in..."

"Woman, seriously. What in the hell would make you think we are dating?"

"You kissed me. Are you going to deny it?"

My stomach churns. I do remember that kiss, and I remember hating every second of it, but how the fuck we went from there to her even thinking in her damn mind that we are dating is what's beyond me. What if she tells that shit to CC?

"You kissed me!" And fuck, now she has me screeching like a banshee.

"You didn't pull away. Listen, Grayson, I know you've been messing around with Claude, but honestly, you can't see her as anyone long-term. A woman like that..."

"A woman like what?"

"A woman with her history. Surely you can't think..."

Before she can go any further, the sprinklers turn on. For a second, we're both standing there stunned and it doesn't hit us what's going on. Actually, my first thought is that it has started raining. Yet when I look up, the sky is a beautiful dusk—not quite dark yet, and it's painted a variety of colors that remind me of home. As the water pressure picks up and I hear the little motorized propellers and feel more of it hit me, I finally realize what's going on. My head jerks up when I hear Cammie screaming. I look at her and she's drenched, her big fancy sequined dress looking just droopy now. Her makeup is rolling down her face, the mascara so dark and runny she looks something akin to a raccoon. I grab her hand, more so she'll stop screaming than anything else. We take off running towards the club. Running however, is a relative term; Cammie is wearing heels—the kind with points on them that could probably kill a man—so it's definitely more like a steady walk-jog. I think we're almost home free when her ankle turns on the grass and she nearly falls. My hold on her and her knee keep her from completely going down.

As much as I don't want to, I pick her up and quickly walk to the entrance. I set her down and she's barely hit the floor before she wobbles forward, picking up her long dress and walking into the entrance. I can do nothing but follow, especially when a wet Riverton and his buddy come up behind us.

I look immediately for CC, just needing to make sure she's okay. The only thing on my mind is to get my girl and get the fuck out of here. I should have known with women it is never that easy.

"Claudia Cooper, you did this!" Cammie screeches, and everything seems to come to a halt as if in slow motion—all the music, the talk, and the chatter. Hell, even the servers stop moving, and all eyes go to CC who is standing there looking beautiful and entirely too close to some fucking man. Cammie pretty much resembles a drowned rat.

Shit.

Chapter Twenty-Five

CC

I can't deny the glee that runs through me as I hear Cammie's familiar and ultra-annoying shriek. I'm talking with Jason again and I school my face to show nothing but dismay. Years of dealing with shit like this makes it easy. As if on cue, I gasp when I turn around. When I see Cammie standing there like the drenched rat she is, I have to admit, it's not that hard. Behind her is Gray and he's wet, but he doesn't look mad. No, there's something else in his eyes—almost humor. Behind him are Cammie's dad and some other man I've forgotten the name of.

I turn my eyes back to Cammie, taking in her ruined hair, the running mascara, and her dress... *Oh my*! Wearing no bra was definitely a bad fashion decision; getting that white material wet made the dress transparent. *Whoops.*

"Cammie! Oh my God! What happened to you?" I ask, doing my best to lace my voice with disbelief and shock. Gray coughs in the background and I refuse to look at him because he might see through me—you know, as easily as I can Cammie's dress.

The girl really should invest in support bras.

"You know exactly what happened to me! You did this!"

"I did? I hardly think I can control the weather, Cammie. We should get you some towels or something to cover you up. I'm afraid you're flashing the whole club, sweetheart."

Behind me, Jason laughs as well as a few others. Damn, did I fail to keep my tone from being sarcastic?

Gray takes off his jacket, which is really wet, and puts it over Cammie, hiding her ta-tas.

"Is my daughter right? Did you do this, Claudia?"

My head jerks around. God, how I hate this man and the fact that he thinks it's okay to talk to me in that tone. I'm taken aback for a minute because honestly, David Riverton has not spoken to me in years. *Years*. But while I'm trying to form words and swallow down the bitterness I have where this man is concerned, Gray tries to defend me.

"Really, David, I doubt CC could turn the sprinklers on for the club. For one, she's only visiting here. Do you really think she would even know where the controls to the lawn are?" Oh, look. He's so cute defending me. It almost makes me feel guilty for trying to drown Cammie. *Almost*.

"Besides that," Jason pipes up, "she's been with me the entire time, and I can assure you that she didn't have time to do anything other than make me a very happy man by agreeing to dance with me." Aww, Jason! Covering for me even though he probably suspects that I did, in fact, turn on the sprinklers—which, by the way, unless someone has found the controls, have probably turned the green grass into grass with mini-rivers running through them by now. I look up at Jason and smile as he puts his arm around my shoulders in support. It kind of shocks me, but the small growl I hear from Gray shocks me more. I look at him and can clearly see jealousy shooting out of his eyes. Inside, the little girl in me is screaming *yes*!

"You'll have to wait for that dance. I need to go home and change, and since CC is with *me*, she's going too," Gray says, his voice hard.

"She can stay if she wants. I'll be glad to escort her home. After all, if I had been her date, I wouldn't have left her all alone in a room full of strangers," Jason says. Yikes, what have I gotten myself into?

"I want you gone!" Cammie says like the spoiled child she still is.

"I don't. Really, David, you need to control your daughter. Making these wild accusations against my friend and now demanding she leaves? It's all childish and very unprofessional," Jason says, and if I wasn't afraid Gray would tear his head off his body, I would totally kiss him right now.

"Yes, well..." Cammie's father begins, looking very uncomfortable. Jason might not be on par with Riverton Metals, but his mother and father definitely are, and Jason isn't exactly a slouch. Gray must get tired of all of this—especially Jason. He comes over and very securely pulls me into him and away from Jason. He locks his arm around me, keeping his hand on my hip. It feels good to be in his arms again, even if he is wet. How does a man get to be so bone-snuggling hot when he's wet? That should be impossible, but Gray feels like a heater right now—my own private heater. *Mine.* One that Cammie can't have. Who knew I could be territorial?

"I'll be taking CC home, since she's my date for the evening, but I think she's at the very least owed an apology."

Geez! Okay, this might be taking it too far.

"What?" Cammie shrieks again. Seriously, this woman's voice is loud. I'm surprised the windows didn't shatter just now. "I most certainly will not apologize! I don't know how, but I'm sure she did this!" Time to pack it up and go home. Not because I want to back down, but because I'm standing entirely too close to David Riverton and my knife is nowhere around with which I would geld him.

"I'm sorry you feel this way. I, however, am rather tired. I'll just be going."

"Lucas, in light of tonight, I think we should have a meeting about your future with Riverton Metals," David says, playing his trump card.

Fear hits me and a shiver runs up my spine. I reacted from the gut. I didn't mean to ruin Gray's chances of getting the endorsement deal he's been working for. Shit.

"Mr. Riverton," I start to say.

"That will be fine, David. We'll talk tomorrow before I head out of town."

"You're going out of town?" I ask at almost the same exact time Cammie does.

"I'm taking CC home to meet my family. We'll be gone for a couple of weeks," Gray says and my gasp is loud enough that it competes with Cammie's.

I'm still trying to form words when he escorts me out of the club from hell, leaving a drowned Cammie there with her mouth hanging open, an outraged David Riverton, and a smiling Jason. Gray takes me out to his car and I'm buckled in the car with the door closing, before I even have time to go over the exchange that just happened.

"I can't go home with you!" I finally tell him, finding my voice once we're a couple miles down the road. "I have a job!"

"Jackson can do it while we're gone. You owe me for the shit you put me through tonight and for probably costing me the Riverton contract," he grumbles.

"Gray," I start, already feeling guilty.

"Just save it until we get home. Once we get there, you can explain what you were doing letting another man paw you in front of everyone."

"What? What are you talking about?"

He slams on his brakes, guiding the car to the side of the road. Thank God I'm wearing a seatbelt or else I'd be thrust through the windshield.

"I'm talking about the fact that you just sent me on my way and agreed with those assholes that I could leave you behind, and then I come back to find you hanging all over another man!"

"Oh good God! You cannot be serious! Jason is a friend! And I encouraged you to go talk business so we could get the damn party over and I could go home. I told you I didn't want to go in the first place!"

"A pretty freaking chummy friend, if you ask me!"

"Did you seriously just say *chummy*?"

"Can it, Cooper. I'm not in the mood for your mouth unless it's on my cock."

"Well, if you quit being an ass, that could be arranged," I huff out before I realize what I'm saying. His eyes narrow and he looks at me. Then, he reaches down and scoots his seat back all the way and reclines it until the head of the seat is practically laying on the back seat. "What are you doing?"

"Waiting for you to put your money where your mouth is," he says, folding his arms.

"Gray... I..."

"Chickening out, Cooper? I expected more from you."

"We're on the side of a road!"

"It's a back road, but if you're too scared to live a little..."

"I didn't say that," I tell him, watching as he unzips his pants. This should be the last thing I do. We need to talk about Gray going out of town, about how he expects me to just pack up and go with him. But as I watch the way his large hand wraps around his even larger cock and strokes it slowly, I know that any discussion we might have has been tabled—at least until we apparently have sex on the side of the road, because if I'm going to give him his, you better believe I'm getting mine, too.

Chapter Twenty-Six

GRAY

I may be unreasonable here, who the fuck knows? What I do know is that I do not like seeing CC with another man near her. The fact that the man had his hands on her and was getting ready to dance with her pisses me off even more. I have this need inside of me to make sure she knows who the fuck she is with. I also have this craving to come deep inside of her, branding her as mine. Which is completely stupid. I will not have a kid. I shove that thought away even as a vision of CC, her stomach round with my child, comes to mind.

"I can't believe you," she huffs, but she's not fooling me. I see the flare of excitement in her eyes. She wants this as much as I do.

"Stop talking," I tell her, stroking my cock. "There's other things you should be doing with your mouth."

"So romantic."

"Keep talking and in a few minutes it won't matter anymore."

"Minute man?"

"I think I've proven how false that is, but for some strange fucking reason, I have the need to come all over that smart little mouth of yours and remind you who you belong to."

"Belong to?" she echoes.

Shit. I know I've said too much, but it's too late to take it back now.

"My mom always had a saying," I tell her, watching as she undoes her seatbelt and moves closer to me.

"I can't believe you're insisting on talking about your mother while you're giving yourself a hand job. You're seriously twisted, Grayson Lucas."

"She always said you never forget to ride home on the horse that brought you to the dance."

She stops just as she's leaning down to my dick. She sits straight up. All at once, a beautiful smile slides onto her face, one so deep that her eyes sparkle. If I was the kind of man who was easily affected by such things, I'd say she could take my breath away in this moment. Then she reaches under her dress, shifting and moving around. At first I'm not sure what she's doing, but when she comes out with a pair of black silk panties in her hand, I understand. I snatch them and watch her as she maneuvers herself to straddle my lap.

"I'd say that's a good saying. Especially since you're acting like a horse's ass," she whispers, but I don't give a fuck what she's saying at this point. I've moved my hands to her hips as she wiggles and settles down on me. My cock slides in between the lips of her pussy. The tip pushes against her and slides up so that it rests pressed against me and her warm, wet, cunt.

"You're wet," I whisper, surprised and thankful as fuck. She rotates her hips, sliding those sweet pussy lips against my cock, then grinds against me. It's all I can do to stop myself from grabbing her and holding her still so I can slam inside.

"I seem to stay that way when you're around, Gray," she whispers.

It's a simple statement and it's not meant to do anything more than just express the truth, but it grabs ahold of me. It burrows deep inside of me and some of the jealousy from earlier disappears, but at the same time, it makes me want to mark her deeper. I want to reach so deep inside of her that no matter where she goes, or what she does, she feels me... she needs me.

She lifts up at the same time her hand wraps around my cock, squeezing it. She positions me at her entrance and I know in a matter of seconds that I'm going to be deep inside of her. I look at her... really look at her. Her eyes drugged with need, her lips wet and glossy, her face flushed, I listen to her breaths as they come in small gasps.

"What are you doing, Cooper?" I ask, truthfully wondering how someone so beautiful could be here with me.

"Riding the horse that brought me to the dance," she answers with a smile right before she slides down on my cock. I groan as my dick pushes into her, the walls of her pussy holding me tightly, branding my dick with the heat of her. It's never been better. Never. Out of all of the women I've been with, they pale in comparison to CC. She's it. *Fuck!* She's it. "And I plan on riding him all the way home," she exhales as she grinds down against me, using my cock to scrape against her and stretch her pussy to accommodate me.

It's a hell of a place to realize it. But right here on the side of the road, with a car going by here and there, my emergency flashers on, and the most beautiful girl I've ever met in my life sliding up and down on my cock, I can't deny it.

I am falling in love with Claudia Cooper.

Chapter Twenty-Seven

CC

"Are you ready?" Gray asks, coming through the front door and acting like he's going to fight a fire, he's in such a rush.

"Ready for what?"

"I told you I was leaving for mom's today for a couple of weeks."

"I know."

"So are you ready to roll?"

"Umm... Gray, I told you. I'm not going."

"Why not?"

"I don't want to."

"C..."

"I like you, Gray. I like you a lot. I'm even getting used to the fact that you whack innocent balls for a living."

"I don't think that's the way to put it."

I smile at him, knowing that would aggravate him. "The truth is, I have a job, a demanding job, and Jackson and I have three engine rebuilds to do this week. I just can't leave right now. I have to work to keep my deadlines."

"I want you with me," he says.

He will never know how much I want to throw caution to the wind and agree. I can't, though, and the fact that I'm using the garage as a reason feels wrong. The real reason is that I'm afraid. We haven't really discussed how the dance went down two days ago. I feel like it was proof that I'm not in the same circles as Gray. It's also proof that I'm not sure I ever want to be.

"Jackson can keep your deadlines. It's just a couple weeks, C. We can make it one if that helps," I'm willing to work with you.

"This is just proof of how different we are. I don't have a bank account, Gray. All I have is my business. I can't ignore it for some man and go traipsing across the..."

"Some man?" he asks, and even I wince. I didn't mean it like that at all. Or, hell, maybe I did. I need him to give up on me because I'm not sure I'm strong enough to give up on my own.

"You know what I mean," I try to defend.

"No, Cooper. I don't know what you mean. Why don't you enlighten me?"

"I don't want to do this," I mutter, unable to look at him. I move to go around him and put my coffee mug in the sink. It's early, but I'll just head out and get to work. And pretend my world doesn't feel like it's crashing around me.

"Do what, exactly? Fight? Meet my family? Be with me?"

"I think it's pretty clear, Gray, that we just don't mesh."

"The fuck we don't. I think if anything, we have proven over and over that we mesh fucking phenomenally."

"Everything doesn't boil down to sex!" I growl at him. I try to leave, but he grabs my arm and pulls me back around to him.

"What is this about? Is it about the dance? Because you never said anything and I thought we had a pretty good bout of make-up sex afterwards."

"Make-up? That wasn't make-up sex, you moron."

"What the hell was it then?"

"Lust! That's all we have. We scratch each other's itches, but we're toxic as a couple."

"Whoa! Hold the hell up here. I thought what we've been sharing has been pretty damn good. How in the hell did we go from having fun and enjoying each other to being toxic?"

"We run in different circles!"

"Whatever, Cooper. You're going to have to come up with one better than that."

"How about the fact that you keep dragging me around people who hate me? People *I* hate? People who did their best to destroy me years ago? I don't want to be in that circle again for any reason, Gray!" I yell, close to breaking down and telling him exactly what he's asking of me. "Not even for you." I whisper that last part, the part that hurts the most. I'm weak and I know it, but I can't handle being around the Rivertons or anyone in their circle. My sense of self-preservation tells me that I can't... *even for Gray*.

"I see."

"I like you, Gray, I really do. But..."

"But?"

"We're just too different."

"I don't think we are at all. I think if you took the time to go meet my family, you'd see that, CC. I think that if you cared even a little bit about me, you'd at least fucking try," he growls, and this time it's him who turns away. Funny how that seems to be the last thing I want after this conversation.

"I do care about you," I argue and mean it. I think part of me is already in love with him. Or at least I think that's what it is. I've never really seen or had that in my life to recognize it.

"Then prove it."

"I can't."

"Can't or won't?" he challenges.

That's when I see it: the hurt in his eyes, the hurt I put there. The weight of that crushes down on me and I almost feel like I'm suffocating.

"It's the same thing!" I lash out in regret, needing to get away because suddenly I can't breathe.

"I never figured you for a woman without a backbone, Claudia Cooper. It's good I found out now, I guess. Maybe I'll see you around," Gray says, and those words combined with the tone of his voice make me jerk my head up to look at him.

"Gray, it doesn't have to be this way. We can keep having fun. We can—"

"What? Keep fucking? Oddly enough, Cooper, I don't want that from you. For the first time in my life, I can honestly say that's not even close to what I want," he says disgustedly.

He looks like a stranger. He barely spares me a glance before he turns around and walks out the door. I'm left standing here wondering what happened. In the last two days, he's joked about me meeting his family, and yeah he told me that he had made all the reservations to leave today, but I never realized he was completely serious about taking me with him. Other than mentioning it to Cammie and her father, he's never once asked me. And now... we've gone from laughing and playing, making love every night to... *this*.

I head out the door and go to my car. I start it up and, on autopilot, I head to the garage. I don't want to think about it anymore because this feels like I just broke up with Gray Lucas. I'm not ready to face that just yet. *I may never be*.

Chapter Twenty-Eight

GRAY

Three Days Later

"Grayson Lucas, you've been moping around here since you got back. What the hell is going on with you?"

My mother's tone is one I've learned I shouldn't ignore. It means she's getting desperate, and when Ida Sue "Love" Lucas gets desperate, chaos ensues. Still, I can't seem to drum up enough energy to care. Everything just seems... flat, lifeless, and colorless since I left CC's home three days ago. God, I miss her. Me, missing a woman? It would be the world's biggest joke except there's nothing funny about how I'm feeling. There's nothing to find humor in when I picture the rest of my life without CC in it. The woman has ruined me.

"Answer your mother when she speaks to you," Cyan says, slapping me up the side of my head.

"Thank you, baby."

"Anytime, Mama," Cyan answers, dodging my halfhearted attempt to swat him back.

"Asshole," I mutter, partly because he's annoying me, but mostly because he's the biggest mama's boy on the face of the planet.

"Grayson Lucas, you stop that or I'll wash your mouth out with soap."

I roll my eyes, though I do it where I'm sure Mom can't see me. The truth is, she says worse than us boys ever thought of—and that's saying a lot. She however, can't stand it for her kids to say the same words in front of her.

"Yes, Mama," I answer, looking out over the yard in front of the large farmhouse I was raised in. It's a large three-story home which has been completely updated, much to Mother's dismay. The boys and I got together while Mom was on vacation and completely renovated the place, giving her all the latest appliances and conveniences. Most mothers would have loved it; ours complained we ruined the charm of the place, though I notice she doesn't complain that the utility room, with a new state of the art washer and dryer, is now downstairs along with her newly remodeled bedroom and large master bath.

There's a large wraparound porch that completely encircles the home—a fact my nephews, when they're around love and make complete use of. It's white with red trim and has a bright red tin roof. The yard is encased with matching red trim and it's quite beautiful when you pull up and see it, but that's not why I love this place and always will; it's the memories. Even when we didn't have two nickels to rub together, this place was the most magical place on Earth. No matter what has happened in my life, being home always had a way of healing me and making things better.

That is, until CC.

"Is Grayson still being moony-eyed over that woman?" Black asks.

"Seems so. I don't get it. I haven't seen a flitter worth that," Maggie says.

"Magnolia Marie! You did not just say that!" Mama yells.

"Sorry, Mama. Terry has taken to using the word and it just slipped out."

"You ruined that boy, naming him Terry. You should have kept the family tradition."

"You mean naming him after where he was created? No, thank you. I don't need a son named Subaru."

"Yeah, cause we all know the story of how Maggie whoopty-do'ed in her Subaru and nine months later..."

Maggie elbows Cyan with a huff. "That wasn't funny the first five-thousand times and it's even less funny now that Terry is three years old, dumbass."

"Ouch! Stop, that hurts! Mama, Maggie called me a name."

"That's because you are being a dumbass. I don't need no grandchild named Subaru. Though you could have named him Cross, dear."

I smile. It's an old argument. Maggie was caught in the back of an old Subaru with Bryant Matthews out on Old Cross Road.

"You really need to make an honest man of that boy, and actually make it work this time," Mama chides her.

"Like you have Jansen?" Maggie comes back.

Jansen is the foreman of the ranch and the unofficial boyfriend of my mother. Mom had her oldest child when she was barely seventeen, which means she will be turning fifty-four in just a week. All of us like Jansen and would love to welcome him completely in the family, but for whatever reason, my mom will not agree to marry him—even though he's asked her a million times.

"Pffft..." Mom waves her off. "At our age," she says, like they're eighty, "we're just celebrating the miracle that we're both still even interested."

"There sure is a lot of celebrating going on around here, specifically in the kitchen," Cyan says, and from the look on his face, I don't even want to know what he saw.

"Praise Jesus," Mom says.

I take a drink of my beer to keep from laughing out loud. I manage to hide my smile around the rim of the can; Mom doesn't need any encouragement.

"Lovey, that damn cow got out again," Jansen growls, sliding onto the edge of the porch, sitting down, and letting his legs hang over the side. He spits out his tobacco and Cyan hands him a beer.

"He just wants his freedom, Jan," Mom defends.

"If he don't stop breaking my fence, I'll give him his freedom. I'll make sure he gets his ticket to the green pastures in the sky," Jan grumbles. Mom ignores him, probably because she knows it's the same empty threat he always gives. Instead, she focuses on the one thing about Jansen that she absolutely does not like.

"I thought I told you that if you didn't give up chewing, Jansen Reed, there would be no more celebrating between us?" she grumbles, hitting his back with a fly swatter.

"You did, but I had a talk with the good Lord about it," Jansen says, looking over his shoulder at her. "He said He'd allow the vice, if I celebrated and praised Him harder. So we're working it out."

"I call bullshit," she says, but she's smiling.

"I'll show you later," he promises with a wink.

"I don't know what's sadder," Cyan says.

"What's that?" Jansen asks.

"The fact that my mom gets more action than I do, or the fact that hearing about it is the highlight of my week."

"Probably both, son," Jansen says.

"Enough about this topic, please? It's almost dinner time and I need my appetite. Besides, I want to hear about Gray and his new woman."

"Nothing to tell, Mags," I grunt, cutting her off.

"Life is short, son. Don't waste it pissing in the wind. One day, you'll wake up all alone and stinking to high heaven with nothing but a basket of laundry."

"That's deep, Mom," Cyan says with a laugh.

"Thank you, sweetie."

"Well, if she's anything like Grayson's usual women, she's an airhead," Maggie says.

"Yeah, we'll probably see more of her than we want in the tabloids soon enough," Cyan agrees.

"She's not like anyone else," I growl.

"Do tell, brother." This comes from White as he comes outside. The screen door squeaks in protest. He leans up against the porch post and looks at me. Shit.

Chapter Twenty-Nine

GRAY

"Mind your own business," I growl.

White is my oldest brother and he's a self-declared permanent bachelor, which is a shame because his best friend is a woman named Kayla—a damn good woman, at that. Plus, everyone knows she's completely in love with White. Well, everyone but him. He doesn't give a fuck about anything other than his next football game, or even riding a bull in his spare time. White lives for the thrill.

Mom jokes she has a child in every profession and she's not far from the truth. Football, golf, baseball, fireman, cop, and rancher. Then there's Cyan. Cyan tells everyone he's still finding himself, but the truth is that he finds himself at the tables gambling most of the time. That's just my brothers. My sisters are just as diverse, from a novelist to Maggie, who's the principal at a local elementary school.

"Come on, Gray, give it up," Maggie says.

I take a deep breath. "Fine. Cooper is smart, funny, beautiful... caring. She's—"

"What kind of name is Cooper?"

"Cooper?" Cyan interrupts.

"Her name is Claudia Cooper. Everyone calls her CC."

"Dude, that's a rough ass name for a girl," Cyan says.

"Oh please, like any of us could talk," Maggie says. "Hello? Magnolia tree, front and center here."

"It was a hell of a Magnolia tree," Mom says. Maggie holds her head down.

We all laugh, even me, and I don't really feel like it, especially since talking about CC reminds me of everything I've lost.

"If she's so wonderful, what the fuck are you doing here without her?"

"White Hall Lucas, watch your mouth!"

"Yes, Mom," he sighs.

"I still want to see the woman who has one of my brothers all twisted up," Maggie says. I flip her off without letting mom see me.

"We may not have to wait long, dear," Mom says.

"Why's that?" Cyan asks, and I just listen to them chatter while I open my second beer. I wonder how long it would take me to get drunk on drinking nothing but beer.

"Because, unless I miss my guess, the woman in question is getting out of that taxi at the end of our drive," Mom says.

My heart speeds up at her words and joy spreads through me. CC must have changed her mind! I'll make sure I reward her later tonight.

"Fuck!" I growl.

"What? What's wrong?" Mom asks, and she must know something is way off from my tone, because for once she doesn't bitch at me for my cursing.

"That's not CC. That's David Riverton and his daughter Cammie," I growl.

"Oh, shit," Maggie whispers while everyone else goes quiet. I hold my head down, wondering how the fuck life got so complicated.

Chapter Thirty

CC

"Okay, so hit me," Mir says, staring at me from across the table. If she only knew how inviting that was right now, she wouldn't tempt me. It's been five days since Gray left to visit his family in Texas. Five days and I haven't seen nor heard from him. I mean, I guess we broke up, so I understand it, but somewhere in the back of my mind, I thought he might try to contact me. I thought I'd get the chance to... maybe rethink things? Get a do-over? Hell, I don't know. Truthfully, I didn't think much past hearing from Gray again. "Earth to C. You get about five minutes to start talking," Mir adds.

"And you'll what?"

"I'll throw such a fit they will kick us out of here."

"That's not much of a threat, woman," I grumble. We're at the new bar that just opened downtown called Drink. It's a small hole in the wall filled with, from what I can tell, college-aged kids and rich snobs who never had a hard time in their life, unless you include chipping a nail or their daddy freezing their trust fund for a few days.

"I thought we both could use a change of pace," she defends, but she doesn't look exactly happy to be here either. "But you're right, it blows. Which is why you have to tell me about Gray!"

"I told you, there's not much to tell," I all but growl, shifting in my seat.

"Oh, please. Last week you couldn't stop talking about him. All I heard was Gray this and Gray that. Today it's over, end of discussion. I'm getting whiplash from the change."

"He went back to Texas to visit his family." I shrug, staring at my drink and wishing I could just go home, curl up on the couch like I have for the last five days, and sleep until I have to get up in the morning.

"So? That does not constitute a breakup. I swear, C, if you kicked him to the curb just because his vine wasn't going to be around to swing through the jungle on, I may kill you myself."

I roll my eyes at her. I decide to talk with her, knowing that if I don't, this is just going to go on all night, and I really need to talk about something else if I'm going to survive tonight.

"Our last date, he took me to a dance."

"So? You love dancing!"

"A society formal at the Riverton's Country Club."

"Oh, shit."

"He was very sweet. Even picked out my dress."

"Okay. So far, I'm seeing no reason to cut the man loose. I mean..."

"It was this beautiful silk and lace, deep red," I interrupt her, "that probably cost a fortune."

"Again, C, not making a connection."

"It was a black and white formal."

"Oh hell."

"Yeah, that's not his fault. I have a very good hunch that it was all Cammie's fault he picked out a red dress."

"What? I mean, why would he..."

"He went to the one shop in Addington to buy formal gear. You know, the one where Cammie's best friend Eliza works."

"Holy fuck-nuggets Batman."

"Pretty much."

"Someone needs to bitch slap that cunt-a-saurus for freaking days."

I think about the sprinklers and start to tell Mir, but I just don't want to get into it right now. As much as I hate Cammie, she's not my problem. I have this sneaking suspicion that it's me that is the problem right now. I let my doubts push Gray away, and the truth is... I miss him.

"I miss him," I whisper out loud.

"Oh, honey," Mir says.

"I got scared, Mir. I like him. I really like him."

"C..."

"Like, really, really liked him," I stress.

"So tell him that."

"He's gone."

"He's in Texas. Not some third world country. Text him."

"But we broke up," I sigh. "Jesus, I feel like I'm back in high school worrying over Clinton Sparks."

"He was an asshole."

"Maybe Gray is," I argue.

"I never thought I'd see the day that Claudia Cooper was afraid to live her life."

"You take that back!"

"Nope. Not going to happen."

"You're such a bitch."

"You say that like it's a bad thing. Now find your lady balls and text your man."

I sigh, looking at my phone. "I could just text him to see what he's doing," I reason, nerves filling my system.

"My freaking Lord, C, you are jinxed."

"What?" I ask, jerking up.

"Cammie and her Witches of Crossville crew just came in. You're jinxed."

"Or maybe my best friend just picked a particularly horrible place to meet," I grumble, because really, this place is just the kind of people Cammie would hang around.

"Point made. Jesus, they're going to sit right behind us. Try not to move. If I have to talk to her, I may projectile vomit," Mir says, and I agree with her. So for the next five minutes, other than making weird faces at each other, we say nothing. Mir makes silly faces imitating Cammie, and I might giggle a time or two, but we remain mostly silent.

Until the topic of conversation changes. "Cammie, where have you been? I was going to tell you about the new shipment of dresses we got in from Paris last week. They are to die for!"

"Father and I just got back from Texas," she says, her voice hitting on every nerve ending I have. Mir mouths the word "Texas" and I stare at her, my fists clenching. It really pisses me off that Gray does business with these people, even if I don't have a say so in it.

"What on Earth were you doing in Texas? It's so hot this time of year," one of the girls says.

"My fiancé is there. He wanted me to meet his family."

My blood runs cold at her words. Her fiancé? Meet the family?

"You got engaged to Grayson Lucas and didn't tell us? I thought he was dating that mechanic," another girl says, and she says the word "mechanic" like it's dirt beneath her fingernails.

"Oh pu-leeze! He was just sewing his wild oats before he settles down. All men do it, but a man like Grayson realizes what kind of woman he needs in his life. We'll make a great partnership. He said so himself."

"He did?" another asks while Mir reaches across the table and squeezes my hand in support.

"He did. Why, before I left, he said I was perfect and then he kissed me and, let me tell you ladies, Grayson Lucas can definitely kiss."

I want to go off. I'm so close to the edge, it's ridiculous. He wanted Cammie to meet his family? He said she was perfect? Who the fuck does he think he is? Was he just playing me for the fool, or because I didn't jump onboard with his plans he replaced me that quickly?

I get up and stomp out. I don't care if Cammie sees me or not. I'm so mad. I'd like to punch Grayson Lucas in his big, fat nose.

"C? What are you thinking? You know Cammie. She's probably exaggerating and you can't put a lot of stock into..." I ignore her, walking straight to my car. "C!" she yells, and I finally stop and spin around to face her. "What are you going to do?"

"I'm going to Texas and punching Gray Lucas in his pretty boy face."

"Oh. Well, yes! Definitely do that! Heck, if I could get off work, I'd go with you! You should go do it right now! Don't let him get away with it a minute longer."

She's entirely too gleeful over this shit for my liking, but she's right. I'm going to confront the bastard and make him sorry he thought it was okay to play me.

Cammie's fiancé! That lying snake.

Chapter Thirty-One

GRAY

"It's a good thing you went into golfing because your fencing sucks," Blue grumbles, wiping the sweat out of his eyes with a rag he's stored in the back pocket of his jeans.

"Bite me," I grumble, holding my thumb which moments before I slammed with a hammer. My mind isn't on what I'm doing. Hell, my mind hasn't been on anything but CC for way too long. She's a fever in my blood and she's infected my system completely. Everything reminds me of her. The color of the sunset reminds me of her hair. The leaves on mom's roses reminds me of her eyes. Hell, the other day I was eating a peach and the taste of it even reminded me of her. God! What the fuck am I going to do? I need to get her out of my head, and soon. I can't go on like this. That much is for sure.

My cellphone rings and I pick it up expecting to see Cammie's number. She's been calling nonstop. It took me two days to get rid of her and her father when they came down here. I still haven't figured out their exact reason for coming here other than Riverton said he was in the area for other business and thought he'd check in on me. Mom hated Cammie and Maggie wasn't far behind her. There were a few times I thought we were going to have an old-fashioned cat fight and my money would have been on my mom. It doesn't even matter how old she is. If Mom had went at her, Cammie would have never known what hit her.

The number showing up on my phone, however, isn't Cammie's; it's Seth's. I know what he's calling about and I've been dreading this conversation. "I have to take this," I tell Blue, and he rolls his eyes at me. Then again, he thinks all cell phones are evil.

"Hey, Seth."

"Don't you 'Hey, Seth' me. Did you tell Riverton you didn't want his sponsorship?"

"Seth..."

"You needed Riverton to grease the wheels here, Grayson! What were you thinking?"

"I was thinking that he and his daughter showing up at my mother's house unannounced and talking down about everything and everyone here was just too fucking much to deal with. So, I told him he could either sponsor me or not. Besides, her father seems to think because I have a big bank account, I'm great boyfriend material. At this point, the farther I'm away from David Riverton and his whack-o daughter, the better."

"Kind of a ballsy move for a fucker who's been literally blackballed."

"Whatever."

"He especially liked the part where you called his daughter a perfect bitch."

"Hey, what can I say? I have a way with words."

"Riverton asked me to inform you that he got a job offer."

"So? What the fuck do I care?"

"He's been promoted to overseer of the championship tour."

"Motherfucker!"

"If you're going to piss off the big dogs, you better expect to have shit thrown at you, Lucas."

"Whatever. Good luck trying to keep me out. All those fuckers can kiss my ass. I came in fifty-one overall the first part of this season and that was with being off for the last two weeks. They can block me. So I have to putt from every shit-hole coming or going, it doesn't matter. I will survive and advance and flip them off while I do it," I growl, fed up with the whole fucking thing.

"Finally, my brother has found his dick," Blue mutters in the background.

"I hope you know what you're doing, Grayson, I really do. You're headed to Nebraska next week."

"The landfill," I groan, referring to a golf course that actually was a garbage landfill at one time. It's a little hole-in-the-wall town that created the golf course to try and get tourism started and save the town's economy. There's one fast food restaurant and two hotels, and those are mom-and-pop owned. I hate the place. I have golfed there before when I was earning my stripes. What-the-fuck-ever. It's tournament time and it's time to prove to all of them that I have what it takes to do nothing but win. Maybe Nebraska is exactly what I need to get over Claudia Cooper.

Even as I say it, I know the hope for that is slim to none.

Chapter Thirty-Two

CC

Adrenaline and anger kept me going for the first half of the trip. The second half of the trip was motivated by constant phone conversations with Mir and memories of Cammie calling Gray her fiancé. Now that I'm riding in a taxi to Gray's mom's house, there's nothing to keep me from running. That fact just gets clearer when the cabbie tells me that he won't drive me up the driveway, but instead stops the car at the end of the main road. When I ask him why, he gives me some kind of vague explanation about a crazy woman shooting at his car because the yellow color scared her pet cow. If I wasn't so nervous and busy second-guessing myself, I would have demanded more of the story.

"Fine, but stay here and wait for me. This won't take long."

"Lady, that woman is nuts. I'm not waiting around for her to fill my car full of buckshot," the cabbie argues.

"Fifteen minutes. You can wait that long, right? I'll pay you double," I bargain, wondering if I shouldn't just turn around. What is really the point of all of this?

"Ten minutes, tops. And I want to be paid first."

"No way. I pay you and you'll leave the minute I get out of this car."

"Lady, I want my money."

"What if I pay you half now, and then I'll pay..."

"What is going on in here? You just going to sit at the end of my driveway all damn day? You're about to give my baby a heart attack."

I look up and there's a lady with my car door open. She's beautiful. She looks around forty, forty-five. She has soft brown hair that falls around her face in a shaggy bob, and she has green eyes that look just like Gray's. This woman has to be Grayson's mother. I was hoping I wouldn't have to meet her. I'm confused, wondering why I'm giving her a heart attack until I realize she's looking at the driver.

"I'm leaving, Ida Sue. I'm just trying to get this woman out of my cab."

"You can't leave! I need you wait until I do what I came here to do!" I plead.

"What is it you came here to do?" Gray's mom asks.

I feel my stomach knot up. "I need to talk to Grayson."

"And why's that?"

"That's something I really should discuss with Grayson alone," I tell her, even though I immediately want to apologize for being snippy.

"You're Claudia," she says, appraising me, and I do my best not to squirm.

"CC," I correct her.

"You definitely have more meat on you than that other girl."

"Did you just call me fat?" She doesn't answer. She grabs the overnight bag beside me and drags it toward her. I grab it to stop her and she looks at me.

"You don't want to get out without your stuff? Heaven knows what this idiot would do with it."

"Listen, Ida Sue..." the cabbie starts.

"I'm not staying," I argue with her.

"Then don't." She shrugs. "But you came a long way to chicken out."

"I'm not chickening out," I totally lie.

"So you were just... what? Shooting the breeze in the cab? We eat dinner in an hour and I've got a roast that needs my attention, so are you getting out, or staying in?"

"Lady!" The cabbie growls, but I ignore him. Instead, I'm looking at the challenge shining in Grayson's mom's eyes. I toss money at the cabbie, secretly enjoying how the money falls apart and scatters over the front of the seat. He's annoying. Then, I give up my overnight bag to Grayson's mom and, once she's standing outside, I slide out and follow her. We don't talk as we walk up the driveway and I feel weird. I feel like I should come up with something to say, but for the life of me I can't think of anything. Instead, I take in the large white farmhouse, the chickens running free, the three cats lying lazily on the front porch. It's all completely different from anything I could have pictured Grayson growing up in, even after all his tales about his family. The strangest thing is watching a baby cow waddle over to the woman and wait for her to pet him. Wow.

"Did you really name your sons after crayons?" I blurt out.

The woman turns around to look at me with a half-smile. "The world needs bright colors to make it more interesting," she reasons, and I can't really argue, even though it seems like the answer has nothing to do with my question.

"And apparently flowers," I mumble, annoyed when she shakes her head and turns away from me.

She looks over her shoulder. "You're a spicy little thing, aren't you?" she says, laughing. "I think I'll like you just fine for my boy."

"I'm not with your boy."

"Then why are you here?"

"I'm here to give him a piece of my mind."

"If you must, dear, but I think Gray would rather have a piece of something else from you."

I can feel my face flame at her words because the first thing that comes to mind is a picture of Gray's body naked and lying on my bed asking me to—I stop the thought by clearing my throat.

"Whatever. I'm telling him off and then I'm going back home to Kentucky and that's that."

"A fine plan, dear."

"Uh, thanks."

"I only have one question," she asks as she throws a stick out for the baby cow. I watch as he goes lumbering after it and doesn't stop until he reaches it and puts it back in his mouth. Did I just watch a cow play fetch?

"What's that?" I ask, momentarily distracted.

"Why did you have to come all the way here to give him a piece of your mind? You could have done that on the telephone, surely."

"Well, I wanted to see his face when I told him exactly what I thought about him," I grumble, and then realizing that I'm talking about her son, I decide to try and soften my response. "No offense."

"None taken, dear. Gray is as stubborn as a horse's ass. It's good to see he's picked a woman who matches him."

I'm inside following her to the kitchen before it hits me that Gray's mom just threw shade at me. Somehow, I get the feeling the woman is a master at putting people in their place. I almost... like her.

Chapter Thirty-Three

CC

"I love your kitchen, Ida Sue," I say lamely. I even like her. In fact, so far, I like everything about this place, and somehow that makes me feel horrible. I needed more reasons not to like Grayson. His family, as crazy as they are, have nothing to do with Grayson himself. The kitchen looks like the kitchen that used to be on television for that old TV show about the family with a huge amount of kids that lived in the mountains of Virginia. I can't remember the name now, but I remember grinning at the end when all the kids were telling each other goodnight and wishing I had a big family. Grayson can't realize how blessed he is.

"Thanks, dear. The kids about ruined it when they remodeled, but at least they kept my kitchen table," she says. I have no idea what she's talking about; the room is a work of art. If this is almost ruining it, I wish someone would do it to my whole house. Plus, her kitchen table, as she calls it, looks like an outdoor picnic table covered in a large white table cloth. It has bench seating only and could probably hold an entire football team.

"I have the tomatoes sliced. I hate to be a bother, but I really need to go find Grayson so I can head back home," I tell her, putting my knife down. In answer, she puts cucumbers down in front of me.

"These too, sweetie. Besides, Grayson's out on the range with Blue. It will be much easier if you catch him here at supper time. Otherwise, you could be looking until dark out there in the pasture and never find him."

"They don't tell you where they're working? That seems like it wouldn't be safe. What if one of them got hurt or something?" I mumble, working with the cucumbers and wondering why things aren't working out the way I had them planned out in my head. I'm thinking the one answer to that is Ida Sue.

"Men. Who can keep up with them?" Ida Sue says just as the back door opens up. I tense, half-hoping and half-dreading to see Gray walk through the door. It's not, however. There's an older man in a black cowboy hat, jeans, and a faded button-up shirt with sandy-blonde hair that has some gray mixed in. Following him is a tall man dressed much the same, but he has shaggy hair, no hat, a faded blue shirt that's more unbuttoned than buttoned, and he looks like walking sex. He has this rumpled look about him that says he just crawled out of bed, or maybe it's just the way those smoky brown eyes look that makes you wish he just crawled out of your bed.

"Damn, Mom, something sure smells good in here," the man says, going to the stove where Ida Sue is standing. He grabs one of the rolls she's putting in a bowl and takes a bite. My eyes are glued to him because he might be the prettiest man I've ever laid eyes on. Jesus, if all of Ida Sue's kids look like Gray and this guy, then the woman should have never stopped. In fact, the country should pay her to continue to reproduce because good golly, Miss Molly, I had no idea they even made men like this. I sure haven't seen them in Kentucky before.

"White Hall, I told you if you didn't stop your cursing I'm going to wash your mouth out with soap. Show some respect. Grayson's lady friend is here visiting us."

White Hall. Definitely a brother, though Grayson left out his middle name. I'm almost scared to ask where the Hall comes from, but considering the story about Magnolia, I have a pretty good idea. White turns around to look at me and those smoky eyes travel up and down my body, and in a way I just know he's not missing anything. Heck, I'm hung up on his brother and still I can feel myself getting warm and tingly. This guy must break women's hearts far and wide.

"I definitely like this one better than the last one. What's your name, sweet thing?" he asks, and I almost want to roll my eyes. Did all the boys learn how to pick up a woman the same way? Gray's "sweet lips" were more interesting.

"I'm CC," I answer, laughing.

"I'm in love," White answers, sliding in beside me and sitting so close I have to move over to make room between us. I shouldn't have bothered because he just crowds up against me again.

"Behave, White Hall. This here is Gray's Claudia."

Gray's Claudia? What does that mean? I'd clear my throat to object, but I don't get the chance.

"Me-maw! Me-maw!" A little white-blonde tornado comes in yelling wearing nothing but a smile. He's running straight for Ida Sue who stops what she's doing, bends down to meet him, and the biggest smile comes on her face. I'm struck again with how beautiful Grayson's mom is. I'm starting to feel frumpy around these people.

"What did I tell you about wearing clothes, River?" she asks, and the name jars me so much that the knife slips and I cut myself.

"Shit!" I growl, holding my thumb out to inspect the damage.

"What did you do, sweet thing? Here, let ol' White have a look at it," White says, taking the knife from me. He looks up and winks at me. "Experience has taught me to watch women with sharp objects. We'll just put this down."

"Experience has taught you that women learn your bullshit fast and you have to be careful," a man says, coming through the front door. He's got blonde hair much like the child and he's also freaking sexy and he's wearing a uniform; sheriff, to be exact. Yeah, I'm definitely feeling frumpy around here.

"Bite me, Luca," White says.

"No, thanks. Haven't had enough shots to protect me from all the diseases you've probably contracted over the years."

"You staying for dinner, Luca?" Ida Sue asks, but she seems a little cold towards the new guy. I definitely detect a chill there.

"Here, sweet thing, you're bleeding," White says, then kisses my hand against the wound, which might be bleeding, but if it is, it's not much. His mouth is warm and the female in me can appreciate the soft feel of his lips, but the guy himself, as cute as he is, is starting to annoy me. I try to pull my hand away but he's not letting go easily.

"No, Ida Sue. Just bringing River and dropping him off. Petal said she was coming here for dinner to meet Grayson's girlfriend," I hear the other guy answer.

This place is chaos because I hear doors open in the background coming from the living room. A couple more people come in through the kitchen door at the same time while White still kisses my hand. The naked kid is asking Ida where Terry is.

But I'm frozen because I heard the sheriff's words. I've been feeling out of my depth and not talking a lot, but before I can stop myself, my mouth picks now to finally work.

"Cammie's coming here?" I squeak because I really can't handle that.

"Who is Cammie?" the sheriff asks.

"I hope to fuck not," the older man joins in.

Then, I hear the voice I'd been wanting to hear ever since I first stepped foot in this crazy house. "White, what the fuck are you doing with CC? Drop her hand right now!"

Gray's voice rings louder than anyone else's, and the room goes quiet. My eyes automatically go to him. How is it that the man is better looking now than he was just six days ago? That doesn't seem fair.

"What? She was cut. I was just giving her first aid. She seems to be having a little trouble breathing now. I'm thinking a little mouth-to-mouth is in order," White says, giving me a wink. I'd laugh if I wasn't scared that Cammie was coming here. In all of my planning of how exactly I was going to tell Grayson off, the possibility of Cammie showing back up wasn't in them.

"If you don't get away from my woman, you'll be sucking your dinner through a straw," Grayson growls. My heart trips inside of my chest. His woman?

"Your woman? I don't see how that can be since you're engaged to Cammie!" I yell at him.

"Engaged to Cam—? What in the hell are you talking about? I wouldn't be engaged to that snake if my life depended on it," Gray growls back, walking towards me. He jerks White's hands away from me. "Back the fuck off, White," he growls quietly. White grins, but nods his head and looks back at me with a wink.

"We'll catch up later, darlin'," he says before getting up.

"Not if you want to keep your face as pretty as you think it is," Gray growls. He's towering over me and I feel at a disadvantage, so I stand up to face him. "Now what the hell are you talking about with Cammie? Have you lost your damn mind?"

"She seems to think you are engaged."

"She what?" he yells, and the anger and surprise in his face makes me feel a little better. I shrug when he looks at me, expecting me to explain further. I'm suddenly not sure what I'm doing here. "I'm not engaged," he grumbles, his hand coming up to touch my hair.

"She says you are," I argue, jerking away.

"Woman, I just left your bed a week ago," he argues, and he doesn't say it quietly. My face heats as I hear the whispering and laughing around us.

"A week is a long time for a player," I tell him stubbornly.

"Not the way you wring a man dry," Gray says, and the laughing becomes almost as loud as the red on my face.

"Gray!" I snarl.

"Everyone out!" Gray yells. No one leaves. "You either leave or you'll see me fucking my woman on the kitchen table."

"If my child says that word one more time, I will cut your peter off so you can't touch your woman again!" a girl's voice yells from the door.

"I got a peter!" the blonde child yells. "It pees!" he yells, then proceeds to show everyone.

Let me tell you, nothing breaks the tension like having a child piss on the kitchen floor.

Nothing.

Chapter Thirty-Four

CC

"What are you doing here, Cooper?" Gray asks me ten minutes later. It took him ten minutes to clear out the kitchen and make sure his nephew's mess had been cleaned up. Speaking of which, he managed to pee on Gray's boot. I like that kid; he's got style.

"I came to tell you that you're an asshole."

"You traveled all the way from Kentucky to tell me I'm an asshole?"

"I was mad."

"Because I'm supposedly engaged to Cammie Riverton?"

"She said you were," I defend, resenting the way he's starting to make me feel... stupid.

"She's fucking nuts," he growls. Well, I can't argue with that.

"So you're saying you didn't ask her to marry you?"

"I don't want to marry anyone!" he growls, and I ignore the fact that, that feels like a slap in the face. I mean, I'm not looking for marriage either, right?

"Don't scream at me!"

"Then start making sense!"

"You're an asshole," I tell him, then stick my tongue out for good measure.

"Don't stick that tongue out at me unless you're willing to use it."

"In case you missed it, I'm rolling my eyes at you too."

"Why are you really here, Cooper?"

I swallow, rubbing my arms nervously. "I got mad."

"Why? You are the one who broke up with me."

"I didn't break up with you. I just didn't want to meet your family!"

"What's wrong with us?" I hear a woman ask.

"Yeah, we're pretty damn good people," White answers.

"White, watch that mouth of yours," Ida Sue grumbles. From the sound of all their voices, you can tell they're pushed up against the kitchen door, listening.

"You're great! I just didn't want to meet you! I wasn't ready for that!"

"Why not?" Ida Sue asks.

"Mom," Gray growls.

"It's a legitimate question, Grayson," she chides.

I hold my head down wondering what in the hell I'm doing. "Because," I groan.

"That's not a good reason, dear. Whenever my kids gave that kind of reasoning, it usually ended up with my spanking their asses," Ida Sue says through the still-closed but useless door.

"Hey, that's it, Gray. Spank her ass."

"I've got to say, that helps iron out Ida when she gets a knot up her ass."

"Eww. Damn it, Jansen," White growls.

"Spanking can help iron out difficulties," Ida Sue says, and moans can be heard echoing for miles.

"Jesus. I belong to a nut-house," Gray grumbles, grabbing my arm and pulling me outside. The kitchen door slams behind us and I can barely keep up as Gray pulls me towards an old painted red barn. I want to argue with him, but honestly I'd rather his family didn't hear everything we say, so I go with him.

I just wish I knew what I could say to get out of this without looking like the jealous freak I am.

Chapter Thirty-Five

GRAY

I pull CC into the barn with me and don't stop until we're in the far corner where the fresh hay has been piled up. I push her against the wall with my body and trap her there with my arms. I look down at her, pinning her with my eyes.

"Okay, Cooper. It's just you and me now." I watch the line of her throat as she swallows. God, everything about her is appealing. I want to move my tongue along the lines of her throat and taste her skin.

"Did you kiss Cammie?" she asks, and whatever I expected, for some reason that's not it. Because I take too long to respond, she punches me in the stomach. "You fucking asshole!" She does her best to push me out of the way. When my woman gets mad, she packs a punch. I grab her fists and push them up against the wall. Her breath is coming in hard gasps and she's pushing against my hold, but I don't let her go.

"She kissed me!"

"Oh my God. You did not just say that to me!"

"Are you jealous? I swear, it was nothing!"

"Are you an idiot?"

"I'm serious. I didn't expect it, and I did nothing to encourage it."

"Fine! Then I'll go out there and kiss White and we'll be even!"

"I love my brother, but if you kiss him, I may have to kill him."

"Are you jealous?" she throws back in my face, and I have to say I am.

"Damn straight. Now that I've had your lips, they're mine."

"Gray..."

"Now that I've had you, CC, you are mine. You need to understand that."

I see the moment fear hits her face, and I know I'm pushing her way too hard, but I can't seem to stop myself. The last thing I expected was to have her follow me here. Now that she's here, I'm going to make damn sure she understands what her being here means.

"You broke up with me."

"I left, but I was coming back, Cooper. You're not getting away from me."

"We were a one-night stand, Gray."

"That's just it, CC. We were. What we are now, what we could be, is so much more."

"Gray, I don't do relationships real well."

"Do you want what we have to end, sweetheart?"

"No..."

"Then take a chance. I don't do relationships either, but I do not want to let go of what we have here."

"We're completely different," she says, but I see a little of the fear on her face fade and I know I'm starting to get through to her.

"Opposites attract."

"What if Cammie's right and I hurt you?"

"Hurt me?"

"In your business, with your whole hitting-balls-in-weird-pants thing," she says and I have to laugh.

"Sweetheart, I can assure you the only way you could hurt me is if you walk away without giving us a chance."

"I don't come from money, Gray. I'm never going to be comfortable around people like..."

I put my lips to hers and kiss her gently to stop whatever she's going to say. Her lips are as tender and sweet as I remember. I drink in the flavor of her and pull slowly back.

"You've met my family, Cooper. Do you honestly think they're anything like the Rivertons?"

"Well, Ida Sue's pet cow does remind me of Cammie a little."

"Oh, that was bad, Claudia Cooper."

"I could show you bad..."

"Right here? In the barn?"

"Let's be honest. Your family already thinks we're having sex. We might as well."

I step away from her. I think she actually thinks I'm a stupid man because her face shows her confusion. She actually thinks I'm turning her down. I pull my shirt up over my body and throw it down on the hay.

"Well, what are you waiting for, Cooper? Strip," I tell her, kicking off my boots. When she starts undressing while smiling at me, something clicks into place. Claudia Cooper is my forever.

Now I just have to prove it to her.

Chapter Thirty-Six

CC

I can't believe I'm doing this. Then again, I can't believe I'm here. Something about Gray makes me do things I would normally never do—like have sex in a barn on a pile of hay in the middle of the afternoon with his crazy family milling around outside. Yet here I am.

I watch him the entire time I undress. I can't go slowly because there's a good chance I'll lose my nerve and an even bigger chance his mom will come out to do something crazy like give her cow a manicure. It doesn't matter because the last article of my clothing hits the ground, then Gray grabs me and kisses me. His body is warmer than I remember, softer, yet strong at the same time. I open my mouth to him, groaning as his tongue pushes inside and takes over my mouth. His mouth slants over mine, our lips caressing, tasting and devouring each other. I've been kissed before, but Gray's kisses are always like nothing I've ever experienced. I could kiss him for hours upon hours and still crave more.

When we break apart, I take a deep breath. My body is literally shaking from the need and the storm he has awakened inside of me. I dig my fingers into his back and hold on as I raise my head to look at him. Gray has to be the most beautiful man on the face of the Earth. Have I said that? It needs to be repeated. The man is so masculine and sexy that it should be illegal. With his hair rumpled and his eyes sparkling with mischief, he is like nothing I've ever encountered. He could charm a nun into spreading her legs.

"What are you thinking, sweet lips?" he asks and I shake my head at that horrible nickname he insists on using. I want to say something smart. I'm already feeling exposed, but before I can stop myself, the truth slips out.

"I missed you," I whisper. What is it about Gray that undermines my defenses and allows these moments of weakness that leave me vulnerable? Gray groans my name, his hand moving down to cup the side of my neck, and he pulls my mouth back to him.

"I've missed you so fucking much, woman," he purrs into my ear. The vibration of his words rock me. Is it another line? If it is, it's a fucking good one.

When his lips slide down the side of my neck and his hands come around to hold my breasts, squeezing them gently, I stop thinking altogether. His thumbs scrape against my nipples at the same time he gently bites my shoulder. A ripple of need pushes through my body, making my knees feel weak. I can feel myself getting wetter as he kisses down my chest to suck one of my nipples in his mouth, feeding my desire. His tongue moves around it, petting it, teasing it and sending shards of electricity through my body.

"Gray," I whimper, torn between never wanting him to stop what he's doing and demanding he just take me.

"I love your breasts, CC. The way they feel in my hands, the way your nipples strain for attention. How they respond when I tease you," he whispers against my skin before taking one fully in his mouth and sucking on it. My head goes back with a gasp, my nails flexing into his skin and scoring his back as desire rips through me. His tongue pushes the nipple to the roof of his mouth, the slick, moist skin tightly sliding against it right before he flicks his tongue over it and puts it in place so he can bite down on it. A small burst of pain scissors like white heat through me.

I feel his hand move down my stomach, his rough callused skin making me feel more feminine than I've ever felt in my life. "Are you wet for me, Cooper?"

For the life of me I can do nothing, not even mumble. My breath is lodged in my throat as I wait to see what else he does to my body. Gray doesn't stop until he reaches my center. The tips of his fingers slide through the sticky moisture gathered on the outside. "Soaked," he grunts, answering himself, right before thrusting his fingers inside of me. "Always so wet, tight, and ready for me. You were made for me, Cooper," his deep voice growls while he slowly thrusts his fingers in and out of me.

"Gray," I plead, my voice weak and filled with need.

"What is it, sweetheart? What do you want?"

I'd answer him if I could, I really would, but words are kind of beyond me. Next time, I'll try and remain in control and torture him like he is doing to me right now. Instead, I do the only thing I can manage, the only thing my brain allows me to do. I reach down and grab his cock. It manages somehow to be even more heated than the rest of him. So hot and thick, it fills my hand and makes my knees want to buckle at the same time. Now it's his turn to groan. I stroke him once, forcing myself to open my eyes and watch his face as I squeeze his cock tightly in my hand. His eyes go inky dark, his breath labored.

"Keep that up and this is going to go pretty fucking fast, Cooper. I've been without you too long."

"I need you inside of me, Gray. It's been way too long," I tell him honestly. It has. In the last few days, I'd wake up in the middle of the night after dreaming about making love with Gray, and I'd want to cry because he wasn't there. "I feel so empty," I tell him, squeezing his dick harder.

He growls and then takes complete control. His fingers leave me and I cry out in frustration. I want to complain, but I can't because he's too busy lying me back on the hay. It pokes against my skin and I have to wonder why you hear so often about people rolling around in the hay because it's not comfortable at all. Then, Gray's body comes over mine. He braces himself with one hand as he pushes against my leg. I spread as wide as I can to make room for him. He positions his dick at my entrance. I can feel the tip of his cock and try to thrust up to bring him inside. He grabs ahold of my hip quickly, preventing it. His hand holds me almost to the point of bruising, but I love every moment of it.

"Hold still for me, Cooper. I'm in control," he growls, the look on his face so intense I shudder in need. I bite my lip, giving a slight nod because words are beyond me. He must understand, however, because he goes back to holding his cock. He moves the tip against my pussy. The slick wet skin glides against me, just skirting the place I want it the most—deep inside of me. Then, it slips against my clit and he moves it over and over in the same spot, pushing against the throbbing nub. My whole body jerks in reaction, my nails biting into the cheeks of his ass. My vision is blurry because I'm so close to the edge, but I can see him smile. He knows exactly what he's doing. A little more of this and I'm done for.

"Oh God," I breathe, my eyes closing as he does it again. Then, before I realize it, he's thrusting inside of me so completely and so quickly that he's seated all the way in before I can even open my eyes. When I do, he's right there, his lips finding mine. I wrap my legs around him. The move pushes him in so deep, I can feel him practically against my cervix.

"Jesus, Cooper, you feel so fucking good," he groans as he sets a rhythm. "So fucking good."

"More, Gray. I need more," I plead, knowing I'm close to coming, but requiring more to send me over the edge. He knows it too and he's purposely holding out.

"You belong to me, Cooper. You're not getting away from me again," he growls, and I swear I can feel his cock rake against my walls when he pulls back out, so tight that the veins of his cock graze me.

That's when it hits me: Gray doesn't have on a condom. I'm on birth control, and we've already tempted fate once before. We can't do it again. Panic washes over me and I push on his shoulders.

"Gray! Stop! Oh God, stop!" It takes him a minute to realize I'm asking him to quit, probably because, greedy whore that I am, I still have both my legs wrapped around him trying to hold him inside. God.

"It's okay, baby, don't get scared on me. This is good. What we have is good," he croons, but he doesn't understand.

"You don't have a condom on. We can't do this. Oh shit, Gray! Get up!" I urge him, unlocking my legs from around him.

"Aren't you on the pill?" he asks, still not moving.

"What? Yeah, of course."

"Then what's the problem?" he asks, sounding confused.

"Hello? The pill doesn't always work, and it doesn't protect you from diseases..."

"I'm clean, Cooper."

"You did a sex tape. You want me to just trust that...?"

"We've already had unprotected sex once. Remember? Besides you trusted me enough to fuck me in the first place," he says, and now he's starting to sound upset with me. That, however, doesn't stop him from starting to move back inside of me. He angles his body and the sensation is so good, I nearly lose my train of thought.

"Gray! You can't come inside of me," I tell him, my voice dripping in panic.

"Relax, I'll pull out and come all over your stomach, but we will be talking about this later. I'm not going to wear condoms with you forever, Cooper. I want you like this again. Fuck, over and over, just like this," he says, slamming into me.

I want to argue, but as he pushes me toward my climax, I can do nothing but hold onto him. I want more of this too. I want it over and over, just like him.

I call out his name as I shatter into a million pieces. I'm barely coming back down when I feel him leave my body, and I want to cry at the loss. I feel his warm cum fall against my stomach and my hand automatically goes there to hold on to it, to rub it against my skin and keep it as close as I can get. I feel a moment of sadness because, although I know I am right, I am perversely wishing it was inside of me, that I could feel the hot spray deep in my body. Shit!

Grayson Lucas is making me break all of my rules.

Chapter Thirty-Seven

GRAY

CC is unusually quiet as we make our way from the barn back to Mom's house. I reach out and take her hand and our fingers slide together. It feels good, and when I squeeze her hand reassuringly, she looks up at me. For a second, I see fear in those green eyes, but then a slow smile breaks on her lips. A smile for me. It's mine, I'm claiming it, just like I've claimed her.

"Wait! Where are you going?" she whispers loudly, sounding as if I'm doing something completely crazy, which maybe I am, because in my head I'm trying to figure out how to talk CC into having sex with me without worrying about the birth control. Any birth control. Just from the panic in the barn alone, I know that's not going to be easily done. Doesn't change the fact that it's what I want. She's mine forever. I'm not giving her up, even if I can't tell her that yet. I know without a shadow of a doubt that if I did, she would run. That can't happen.

"We're already late for dinner. Mom will skin us both alive if we don't get in there pretty soon."

"I can't go in there!"

"Why not?" I ask, thoroughly confused.

"We just had sex!"

"Sweet lips, not to point out the obvious, but I think they all know that."

"But I have your protein sauce all over my stomach!"

"Protein sauce?"

"You know what I mean! I'm all sticky!"

"We wiped it off. It's fine. You're being crazy over nothing. Besides, you made me put it there. I would have much rather had my little soldiers swimming inside that sweet little body of yours and eventually dripping down your thighs to remind you of everything we did."

"Your little soldiers need to stay far away from my insides, Grayson Lucas."

"We'll see," I tell her, frowning. Getting in her unprotected might be a little harder than I anticipated.

"We'll see? There's nothing to see!" she practically shouts.

I ignore her, instead choosing to open the door to the kitchen and gently, but firmly, pushing her inside. She stumbles slightly before looking over her shoulder and shooting me a look to kill. I grin just to piss her off more.

"What are we seeing?" White asks.

"Cooper doesn't want to have a baby with me," I tell him like that's something I discuss every day. The room goes silent, but I ignore them all. They don't get it. When I decided CC was mine, all of my normal routines were thrown out the window. I'm not interested in other women. I'm not interested in trying to burn her out of my system. I want to keep her attached to my side. I want to make sure she can't get away. I can't give her those reasons out loud yet because my CC is as skittish as a young colt. I'm not going to make a big secret about shit, either. She needs to hear some of it. She needs to get used to it because I'm going nowhere.

"I can't believe you," she huffs in my ear for me alone. "Ignore him. He hit his head on a stall door in the barn. He's obviously delirious," she says louder for everyone to hear. Everyone remains silent, most likely because they know I'm totally serious.

Mom reaches over and takes a piece of hay that was stuck in

CC's hair. "You seem to have hay in your hair, sweetie. You really should have picked the kitchen table. That hay can be mighty uncomfortable. And the barn usually has mosquitoes big enough to carry a body off," she says.

"Umm..."

"And you needn't worry. Jansen made sure this table could hold up an army. It's sturdy enough to handle anything you two do."

"Umm," CC says again, probably not knowing what to say. Mom has that effect on everyone, and has it often.

"There's a lot of good memories on this table. It's our favorite worshipping altar," Jansen agrees.

"You guys, really? I eat off this table!" Cyan growls, being the lone Lucas sibling who still lives at home.

"So do I," says Jansen, grinning and winking at Mom.

Everyone moans at the yuckiness of thinking of our Mom like that. Hell, my own moan joins in.

"You have a very strange family, crayon man."

"If I had a dollar..." I sigh, then put some roast on CC's plate before adding some to mine. I do the same with the mashed potatoes.

"What if I didn't want mashed potatoes?" she asks, then reaches over to get a roll and put it on my plate.

"You love mashed potatoes. The waitress at the diner always makes sure you get a double order and you eat every bite," I tell her, pulling off a piece of the roll with my fingers and popping it in my mouth.

She turns to look at me, studying my face. "You notice things like that?"

"I notice everything about you, Cooper."

"Why?" she asks, sounding really confused.

"Because you matter," I tell her, kissing her briefly on the lips. Then I return to eating, leaving her to think while I get lost in the conversations going on around us. I figure I've given her enough to think about.

Rome wasn't built in a day. Tomorrow, I'll push a little more.

Chapter Thirty-Eight

CC

"This was your room growing up?"

"What gave it away?"

"The naked girl posters."

"Well, this was also Green's room, so those are his, and I'd like to point out that some of them are wearing clothes."

"Like... those two over there?" I point to the wall across from the bed.

"Well, those are Green's. Really, they all are, except Sophia Loren there. That one is all mine."

"You're kidding, right?"

"Hell no! That woman is trophy-boner worthy."

"Okay, first of all, talking about other women inducing boners while in bed with me? Yeah, that should never happen again."

"Point made, sweet lips," he whispers, rolling over me so his body covers mine. He kisses along the inside of my neck and, just like that, I have to struggle to remember what we were talking about.

"Second, what is a trophy-boner?"

"It's what you get from me every fucking time without even trying," he says, grabbing my hand and pulling it to his dick. He wraps my hand around it, putting his own on top of mine. We stroke his cock together while looking into each other's eyes.

I grin. "That is impressive."

"And you and Sophia Loren are the only two women to ever get me this hard," he whispers, biting on my earlobe.

"Oh my God! You do realize that she's, like, one hundred and eighty now, right?"

"Sacrilege! She's like eighty, eighty-one tops."

"It scares me that you know this."

"Hey, I get invested when it matters," he murmurs, sliding down my body and kissing my stomach. I reluctantly let go of his cock, but only because his mouth is headed in a direction I'd definitely like to have it. I close my eyes and enjoy the way his lips graze against the skin on my stomach and the small kisses he places along my hip bone.

"Cooper, I have a favor to ask you."

"What's that?" Something in his tone pulls me out of my happy place.

"I want you to go to Nebraska with me."

"Nebraska?" I'm completely alert now. My body stiffens and Gray must notice because he sighs and pulls up so he can lie beside me. He picks up my hand and pulls it to him, letting his fingers trace around the bones in my wrists as he massages my palm.

"That's where my next tournament is. I've been on break for a couple of weeks because of tendonitis in my shoulder. I have to go to Nebraska, and I really want you with me."

"They play golf in Nebraska?"

"Yes, though everyone wants to avoid the course I'm on."

"I thought in golf you could pick and choose what tournaments you play in? Or did I read that wrong?"

"You researched golf?" he asks, turning to look at me. I shrug uncomfortably. If he knew how much he consumed my thoughts, he'd probably worry. He kisses the tip of my nose and grins like a big kid on Christmas morning. "That deserves a reward, Claudia Cooper."

"Yeah, yeah. So why are you going to Nebraska and not one of the big time golf courses?"

"Do you know where those are?"

"South Carolina? Georgia?"

"A big reward..."

The way he says that combined with the look in his eyes causes my insides to spasm.

"Explain now. Sex later."

He sighs like I just took away his favorite toy, but he does it still smiling. "Okay, well, ideally when you are a ranked golfer, you can pick and choose."

"Yeah, and you can't convince me—"

"Unless, of course, you tick the wrong people off and then your invite gets misplaced, your inquiry gets ignored, your mail gets lost..."

"Holy shit."

"In short, you get blackballed by the powers that be."

"What did you do?"

"We don't need to talk about that right now," he says uncomfortably.

"I think we do."

He sighs at my answer and looks at me for a minute, then lets me have it. "Remember the tape with the two girls?"

"I'm trying to forget. That should be another topic, by the way, that we don't talk to each other about in bed. Or ever, really."

"You brought it up. It's just that one of those girls happens to be the daughter of one of the major tour promoters and sponsors."

"Jesus, Gray. Haven't you heard the saying 'don't shit where you eat'?"

"You've been hanging around my mom a little too much."

"So Riverton's sponsorship meant his money would make things easier..."

"Well, more like he had influence with most of the powers that be. With him in my corner..."

"You could go back to playing at the fields you love..."

"And hopefully winning to further my rank."

"And here I thought golf was boring. It's reading like a made-for-TV movie."

"Anyway, telling Riverton and Cammie to go fuck themselves—though, in nicer words—kind of nixed any thought of that working out. Hell, it probably made a bad situation even worse."

"They are vindictive assholes."

"So, Nebraska it is, and I want you with me."

"Gray..."

"C'mon, Cooper. Come to Nebraska with me. I want you by my side."

I study his face. I should say no. I have a business I've already neglected enough by coming here. I have obligations. There's a million reasons I should say no and, honestly, only one reason I should say yes.

Gray. Gray is the reason. Gray with his wicked smile, his sexy laugh, his outrageous behavior and crazy family. Gray who makes my body melt and my heart feel light. Gray who knows that I love mashed potatoes.

"Okay."

"C'mon, Cooper," he persists. "I promise that if you... Wait. What did you say?"

"I said okay, I'll go to Nebraska with you."

"Fuck yeah! You won't regret this, sweet lips."

"On one condition," I add, interrupting him.

"What's that?"

"I want my reward," I tell him. "Now."

Then I watch as a smile spreads across his face and he moves his hand between my thighs. That's when I stop worrying about everything.

Chapter Thirty-Nine

GRAY

One Week Later

"What's this?" CC asks.

I look up to watch her walking to the table. She's wearing my t-shirt and nothing else and my dick instantly tents the gym shorts I'm wearing. Maybe I can talk her into a second round.

"My woman coming towards me to offer her pussy?" I say hopefully and only half joking.

CC stops, looks up from the paper she's holding, and rolls her eyes at me. "You are a horn dog."

"You haven't seemed to complain much lately."

"I know. I think the Nebraska heat has gotten to me."

I reach up and pull her down on my lap. She moves so she can straddle me and my hands rest on her hips, moving her body so the hard ridge of my cock nestles against her center. She's wearing nothing under my shirt and I don't give a fuck if an earthquake hits at this point—there will be a round two.

"You mean the Gray Lucas heat," I tell her, moving my hands to the tops of her thighs and letting my thumbs drop down to tease the inside, so close to her sweet little cunt that I can feel the heat rolling off of her.

"Is that like the clap?" she asks, smiling sweetly. If there's one thing CC does, it's constantly keep my ego in check.

"I really need to start spanking your ass," I grumble.

"Right now, you mention that and all I can think of is Ida Sue bent over the kitchen table..."

"Quit trying to kill my boner, woman."

"I'm thinking that's not possible with you. But back to what I was saying," she says, picking up the paper. "The main story in the sports section of the Nebraska Gazette reads, and I quote: Grayson Lucas proves why he's the hot young stud of the golf course."

"Jesus," I grumble, pushing the paper out of her hands and pulling her into my body. Then, I burrow my head into her neck. God, she tastes so sweet here—like sugar. I could spend hours nibbling, biting, and kissing nothing but the spot where her neck and shoulder meet. I run my tongue up her collarbone and then gently knead her neck with my teeth, groaning as her hips shift and she grinds against my hard cock. I feel her fingers thread through my hair and she holds me close. "I can't get enough of you, Cooper. I don't think I ever will," I tell her with stark honesty. I've spent this last week trying to show her how much I love her. I haven't said the words. It's a fucked up mess that the man who meant to always stay single now finds himself in love with a woman who is so freaking scared of commitment it oozes out of her pores. It's probably fate's sadistic karma. Somehow, I will make her see what we have. What we are together is a once-in-a-lifetime thing.

In the past week, she's thrown up some of my tabloid exploits. I've laughed them off, but even that's getting tiring. I want to tell her that's all in the past. Hell, since meeting CC, I haven't looked at another woman. I don't see them and that's the truth.

"Gray," she whimpers, sliding back and forth on my cock. My dick slides in just the right spot and I wish to fuck that I wasn't wearing my shorts.

"I'm going to fuck you, CC. I'm going to bend you over this table and fuck you so hard that the people in the next room will hear you crying out my name." I can feel the way her body quakes at my words, her fingers tightening in my hair almost to the point of pain, and she moans while she continues trying to ride the hard outline of my dick. "Is that what you want, baby? Do you want me to push that pretty face of yours down on the glass of this table and hold you in place while I feed your hungry pussy every inch of my cock?"

"Oh fuck," she whispers, her hands moving from my hair. I raise up from where I'm whispering in her ear to watch her hands move under my shirt. I grab the collar on each end and pull, ignoring the buttons that fly, interested only in exposing her lush breasts. I watch as CC toys with her nipples, her hips undulating against me. She's fucking gorgeous and she's very close to making herself come. That can't happen, even if she is using my body and my hard-as-a-rock cock to get what she wants. I watch for another minute because I'm a man and this is the fucking hottest thing I've seen in my life. Then I grab hold of her and stand up in one swift movement.

"Gray!" she whines, her body shaking since she was so close.

I ignore her protest and, instead, rip the shirt from her body. I should make a rule that she doesn't wear clothes when we're in the hotel room together; it slows me down too fucking much. I use my hand to push everything off the table. The vase and flowers crash first with a heavy thud on the carpet, followed by the breakfast dishes we used earlier. I ignore the noise, shifting us around so she's in front of me. Then I push her against the table, bending her over. Her hands go out to steady herself. I'd worry I'm going too far if it weren't for her ass pushing out against me, demanding more.

"Hurry, Gray," she urges.

Fuck, she really is perfect for me.

Chapter Forty

CC

He pushes me down on the cool glass of the table and I gasp as my breasts press down and my nipples caress the cold surface. I feel Gray close behind me, his hand pressing down on my back to keep me in place. He needn't worry; I'm not going anywhere. Hell, I was supposed to go back to Kentucky, and instead I'm planning on going with Gray to Arizona. If I'm completely honest, I'm already wondering if Jackson can take over longer. I have it bad for this man, and as much as it scares me, I can't seem to push him away.

He keeps one hand on my back and I feel his other on the inside of one of my thighs, pulling it so my legs are apart. Then I feel him behind me, completely naked. His legs press against mine, and I can feel his cock slide against my ass as I wait for what comes next.

"So ready for me. Are you willing to admit you're mine yet, CC?" he asks, his voice hoarse. A million butterflies move in my stomach at his words. He's been pushing and pushing for me to give him this. I haven't. I want to say it out loud because inside I know it's true, but I just can't seem to.

"Stop talking and start fucking," I growl, but break off when his hand connects with my ass. Fire lances through my body. "Gray!" I yell, but he spanks me again. I breathe through it as his hand connects again. "What do you think you're doing?" I ask just as another one is delivered.

"You're mine, CC."

"I'm not..." I start to deny it, but the words refuse to come out. In the end, I whimper as his hand slaps my ass again. Somewhere while he delivers his punishment, it changes from pain to... an added pleasure.

"You are mine, CC. Your body knows it, you know it. You just need to admit it," he whispers against my ass as his tongue moves over the hot, tender skin. His lips place small kisses along the spots he has spanked and his hand moves down to find my pussy. "You're so wet for me. I think my Cooper likes being spanked." God. He's right. I'm soaked and I'm aching to have him inside of me. "Your pussy is holding onto my fingers so tight, it's going to break them," he groans. His fingers move in and out of me, hard and fast. Gray's right. I'm clenching my muscles so tight on his arm trying to keep his fingers exactly where I need them to come. I'm riding them with all that I have, needing to come so bad, I'm almost mindless.

Suddenly, he takes his hand away. I try to rise up and complain but he keeps his hold solidly on my back, forbidding me to move. Then all at once, I feel the head of his cock sliding in the slick cream at my center. I can feel him at my opening and I whimper, needing him to push inside, to end this torture. When he does nothing, I all but snarl. "Gray! Stop torturing me!" My demand is met with a tight laugh, but even through it, I can hear the need in him.

"I don't have a condom. Are you going to let me fuck you raw?" he rumbles behind me as just the tip of his cock presses inside of me.

"Damn it, Gray," I growl because he's been trying for a week to get me here. He thinks I'm being crazy, and a part of me thinks I am too. My whole life, no one sticks around though. Even people who care about me leave. Banger left. He may not have meant to, but he did. Letting Gray in completely is opening myself up to more pain, and I don't think I can handle the pain that would be associated with losing Gray.

"Tell me, CC," he growls.

"Yes, damn it. I want it too," I growl, trying to ignore the tear that falls from my eye. It's not because of what we're doing; it's the fear of losing Gray... because I might love him.

All thought flees when he thrusts inside of me completely. When he sinks all the way in, he holds himself still. I feel his body stretched over me, his breath near my back. I close my eyes and memorize the feel of him everywhere—the feel of him inside me. Proving how well Gray knows me, his next words grab ahold of me and do not let me go.

"Don't be afraid, CC. I'm here, baby, and I'm not going anywhere," he whispers. His hand pets my back before tangling in my hair. Then his other hand reaches around and zeroes in on my clit. He begins slowly manipulating it with his fingers and then starts setting a slow pace with his body.

He fucks me slow and steady and the emotions are thick, my breath stalling in my chest when I hear him moan and feel his hot cum pour into me.

"Never letting you go, baby. Never letting you go..."

His words are the last I hear before I completely fragment into a million pieces with the largest orgasm I've ever had in my life. My entire body shakes and I squeeze my eyes shut. Then I bite my lip to keep from begging him to promise me he'll always stay.

Please, God, don't let him be lying...

Chapter Forty-One

GRAY

"Cooper? Where are you? I have something I need to run by you!" I yell, coming through the hotel room. I don't know how I've managed it, but somehow I've kept CC with me for two weeks. We've traveled through Nebraska, Arizona, and North Dakota. Now we're in Mississippi. I've won each of the courses—and rather easily. What's even better is that the press has been following me more and more. In fact, last tournament, more fanfare showed up in North Dakota to watch me work my magic than actually showed up for some of the premiere tournaments and talent. I don't really give a fuck. However, it does mean one thing: Now the assholes in charge have set up a dinner with me. They've talked to Seth and they want me onboard in Hilton Head next week. Seth's urging me to play ball. I want to say I don't give a fuck. The truth is, however, that the competitive side in me realizes these tournaments are where the real talent is. The men who eat, drink, and sleep golf. The men who leave it all out on the green. In my career, I've had one motto: To be the best, you have to play the best. That competitive drive is what got me this far and I can't ignore it now.

All of that boils down to the fact that I'm meeting a bunch of stuffy suits for dinner tomorrow night, which would be easy, but it worries me how CC is going to react. Even I have to admit I'm nervous about it. Dinners haven't exactly gone well with me and CC. Worse, Riverton will be at this meeting. I can only hope that Cammie doesn't show up. It's going to take a miracle to talk CC into going to this damn dinner as it is—a miracle I'll never pull off if I can't even find her. She's not in the main room or the attached kitchen. The bedroom is empty, too.

"Cooper!" I yell again, starting to get worried.

"In here," she calls from the bathroom. I open the door and what I see makes me feel like a hand is squeezing my heart. CC is in a bubble bath, her flowing red hair pinned atop her head, but a few curls have fallen down to frame her face. Her body is wet, shiny, and perfect, and I get just enough of a glance before the bubbles curve around and hide her from me, making me want more.

"Damn, there's a vision for a man to come home to," I tell her, and I'm not joking. At all.

"Except we're not home, Einstein. We're in a hotel."

"Honey, with a body like that, it doesn't matter where we're at," I tell her, but I am mad at myself. What I really want to tell her is that anywhere she's at feels like home to me. I can't say that. She may be thawing out some, but she's definitely not ready to hear me tell her how I really feel... what I really want.

"So much flattery. Now can you get out of here so I can finish my bath?"

"Um... go ahead and bathe, I'm not stopping you," I tell her, leaning on the bathroom door and crossing my arms. Fuck no. I'm not about to leave. I'm not stupid.

"Okay, let me rephrase that: Leave so I can finish my bubble bath without you bothering me."

"I'll be good. You won't even know I'm here."

"Yeah, sure. Your tongue is sticking out, pervert."

"What? I'm innocent."

"Whatever. You would think you'd be worn out especially after this morning."

"This morning was just an early workout. You should know your man by now, woman," I tell her, and she gets this look on her face that stays there for all of a few seconds. Then, she just shakes her head at me.

"Why are you back early? I thought you said you were going to go by the course and scope things out."

"Well, Seth called."

At my words, CC sits up a little taller in the tub, which is good for me because it reveals her breasts. My eyes are glued to them, watching as the water and bubbles stream slowly, running down her breasts until her nipples are revealed.

"Are those assholes messing with you again? What the hell can they do now? Jesus, someone needs to teach these fuckers a lesson. I might be the one to do it. What are they doing?"

I can hear her talking, but honestly I'm paying very little attention. My eyes are glued to her body and my cock is throbbing. I've always enjoyed sex, but having CC is making me a self-proclaimed sex addict.

"Gray! Eyes up here, moron. What bullshit are they pulling now?"

"Moron? Words hurt, Cooper."

"I'm going to hurt you."

"I've never been into dominating women, but for you, I'd be willing to try."

"I know it's hard, but will you try and be serious for a minute?"

I crouch down by the tub, folding my hands on the edge and smiling at her. "Well, I am pretty hard."

"I know when there's a naked woman in the room, your brain cells dissipate, but let's try. What are those assholes pulling now?"

"God, you're sexy when you're all set to defend me."

"Right now I'm thinking I might rather kill you."

I grin. Shit, this woman never stops giving me what I want.

"They're not doing anything, sweet lips. They want to meet with me."

"Of course they do, because they realize you're the star. They need you. I swear, assholes with money are all the same."

"Hey now."

"You know what I mean," she growls. "So when do you meet with them?"

"They want to meet for dinner tomorrow night."

She is silent for a few minutes. Then, she takes a deep breath and her hand slides along the side of my face. "You got this."

There it is. CC giving me her support. CC believing in me. I don't think she even realizes she does it, but she does. I notice, and that's just one small thing in a million larger ones that makes her special, that makes her the woman I plan on keeping.

"We got this," I correct her, giving her a gentle kiss on her lips. "I thought it would be harder to talk you into having dinner with them. It means a lot that you..."

"Wait. What are you talking about? Why would I be having dinner with them? It's a business dinner. There's no reason for me to be there."

"There's every reason. I want you there. Hell, Cooper, I need you there."

"Gray, I don't get along with those kind of people. If there's anything our time together has taught us, it's that."

"Bullshit. We're a team, CC. You and me against them all."

"Gray..."

"I need you, CC."

She closes her eyes, and guilt hits me. I know she's given up a lot to come with me. I know this is hard for her. I'm a second away from telling her it's okay when she surprises me.

"Okay, fine," she says.

Elation strums through me. "You mean it?" I ask, sounding like a little kid.

"Yeah. I mean, how bad can it be? At least Cammie and her father won't be there," she says.

And here is my first huge mistake: I remain quiet. I don't confess that Riverton will be there.

Instead, I say, "You amaze me." I push the guilt down, then pull her in for a kiss. Our tongues dance. Her arms go around me and she gives herself over to me. I push in closer, intent on climbing into the tub and taking what's mine.

"Gray! What are you doing? You'll get all wet!"

"I don't give a fuck," I tell her, and I don't. I need this. I need her. And I really don't want to think about what's going to happen if Riverton and Cammie are at that meeting tomorrow night.

Chapter Forty-Two

CC

"Are you sure I look alright?" I ask Gray for the tenth time, which is crazy since I know I look good. I'm also confident in the dress I'm wearing. I spent all day researching places on the web so I would find the perfect dress to wear. We're having dinner at a very uptown restaurant. It took us two hours to drive here. I guess the assholes didn't want to eat in the small town they had condemned Gray to compete in.

"Sweetheart, you look beautiful," he says, and the softness in his voice almost undoes me. I'm wearing a black cocktail dress. Classic, chic, and definitely not something that will embarrass me or Gray. I went to a spa and had my hair tamed and fixed. If there is one thing about my outfit that Gray doesn't like, my hair would be it; he loves my hair and misses the curls tonight. I'd never admit it, but I kind of do, too. I take a breath at the hostess table, trying to make sure my dress is straight and I haven't done something stupid. I look behind me thinking I will find toilet paper stuck to my dress from when I went to the bathroom, but there isn't. It doesn't make a damn bit of sense, but then again, I'm not exactly making a lot of sense tonight. "Stop fidgeting, Cooper. You're beautiful. You're the best looking woman here tonight."

"You haven't seen the other women," I tell him.

He pulls my face close to his, so close that our foreheads touch. His hands gently cup the sides of my neck and his eyes look deep into mine. “Since the moment I met you, Claudia Cooper, other women ceased to exist for me.” His words, so softly delivered, pierce my heart and squeeze it so tight it’s hard to breathe.

I fight through it, my hand going to cover his on my neck. “That’s a really good line, Grayson Lucas.”

“There’s not a line in it. I’m so fucking proud to have you on my arm, Cooper. Never doubt that for one fucking minute.”

Can you stop breathing from the force of words alone? The thing about it is, his words seep into empty parts of me and fill up holes that have been there for years. I have no defense. I’m just here, exposed.

“If you make me cry, I’m going to kick you in the nuts,” I try to joke, but my voice is broken, giving away the emotion he has evoked.

His beautiful lips slowly smile. “Got it. No more sappy stuff.”

“No more sappy stuff,” I agree, and he kisses me quickly before pulling away.

“Do you have reservations?” the hostess asks, and Gray looks at me strangely, clears his throat, and takes my hand. He squeezes it reassuringly and I’m starting to get a bad feeling.

“It should be under Riverton,” he says quietly to the hostess, but he’s looking at me.

My face goes pale. I know it does because I can feel the cold clamminess spread. Riverton? What the fuck? He knew Riverton was going to be here and he didn’t warn me? Gray knew I thought he wouldn’t be here and he let me believe it. I jerk my hand, trying to get it free from his hold. He doesn’t let go, however, and before I can say anything to him, the devil himself picks that moment to walk up.

“Grayson, how nice to see you again,” he says, and I don’t know which one of the two I would rather kick right now. It would be a tough call.

“David, you too,” Grayson says, shaking the devil’s hand.

"We're seated this way," Riverton says, ignoring the fact that there's a hostess who gets paid to do that. He doesn't acknowledge me on the way there, which is fine as I'm more than used to that. I prefer it, really.

"I'm sorry, sweetheart," Gray whispers as we're walking behind Riverton.

"I'm not talking to you," I whisper back.

"If I had told you, you wouldn't have come."

"So you lied."

"No, I just didn't correct you. It could be worse," he adds just as we get to the table.

That's when I see her: Cammie Riverton. She stands up and beams at Gray, wrapping him in a hug that, to his credit, he doesn't return.

"Grayson! I've missed you," she says, and the fact that Grayson doesn't return the hug and pretty much ignores what she says might be the only thing that saves his life.

At least for now.

Chapter Forty-Three

GRAY

"Cammie," I all but growl. Fuck, it was going to be hard enough to get CC not to hate me over Riverton. The fact that Cammie is here will just make everything fucking worse.

"Oh, Claudia. I didn't realize you would be here," Cammie says, her voice dripping with distaste.

I feel CC stiffen beside me and I hate myself all over again for putting her through this. My woman is brilliant and completely in charge—unless these idiots are involved. They make her feel out of her depth. I get the feeling that Cammie Riverton is a real expert at it.

"Odd, I could say the same about you," CC returns, and when I look up, she's staring at me. I'm not sure what to call the look on her face. I knew I would be in trouble, but her look is something else altogether. I wouldn't even call it anger, which is what I expected the most.

"I'm afraid we don't have enough seats," Cammie says, saccharinely sweet.

"Here, sweetheart. Sit here and I'll get the waiter to bring us another chair," I jump in, shooting Cammie a look of disgust. Not that she gets it.

"Aww, thank you, Gray," CC says, sitting down. "It's so nice having a boyfriend who does these little things to show how much he cares," she adds, and that might make me feel good if I didn't feel the bad vibes coming off of her. I quickly find another chair. Cammie slides over to give room to put a chair in between her and CC. That's not happening. I gently nudge CC next to Cammie and sit close beside her with Neil Brayden, another investor, on my other side.

The next few minutes are consumed with everyone ordering food and getting settled. CC says very little, but right now I'm calling it a win that she doesn't get up and walk away. I'm doing my best to ignore Cammie's little digs she's adding to the mix; all are designed to make CC feel unwelcome, or to talk about things she has no idea about. All this time, I thought Cammie was ditzy, mostly an airhead, but I'm starting to see the error in assuming that. Small talk continues while we wait on our food. It's stilted at best. I never thought I'd be so glad to have a waitress come and interrupt us as I am in this minute. I've got my arm wrapped around the back of CC's chair, the message clear: I'm with her. I'd feel better if she would at least acknowledge me.

"Are you okay, sweetheart?" I ask, trying to get her involved—at least with me, if nothing else.

"I'm fine, darling. Why wouldn't I be?" she asks, and the sweet, innocent routine is definitely fake. She turns around to talk to Cammie. "He's always so attentive, worrying to make sure I'm okay," she smiles. I squeeze her shoulder reassuringly. She remains stiff, but doesn't pull away.

"I care about you, sweetheart. I just want to make sure you're okay."

CC looks up at me, and that's when I see it: hurt in those big green eyes. For a minute, she lets her guard down, and I can see it clearly. Acid churns in my stomach. I can deal with her anger, as that's what I was expecting, but what I see is pain and hurt. That's more than I can handle.

She turns over and leans into Cammie like they're the best of friends. That should warn me what to expect. Sadly, it doesn't.

"He's always doing this. It drives me crazy."

"Gray's a very thoughtful man. I'm sure he's just being kind," Cammie says as if she's offended on my behalf. "You should be grateful," she adds, reaching over to pat my hand. I pull it back immediately, but it doesn't seem to faze her. "I'm sure the men you're used to dealing with aren't like that, only there because of what you give them. But a real man is different, Claudia. A real man expects a more adult relationship with a woman."

I start to interject, but CC responds before I can. "You're most likely right. Though Gray and I do have the adult part down, most of our talking is done in the bedroom. Isn't that right, dear?" she asks, smiling at me innocently. I hear Brayden cough, nearly choking on his food. Riverton's indrawn breath is larger than it should be and almost overpowers Cammie's gasp. Me? I'm torn between holding my head down, banging it on the table, or laughing. Still, CC doesn't know who she's with if she thinks she's going to wiggle her sweet little tongue and get back at me. I know how to deal with this. This I can handle instead of the pain.

"Really, Claudia," Cammie says, sounding scandalized.

"I just like to make sure my woman is happy," I tell her before Cammie can say something else. "So gentlemen, I'm sure we're all anxious to get home. I know I am," I say, looking at CC and leaving nothing about my intentions hard to read. "How about we get down to the real reason we're here?"

"Maybe they would like to finish their dinner, dear."

"I'd like to get home and make sure my woman is happy."

"Your woman seems to have developed a headache," she says, and Brayden laughs out loud. CC gives him a genuine smile that, oddly enough, makes me want to punch the man.

"Grayson, you never pull any punches," Cammie croons. "It's one of the things I so admire about you. You've been doing outstanding on the greens. You practically bury every opponent. And your form is so outstanding. A mark of a champion."

"Thank you, Cammie. It has been a good tournament. I'm

looking forward to South Carolina. The competition there promises to be more challenging."

"Oh, I'm sure you will handle it and come out on top. It's one of the many things you and I have in common. Competition just fuels us. We find something we want and we don't stop until we get it," she says. I start to respond, staring at my food and wishing this was over and done. I should have ignored Seth's orders and just kept going like I was. I would have made it to the Beach on my own. My head jerks up when Cammie screeches like a wet hen. Her pale beige gown has a crimson red slowly soaking into it. I look over at CC and she's holding her wine glass—now empty, and doing her best to look innocent. She's failing.

"I'm so sorry, Cammie. Here let me help you dry that up," she says, grabbing her napkin and moving it to Cammie's breasts to try and dab the liquid.

Cammie yanks the napkin out of CC's hand in outrage. "I think you've done enough," she growls. "Really, I know you don't get out of that garage very often, but you could try to be a little civilized!"

CC pulls back and a look comes on her face that I've not seen. She looks almost calm. "Funny thing. You're right. I didn't get much of a chance to be accepted in the civilized world," she says, her voice a funny tone. She's not looking at Cammie, however; she's looking at Riverton. "A fact I've never been more grateful for than I am tonight. Mr. Brayden, I'm sorry we met under such strained conditions, as I think I would have enjoyed meeting you."

"It was my pleasure, Ms. Cooper," he says, standing up when CC does.

"Yes, well, I think I'll just be going. My headache seems to be worsening," she says, and I stand up to join her. I pull her chair out, putting my hand at her back. There are things we need to discuss.

"Lucas. We haven't discussed the upcoming matches. I think it would be in your best interest to stay."

"I'm afraid..."

"Yes, Gray, you should stay. Don't let me ruin the night for you. I'll just grab a taxi," CC says, already turning away from me.

"No, sweetheart. I'll get you home and make sure you're okay. You are my priority," I tell her, making it clear to everyone—or at least trying to.

"Listen to Claudia. She's making sense. Business should come first. She'll be fine. We'd like to talk to you about becoming the face of the tour." He's dangling a large carrot that pretty much has never been done before. Favoritism is rarely shown except in carefully controlled media shots. At one time, this offer would have been a major score. Right now, I find I don't give a damn.

"Yes. Mr. Riverton is right. I know exactly how businesses are. I'm afraid I have to return to mine tomorrow."

"Oh, that's right. Cammie was telling me you run a garage?" Brayden says.

"I own it, and I've let it go for way too long, really," CC says. "Way too long," she says again. She reaches up to place a cold kiss on my cheek and then leaves. I should be chasing after her, but I feel like I just been sucker punched.

She's going back to Kentucky?

Chapter Forty-Four

GRAY

"Where have you been?" I ask CC as she opens the door to our hotel. I've been sitting here on the couch staring at the door since I got back. I tried to rush out and catch her at the restaurant, but she disappeared much too quickly. I came home to find an empty hotel. She didn't answer her texts and her clothes were still here, so I've just been waiting. It's a fucked-up feeling and I'm pissed off she ran instead of facing this head on.

She looks at me but doesn't respond. In fact, instead of answering me or talking to me at all, she ignores me and walks into the living room. I follow her like a damn dog, and that just pisses me off more. *When the hell did I start chasing a woman?*

"I asked you a question," I tell her, standing. I watch as she gets her overnight satchel she's been using and starts pulling stuff out of the dresser drawers and shoving clothes into her bag.

"I heard you," she mutters, not bothering to look up. I walk over, and when she turns to go back to the dresser, I pull the clothes out.

"An answer would be nice," I tell her as she comes back to the bed. She looks at the clothes laying on the bed and then back at me. Then, she throws the clothes in her hand at me.

"You want an answer? You're a selfish asshole!"

"I'll admit to that. You want to tell me why you're leaving?"

"*Because* you're a selfish asshole!"

"I've been that from day one and you've still hung around."

"Because I was stupid!"

"Sweet lips..."

"Don't you 'sweet lips' me! I can take a lot of shit. But you made me trust you and then you turned around and lied to me."

"I didn't lie exactly."

"You did! Lying by omission is still lying. You let me walk into that den of vipers unprepared!"

"You wouldn't have gone otherwise!"

"That was my decision! Which is why you should have told me!"

"I wanted you with me!"

"So you voluntarily made a decision that threw me to the damned wolves?"

"I wanted to prove to you that—"

"Prove what? That you're a selfish prick? Are you even listening to yourself? You aren't even apologizing! It's all I want. Let me tell you what *I* want, Grayson Lucas. I want a man who respects me and realizes that I put my whole damn life on hold to support him. All I wanted was you to be honest with me."

"I didn't lie!" I growl, but I know it's weak.

"Fuck you." She's finished stuffing the clothes back in the bag, so she throws the strap over her shoulder and moves to walk around me... away from me.

"I was an idiot. I'm sorry, CC. I didn't mean for it to go down like this."

"What on Earth did you think would happen? Hasn't the past shown you that I'm oil and water with the Rivertons by now?"

"I wanted to show them that you're mine. Shit, CC, I don't know. I knew they would be crawling tonight, asking me to reschedule into the bigger tournaments and I just... I wanted you there to share that with me. I wanted us to be there together like a team."

She studies my face and I let her. I want her to see the truth there. I didn't mean for this to go bad. I wanted to show that we were a team. I fucked up.

"If you wanted us to be a team, you should have told me the truth."

"You aren't telling me the truth," I tell her before I can stop myself.

"What are you talking about?"

"There's something between you and the Rivertons. More than just you and Cammie hating each other. If tonight showed me nothing else, it showed me that."

"There's a difference between lying and just not telling you something because it's none of your business."

"You are my business," I tell her.

"Not anymore."

"Wait, just like that you think it's over? Fuck that shit, Cooper. We're having this out, then I'm stripping you bare and reminding you just how well we match up."

"Sex is just sex."

"The hell it is. What we have is special, Cooper. You have to admit to that much."

"What I have to admit is that I can't trust you!"

"Oh, for Christ's sake! I made a mistake, I admit it! But—"

"It was a big damn mistake. You kept something from me that I needed to know. I walked into that restaurant and got blindsided!"

"Why do Cammie and her dad matter? They're idiots! They aren't worth this shit."

"You just don't get it!"

"Then explain it to me, Cooper, because I'm missing something here." I take a step back and bottle the frustration I'm feeling. I want her to stay. I don't need to give her more reasons to run because I know my woman and she has that look in her eyes that tells me she's close to running.

"My whole life, the Rivertons have done nothing but make me

feel like trailer trash... the dirt under their fingernails. I thought Cammie was my best friend and I got to school one day and the shit she pulled, the things I learned... it nearly destroyed me."

"Destroyed you? You told me you were in the fifth grade when the two of you started having problems. What in the hell could happen in the fifth grade that could destroy you? I get that I should have told you things, CC. I do. I fucked up. But don't be melodramatic here. What's in the past is in the past. It doesn't have to color the people we are now. It doesn't have to interfere with the lives we have."

When I finish talking, CC looks white. Her whole body is tight and I can see small tremors in her hands as she holds her arms close at her chest. I feel like the biggest bastard in the world.

"You have no idea," she whispers, sadly.

She's right. Before I fuck up everything else, I drop down on my knees in front of her. I brace my hands on her hips and I look up at her.

"You're right, sweetheart, I don't. But I'm asking you not to write me off. I fucked up. I keep fucking up, but I need you to give me another chance."

"Gray..."

"Please, CC. I won't make you regret it."

I stay there on my knees hoping she softens. If she doesn't, I can see myself following her back and telling the tours to fuck off. That's how far gone I truly am—and I don't even care. In fact, I'm embracing it. *CC is it for me*. I just have to get her to believe in that.

Chapter Forty-Five

CC

He has no idea how bad he hurt me. He doesn't truly know the history between me and the Rivertons, so on one hand, I can't truly be upset with him. In his mind, he thinks it's a simple case of spoiled rich kid versus blue collar bitch. On the other hand, he purposely set tonight up and, after two dinner disasters where the Rivertons were involved, he should have been completely up front. I can't help feeling betrayed.

"Stay with me, Cooper," he urges again.

I need to make a choice. Am I dreaming to think that Gray and I could work out? To look at us and the lives we've led, you would think we're completely different. But spending time with him, especially when it's just the two of us, it doesn't feel like we're that different. When I look at his crazy family, I kind of feel like I fit in. They like me. Even Maggie has taken to calling me here and there to talk. I like her. She's crazy and sweet—a lot like her mom, though maybe dialed down a notch on the crazy.

"I'm not a drama person, Gray. I had enough of that when my mom was around and then when she left. Banger did more than just take me in; he gave me peace and a home."

"I promise, CC. I'll tell you everything from now on. No more secrets." His words make my stomach tighten in nervousness.

Some secrets should never come out. It's the moment of truth. Do I give him the ugly truth? Or do I hold back? Sometimes, it's best to let sleeping dogs lie.

"I'm not asking you to tell me everything about your past, Gray. I'm sure we both have things we want to forget. Don't make it sound like that. I'm just asking that before you let me walk into a situation like that, you give me some damn warning," I huff. I'm feeling really uncomfortable. I just want this conversation done. There's a big part of me that wants to go back to Kentucky, back to the safety and the life I've built there. I'm not ready to let go of Gray, though. He's important. I... care about him.

Gray leans in and kisses my stomach.

"Does this mean you're going to South Carolina with me?"

"No," I sigh, my fingers curling in his hair.

"Cooper, damn it. You can't let what we have, all of it, just go without even giving me a chance," he growls, getting up and turning away from me, frustration thick in his voice.

"I need to get back to Kentucky, Gray. I have a life there... a business there. I was planning on going back soon, anyway. Tonight just sped the decision up."

"I need you with me," he says, turning around to look at me. I immediately want to give in, but life taught me a long time ago that it's better to live cautiously.

"I'm not breaking up with you, Gray. I'm going back home to check on my business and house. Heck, I need to make sure that Miranda hasn't killed Cat."

"That mongrel is too mean to die."

"Lay off Cat," I tell him with a slight smile.

"You'll come back?" he says, and fear grabs ahold of me, beating in my chest. He wants me back and that feels amazing, but what happens if I let him completely in and I lose him?

"Not for South Carolina, but if you keep winning, maybe I'll come admire your trophy."

"You're not fooling me. You're totally talking about my dick."

"Or at least your boner," I agree, breathing a little easier.

"If you don't come back, Cooper, I'm coming to get you. You need to understand that. I'm not letting you go. I'm keeping you."

His words break through the fear in my chest—*at least a little of it.*

"Keeping me? Careful, you sound a little caveman there." He walks over and picks me up. I squeal, trying to brace myself on his shoulders. "What are you doing? Put me down before you hurt yourself, you big dummy!"

Gray just laughs at me and then tosses me on the bed. I land horizontally on it beside my packed bag he must have tossed there earlier. Heck, I hadn't even realized it wasn't on my shoulder anymore. He pushes it to the floor and grins down at me, taking his shirt off over his head and throwing it on the ground.

"Me Tarzan. Me fuck Jane senseless. Jane be too tired to get on plane," he grunts, kicking off his shoes.

"That's your plan?" I ask him, laughing.

"It good plan. Jane shut up now and Tarzan take her for a ride on his grapevine."

"You are seriously, *seriously* deranged," I laugh, but I'm sitting up and taking off the clothes I threw on when I got back to the hotel. Gray works faster than me and by the time he has his own clothes off, he reaches down and helps me kick out of my jeans and underwear. He wraps his arms around my hips and pulls me down on the bed. Without warning, he buries his face between my legs. I cry out just as his tongue begins working its magic. When I feel it stroke against my clit, I forget about everything else and just let myself get lost in the sensations that only Gray can create.

"That's it, baby. Lay back and ride my fucking face," he groans, and this is one time I lay back and give Gray control without worry.

I do exactly what he tells me to. I ride his face. *Tarzan good.*

Chapter Forty-Six

GRAY

"That was outstanding, Gray. You're really racking up the wins."

"Thanks," I tell Riverton, wishing he'd leave. Something about the man rubs me wrong.

"The way you've been tearing it up, you'll need that week off you wanted before the next Florida match. Your official invite to the king of them all came today, by the way. Just four weeks away," he says, like he had much to do with it. I've busted my ass and racked up win after win and climbed so far in the standings that the invite is an afterthought. The only thing he's involved in is making the courses a little smoother and nicer. I finish this match here and then I get a week off. I return to Florida for one more match and the competition there will be the best of the best. I'll need to be on my A game to make it out with my top fifteen rank intact. I'm currently twelfth in the standings, which is a fucking huge accomplishment. But I want that trophy and that green jacket. Then, I'll feel like I've made it to the top. It's so close I can almost taste it, so I'm chomping at the bit to get rid of the Florida matches so I can look towards Georgia. "What do you say we have dinner and celebrate?" Riverton adds, and that's the last thing I want to do. I am supposed to be on the course early in the morning and get this damn tournament done, then I am hopping a plane to Kentucky and getting back to my woman.

"I got an early call in the morning," I tell him. "I probably should get back to the hotel and pack. I'm leaving right after the tournament."

"Nonsense. A quick dinner will still get you back in plenty of time. Actually, you know what you'd enjoy? The boys and I have a poker game coming up at the local club. That's just the thing to help you unwind before tomorrow. What do you say about joining in? Brayden was called out of town and it left an empty chair."

"I don't know..."

"It's good to rub elbows with the tour members, son," he warns, instantly annoying me. Still, if I go home, all I'll do is jerk off to the memory of CC and God knows I've been doing that enough since she's been gone. I haven't had her in two fucking weeks. I've never missed a woman before CC. I absolutely ache for her. Memories of her laugh and smile haunt me. Thoughts of being inside of her keeps me from sleeping. Hell, I think part of the reason I've been doing so good on the course is that I've been working on pure frustration.

I've been talking to CC every night and the only thing that manages to make me feel even a little bit better is the fact that she seems to be missing me, too. So much so, she's talking about coming to Georgia to the big tournament to, in her words, mop the floor with those other ball whackers.

I love that woman. Just thinking about our conversations makes me smile. Now, if I just knew the right way to tell her I love her and need her in my life. When I told her I was keeping her, she didn't react exactly how I wanted her to. I figure if I even try to bring up the word "love", she'll run hard and fast.

It's crazy, actually. Before CC, women were lining up for me. If they thought they could hook me anywhere close to the way CC has me right now, they would have been jumping for joy. CC would be running for the hills. I don't doubt that at all.

"I can stay for a couple hands. Just a couple, though. I have a phone conference with CC later tonight."

"A man in your place who's on the verge of hitting his hard earned dreams? You shouldn't be tying yourself down to a woman who won't be able to further your career or appreciate your achievements."

"CC is all I need," I correct him, and turn the subject back to safer ground. I'm not discussing CC with Riverton. I hope I'm not making a mistake.

As the night goes on, that's one line that keeps repeating—I hope I'm not making a mistake—and when I leave late that night and Cammie shows up to pick her father up and comes running up to hug me, it just repeats louder.

The only saving grace is that I took Riverton's money in cards, but as I endure Cammie's hug goodbye, I don't think even that makes it worth it.

Chapter Forty-Seven

CC

"I can't believe this is what we've been reduced to," Jackson growls, but he plops down on the half-broken sofa in the break room, pops open a beer, and stares at the TV screen, despite his complaining.

"No one is twisting your arm to make you watch golf." I shrug, taking a bite out of the pizza. The gooey cheese and garlic spiced crust burst on my mouth and I can't stop from moaning. I'm starved. We've worked straight through all day so we could close early for one reason and one reason only: to watch Gray on television. This is his second-to-last match before the big one, the one all the money is riding on. He doesn't need to win to have a good standing, but he wants to, and I can understand it. He wants to beat everyone that crosses his path. When they say he's the best in the sport, he wants there to be no question.

"Hey, if watching this shit makes you quit moping around here with that hound dog look on your face, I'm willing. You're starting to scare off some of the regulars," Jackson mumbles.

I push a bag of chips and a can of bean dip into his hand. I'm not the dishes-and-fancy-crab-dip kind of girl. Besides, it's a fucking garage. Then, I plop down beside him with a can of my own French onion dip.

"Have they shown Gray yet?" I ask.

"Nah. For some weird reason, there seems to be other players out there. Strange, right?"

"Sarcasm can be an ugly thing, Jackson."

"So can anxious, love-sick girls."

I ignore the flutter in my chest as he mentions love and, instead, choose to stick my tongue out. Jackson just ignores me and takes a drink of his beer. My attention returns to the television. I've never been one to watch golf. It all seemed rather boring and all too quiet. Sports are supposed to be full of screaming fans, marching bands, fly balls, touchdowns, or even a dunk. Somehow, hitting a little white ball into a hole seemed stupid, or like something I do on vacation from time to time, but the hole is usually the mouth of a clown, or a windmill—anything to make it interesting, because otherwise I'd be bored as hell and, hence, not watching. But here, the attraction is not a clown, an elephant, windmill, or anything else. It's all Gray. I think my breath lodges in my chest when the camera zooms in on him. He looks so good, though different. He's wearing relaxed slacks, not his usual jeans. His t-shirt has been replaced with a polo shirt. He's got a hat covering his beautiful hair. It's not that he looks bad, but he doesn't look like my Gray. Even when I was on the road with him, he didn't seem this different. I shrug it off. It's just been awhile since I've seen him. That's all it is.

I'm sadly glued to the television as Gray moves from hole to hole, zooming to the top of the leader's board. At one point, I think I even cheered out loud. The same can't be said for Jackson, who is snoring. I threw chips at him once to get him to stop, but he shoved it off his face with his hand and went back to snoring.

At the last hole, Gray struck once and got so close to the hole, I'm sure he could almost taste it. He's standing at it now, ready to baby it in the hole. I watch as he chooses his club and I'm literally sitting on pins and needles. The camera zooms in on him, the wind ripples through his hair, and I'm holding my breath as I watch him swing and connect with the little white ball. It rolls towards the hole... and sinks. Cheers erupt, and I'm not any different as I screech out in celebration, waking Jackson up. I immediately want to call him and congratulate him.

I reach for my phone just when I see Cammie running out and hugging him. I want to bust the television screen. Gray returns her hug, though I can't say he was overly friendly. He's shaking hands with some of the other men and players. I'm still frowning at the television, wondering how I can kill Cammie Riverton from afar.

The reporter pulls Gray to the side and I breathe a little easier because it cuts Cammie out of the picture enough that she doesn't show up on my screen.

"That was outstanding, Gray. Can you walk our viewers through that last hole and how you rebounded after getting that bogey early in the match?"

"It's all a blur, honestly, Pauline," he says, laughing easily. "I just went into competition mode. I want to hurry and get this match done because I'm heading to Kentucky to spend the week with my woman."

"Does this mean that golf's most notorious bachelor is off the market?" she asks.

"Completely. My heart belongs in Kentucky. Now if you'll excuse me, Pauline, I have a plane to catch," he says, and then, adding with a wink, "See you soon, sweet lips."

My stomach flutters. What did Gray just do? Oh my God! Then I fall back on the couch giggling like a school girl. Jackson's glares from my waking him up again can't even stop the happiness surging through me.

Holy crap! I think Gray really likes me!

Chapter Forty-Eight

CC

I'm more than half asleep when I hear it: a noise coming from the living room. At first I think I dreamed it because I don't hear anything else right away. I sit up in bed and do my best to focus my eyes in the dark. There's a faint light in the hall coming from the bathroom, and it helps keep me from being completely blind. I reach over beside the head of my bed and wrap my fingers around the baseball bat I keep there. My fingers tighten against the wrapped handle as I wait. I hear the noise again. This time, it's definitely real and definitely coming from the living room. I can no longer write it off to just sleeping.

I carefully get out of the bed, clutching the bat as tight as I can. My heart is pounding in my ears and bumping so hard against my chest, it's a wonder I can breathe. Quietly, I walk through the hallway. As I near the end of it, I can make out a shadowy figure standing by the couch, bending over. I pick up my speed, walking quickly and forgetting silence in hopes I can attack fast and hard. He has to have heard me because he jerks up just as I swing with the bat, claiming the lamp on my sofa table. I close my eyes tight as I hear my lamp shatter, then wait for the dull thud of hitting the person breaking in.

That sound never comes because the bat is jerked out of my

hand. I try to hold on and wrestle with it, but it only succeeds in bringing me closer to the person. So, instead, I let go all at once. I hear a muffled, "Motherfucker!" before the figure goes barreling back and falls on the ground.

I take off running towards the front door, deciding there's no way I'd win in a fight with this asshole. If it had been a woman, sure, and even some men, I think I could take on. But this man was strong when we were fighting over the bat and his voice was very male. Banger didn't raise a fool. Run now, live tomorrow.

"Jesus Christ!"

I stop with the door halfway open. I know that voice. I hit the light switch by the door. It takes me a few minutes before my eyes adjust, and when they do, it's to discover Gray lying there looking pissed—but somehow still sexy as hell. He's sprawled out on the floor, which I can only assume is where he landed, and he's sitting among the broken glass of my favorite lamp.

"Gray?" I'm sure I'm hallucinating. Heck, maybe I am still asleep.

"Fucking hell, Cooper. Are you trying to kill me?"

"What? No. I mean... Wait... What are you doing here?"

"I caught a red-eye so I could get home to my woman sooner! Now I'm thinking I shouldn't have bothered."

I close the door slowly and lean on it while I still my breath.

It's just Gray. Gray, home early. Gray, coming in the door at four in the morning to surprise me. Gray, missing me so much that he took a flight out of Florida to get here. Gray, calling me his woman. As soon as I kill him for scaring the hell out of me, I might finally admit that I'm... in love with him.

"You almost gave me a heart attack!" I growl, trying to ignore the way my heart is still pounding. I have a feeling it has more to do with the thought of being in love with Gray Lucas than it does still being scared from thinking someone is breaking in.

"Yeah, well, you almost killed me, so I guess we're even," he grumbles, slowly getting to his feet. I watch him for a minute before walking to him and taking his hand in mine, palm up, and trying to see what he's looking at. I wince as I see little slivers of glass all over his skin and some of them sticking in it.

"Shit, that doesn't look good."

"It doesn't feel good either," he grumbles.

"Let's get you into the bathroom and I'll clean the glass off of you," I tell him. As we walk down towards the hall, I look back at my shattered lamp forlornly. "I really loved that lamp," I sigh.

"You would have never known it. I think you could probably give my brother lessons in swinging a bat there, Babe Ruth."

"Bite me. You owe me a lamp. It won't be easy to find one that I like as much."

"I'll give you something besides a lamp you'll like better," he says, grinning.

"You're horrible. Besides, that will be *hard* to do, but I'm lonely so I'll let you try."

"I'll show you hard."

"You never stop, do you?"

"Not even when you beg, but there is just one thing that's going to have to happen first."

"Oh yeah? What's that?" I ask him as we make it to the bedroom and I head in the direction of the adjoining bathroom.

"You're probably going to have to dig glass out of my ass first, sweet lips."

I look around at his behind and wince when I see one particularly big shard sticking through the jeans.

Yikes.

Chapter Forty-Nine

GRAY

"Ow! Damn it, woman, leave some of my ass back there, will you?"

"Oh, good Lord, you're acting like a little girl. There's no way that could hurt."

"Easy for you to say. It's not your ass all bleeding and cut open. I may need a blood transfusion," I exaggerate, hiding my grin as I bury my head in my hand so she can't see. We're lying on the bed and, even if all CC is doing is bandaging up my ass, I'm completely naked and she's in a t-shirt (mine, by the way; she's totally wearing my shirt to sleep in while I'm gone, and I call that a fucking win) and I'm happier right now than I have been since she left.

"Oh my God, men are such babies," she says as she slaps a Band-Aid on my butt. "There. You're finished, whiny boy."

I roll over and pull her down against my chest. For a minute, I can do nothing but stare at her. It's been weeks since I've seen her, but I must have forgotten just how beautiful she is. Right now as I'm staring at her laughing face, her eyes glowing, her cheeks red, her lips moist and plump and begging for attention, the curve of her neck, the gentle sway her breasts make with each breath, I'm completely and utterly hypnotized by her. I'm owned by her. The man I was before I met her seems like a different person. I never want anyone in my life but this woman. I want her when I'm old. I want babies with her. I want to fight with her and, fuck, I really, really want to make it up with her. I want her face to be the last thing I see before I go to sleep and the first thing I see when I wake up. I'm dying to tell her that, but I hold back, still unsure of her. In a lot of ways, CC is like a frightened doe, ready to take off and run at the first approach. Keeping that in mind, I give her the only words I feel like I can right now. They're thick with unspoken emotion; I can't help that.

"I've missed the fuck out of you, Cooper."

Her eyes dilate and she licks her lips nervously. Just the simple move of her tongue sliding against her lips to moisten them makes my cock push against her leg, begging for attention.

"I've missed you too, Gray. Very much," she says quietly, and just like that, I feel like I have the world at my feet.

"Show me," I dare her, and I stare at her lips as I wait to see what her next move will be.

"Show you?" Her hand comes up so that her thumb moves back and forth on my bottom lip. I suck it in, letting my tongue graze over it, kissing it gently before releasing.

"I'm tired. It was a long flight."

"Poor baby."

"Yeah. I'm too tired for anything, but I want it."

"You want... it?" she asks, and I hear the laughter thick in her voice now.

"Oh yeah. I definitely want it."

"I see. So what do you suppose we should do? I mean, maybe you should nap before you get it."

"I could. But I like my plan better."

"And what is your plan, dare I ask?"

"I'm just gonna lay here and let you have your wicked way with me."

"Is that right?"

"Yep. That's it."

"That sounds kind of boring for... me."

"I have confidence in you. I think you'll make sure you get yours, too."

"How do you suppose I should start?" she asks, and I know she's trying to sound deadly serious, but the slight laugh in her voice gives her away.

"Surprise me," I tell her, then I lay completely back on the bed and see what she does next.

It's fucking good to be home.

Chapter Fifty

CC

I study him for a minute. The smile on his face, the almost childlike happiness that oozes from him... and it feels good. It feels really good. Almost as if I'm the reason for it. For that reason alone, I feel another piece of my defenses completely fade away. I touch my lips to his, bringing them together gently, slowly. He tastes minty and warm with a touch of spice that I can only describe as Gray. It's a taste that I know I won't forget until the day I die. Gray takes my kiss and, though he drinks from my lips, he doesn't offer his tongue or take it deeper. When I pull back, he's smiling at me. If it wasn't for the way his breath and heart rate have noticeably picked up, I wouldn't be sure I affect him the way he does me. But the evidence is right there, and that gives me courage to touch his lips again, letting the tip of my tongue run along the outside of them. I push a little harder and my tongue slips inside. I immediately search his mouth for a deeper taste, for something to satisfy the need inside of me that is already raging with little more than a kiss.

I find his tongue and caress it with mine, slowly at first, but as more of his taste hits me, I lose myself in it and whimper as our tongues begin dancing. Gradually, our kiss becomes more heated. Less about remembering and savoring and more about need. We break apart and I take oxygen into my lungs, but my eyes are glued to his. I can't tear them away even when I slide further down his body so that my lips can find his nipple. I capture it gently between my teeth, rolling it carefully. His hand comes up and tangles in my hair, tightening in it. I smile at the way I can so easily tell I'm getting to him. As a reward, I suck hard on his nipple, bringing it all the way in and using enough pressure so that it's pressed against the roof of my mouth. His hand tightens to the point that it's almost painful. I pull away anyway, kissing my way down his ribcage and even lower to that fantastic V outline pointing the way to his cock. His body is so well defined, it's a work of art.

I drag my tongue along the outline, letting my teeth follow the same path as I give little love bites for the simple reason that the taste of him makes me feel powerful, sexy, and happy. I move further down so I can kiss his cock. It's straining towards me, and I reward it with a gentle kiss on the head. That's all I meant to do, but the taste of his pre-cum hits my tongue and the musky smell of him enters me, and I can't stop myself from holding his cock in my hand and letting my tongue slide against the head and burrow into the small opening trying to find more of his pre-cum, needing his taste. Gray groans, and he must be tired of being passive because now his hands are digging into my hair harder as he urges my head down on him. As much as he takes control, I'm the one feeling powerful here. I give in and suck him deep into my mouth, stopping before I can take all of him in, because his cock hits the back of my throat. He stretches my mouth, so swollen with need that I can barely close my lips around him. As I back him out and leave him with another gentle kiss on his head, Gray moans. His hips buck as he begs for more of my mouth.

I'm not in the mood to give him what he wants, though. Now, my needs come first. I have been craving him these past few weeks and I'm not about to deny myself a moment longer. I shift so I can move my leg over him, straddling him. I can't stop the growl that comes out when I settle against him and his hard, hot dick slides between the lips of my pussy effortlessly.

"Fuck, baby, I'm glad you don't wear a lot of clothes to bed," he growls, and just to prove he's telling the truth, he pulls the shirt over my head. I raise my hands, helping him. I'm eager for there to be nothing between us. His hands immediately come up and palm my breasts, kneading them—his touch, rough and eager, and his skin hot. I shift against his cock, rotating my hip and sliding so that I hit that perfect stroke—the one that eases him right against my clit and lets me ride him without taking him inside.

"God, you feel so good, Gray," I whimper.

"You're soaked for me," he growls, his hands biting into my thighs as he tries to pull me even tighter against him. He's right. You can hear the suction between us as his cock forges through my cream. I ride him like that a few more times, gasping as his head rakes against my swollen clit, painting it with a mixture of his pre-cum and my own juices.

That's the trigger that shows me I can't take anymore. I rise up on my knees, reaching under me to hold his cock. I position him just outside and look at him. I want this connection with him as I slide down his shaft. I carefully lower on him, taking my time to savor as he stretches me. My eyes close as he finally goes inside of me, filling what has been way too empty since I left him. Once I take him in as deep as he will go, so deep it makes it hard to breathe, I just stay there. I'm afraid to move, afraid to breathe. I want to savor the way he stretches me completely, the way we fit together, and just enjoy the peace of finally having him here with me. I'm not sure how long I'd want to stay like this, but Gray takes that choice out of my hands when he grabs my hips and grinds me against him. His cock flexes inside of me, raking against my walls and making me feel so full that I'm not sure I'll survive.

"Gray," I gasp. I brace my hands on his shoulders and slowly stretch out on him while his cock is still buried deep inside. The movement angles his cock in just the right spot and moves him so far inside, he's touching spots of me that have never been touched before. He's... claiming me in a way I've never experienced.

"It gets better every time," Gray whispers right before his lips claim mine in a slow kiss. Our tongues mimic what our bodies do, slowly moving, relishing each other, cherishing each other... loving each other. We come together as our orgasms slide out of each of us as if we're in tune, as if we're one, and as I give myself over to it, I know I will never be the same again.

I love Gray Lucas. I love him.

Chapter Fifty-One

CC

"Loverboy is back with pizza," Jackson calls, and I smile. Gray's been back for three days and it seems all I do is smile. Jackson likes to give us both a hard time, but I can tell he likes him too. What's not to like? Gray's good-looking, dependable, funny, sweet, gentle when you need it, but not afraid to pull your hair... "Claude, did you hear me?" Jackson calls out again.

"Yeah, I heard you. Be there in a minute," I yell back. You just caught me daydreaming about the man I'm head over heels in love with. That part I don't yell back. Still I hear it inside, and though the fear is there, it's getting easier and easier to breathe through it. I worried that Gray and I wouldn't be able to work because we are so different, but with every day that passes, I think I worried for nothing. Gray may have to work with the likes of the Rivertons, but he's not like them. He's more like his crazy family, which I love. Even meddlesome Ida Sue who has taken to calling me once a week. She says it's just to check on me, but I can read between the lines enough to know that it's to see if I'm still boning her son. It makes it easier to figure out when she ends every conversation with: "I'll talk to you next time, dear. Are you and Gray still shagging each other's brains out? You know, the world is a better place if there are more kids in it."

It used to unnerve me, but now I think of Ida as June Cleaver from the television classic Leave It To Beaver. Well, June Cleaver if she was a flower child who believed in free love. "Kids, you left your bong on the floor! Don't forget your condoms tonight for the orgy. Your father and I will be there too! I'm making your father take those pills so he doesn't get performance anxiety." I laugh as I imagine my version of the television show, going to the old sink in the garage and washing my hands.

"What's my woman laughing about?" Gray asks, coming up behind me and wrapping his arms around me as he kisses the side of my neck.

I finish cleaning my hands and lean back into him for a minute, just letting him hold me and enjoying the moment. "Orgies and free love parties," I whisper, grinning.

Gray's lips freeze on the side of my neck and then he bites the skin there. I inhale at the sting.

"You can fucking forget that shit," he grumbles, burrowing his head against the back of my neck and holding me tighter.

"What? I thought you liked that kind of thing? I'm not the one with the sex-tape out there, after all."

"That was before," he mutters, his hand moving down my stomach and trying to push up under my shirt. I help him because —let's be honest—anytime Gray's hands are on my bare skin, I'm good. I turn to the side a little though, wanting to see his face.

"Before what?"

"Before you, Cooper. You've reformed me, made me a better man."

"Is that a fact?"

"Well, yeah. That, and I ain't fucking sharing you with anyone. My dick is the last dick that pussy is ever going to squeeze the baby juice out of."

"Baby juice?"

"Mmm-hmm," he mutters, his lips on my neck.

"There's my caveman. I thought he had gone all civilized on me."

"I would have thought last night proved that theory wrong," he mutters, and my freaking ovaries actually flutter when I think about the dirty little things he did to me last night. I'll never look at that showerhead in my bathroom the same way again. Not to mention the mirror in my bedroom.

"You might should let go of me because you're going to get filthy," I warn him, suddenly remembering I just changed oil in a Toyota.

"Maybe I want to get dirty with you," he says, but lets me go. I turn around to look at him and it hits me again that this man likes me. I apparently switched into another universe at some point. I hope I don't have to leave. This world is much better.

"Later, Romeo. I need pizza first."

"I thought I could give you your first golf lesson."

"Umm, you do know I don't especially like the game, right? Though, if you want to go out to the mini-golf park, I am killer on that course. Especially the windmill hole at the end. I always manage to get in with just one stroke."

"Impressive," he jokes, but he's reaching over and taking my shirt off. I halfheartedly try to stop him.

"The trick is to get the ball under the little bridge. Most people try to go over top, but it never works," I tell him, wondering exactly how to get away with having sex in the middle of the day in the garage where customers—and not to mention Jackson—could walk in at any time.

"I will have to learn from your ways, oh wise one," he mumbles, reaching around to undo my bra.

"Gray! We can't do this here. Jackson—"

"Took his pizza and his six pack I brought him and went into the office."

"But he could come in and there could be customers..."

"You need to learn to live a little, Cooper. Life is way too short not to enjoy yourself once in a while."

"Enjoy myself?"

"And learn new things."

"Like golf?"

"Exactly," he says, dipping his finger into the oil I just drained into the container beside him.

"Umm, Gray? What are you doing?"

"Getting ready to give you your first lesson," he says, trailing his finger between my breasts and down my stomach. The sensation of the oil is cool and a little slimy, but his finger on my body and the way his breath hits my skin has a way of putting me on edge and instantly making me need him. I'm quickly becoming addicted to anything he wants to give me.

"This line is like the fairway on a golf course."

"A fairway?" I whisper as he moves the oil over my nipples.

"The fairway is the beautiful trail straight to the hole," he explains, unbuttoning my pants and pushing them down my hips.

"I don't remember breasts and nipples on a golf course."

"Those represent the small mounds on the course that can distract a driver."

"Small mounds?" I ask, laughing.

"Well, I thought huge jugs didn't sound as classy."

"We can't have that," I tell him, letting my fingers move into his hair as he leans down on his knees in front of me.

"Now I'm going to tell you the secret to golf, sweet lips," Gray says, kissing my thighs.

"What's that?" I whimper, willing my legs to remain strong as I feel his breath so close to where I want his mouth the most.

"Every man wants a hole in one," he murmurs, dragging his tongue along the inside of one of my thighs.

"Gray..." I whimper, my body thrusting towards him, needing more than what he's giving me. "I don't think that's a big secret."

"True, but I'm going to tell you exactly how to get it."

"You are?"

I gasp as his hands move back to my ass and I feel him place a gentle, sweet kiss at the top of my pussy. My fingers tighten in his hair as I pull him closer, wanting to feel his tongue on my clit. I need the sensation I get when his entire face moves between my legs. I need so much more than what I'm getting and it frustrates me.

"You have to become one with the hole, meld with it."

"Gray!" I cry as I feel him flatten his tongue and part the lips of my pussy, letting it drag against the sensitive skin there.

"That hole has to become all you think of. You can't let anything distract you from driving inside of it," he tells me.

"Baby, please. I need you to..."

"You can't let yourself get distracted even when there's an area above throbbing and begging for attention," he murmurs, his voice muffled when he moves his tongue to my clit, stroking over it once, twice, three times, and then without warning, he sucks my clit into his mouth—hard.

My hands move down to Gray's shoulders and I hold on, my entire body shaking. I know I'm close to shattering into a thousand pieces. I won't be able to hold back. I'm not even going to try. I growl in annoyance when he pulls his head back. I lock eyes with him, and find that his are full of desire and mischief. He stands back up without giving me what I really want, and it pisses me off. I didn't ask for him to get me all worked up and then leave me all horny and needy. I'm about to go off on him when I watch him unbutton his jeans.

"What are you doing?" I ask, even as he pushes his pants down and moves back to me.

"Showing you just how good I can drive to the hole," he tells me, grabbing my leg and wrapping it high on his hip. "And all you have to do is hang on and enjoy the ride."

I don't respond. I can't because he thrusts inside of me and all thought is gone. Nothing is left but sensation, pleasure, and need. Everything else ceases to exist. The garage, customers, the work, Jackson, it all fades away as I lose myself into the man who owns me. Everything is gone, and all that's left for me is Gray.

Chapter Fifty-Two

GRAY

"Do you think we might be having too much sex?" CC whispers as she sits back in the seat beside me on the plane. I just got back a minute before her. I think we played it all rather smoothly, really.

"Is there such a thing?" I ask her with a grin. "Besides, you weren't complaining when I had you pinned against the door of the bathroom."

"You couldn't help but pin me. There wasn't enough room in that bathroom for two people."

"I think we need to go back in there. You didn't complain as much. I mean, seriously, is this the thanks I get for making you a member of the mile-high club?"

She leans over and kisses me sweetly on the lips. "Thank you, Grayson Lucas, for inducting me into the mile-high club."

"Much better. You're welcome, sweet lips."

She laughs and pulls away, rolling her eyes at me. "What do I make, anyway? Your, like, fiftieth inductee?"

"Ouch. I can't remember. Since you came in my life, Cooper, I can't remember a fucking woman before you."

"That would be a better line if you said you couldn't remember *fucking* a woman before me. Grammar is very important, Tarzan."

"That's what I meant. Stop being a pain in my ass," I grumble, watching as my fingers play in her hair. I'll never get enough of the beautiful auburn-gold color. It's natural, unique, special... just like the woman who wears it. "I love your hair."

"I like being a pain in your ass and I'm glad because, well, it's kind of stuck on my head, ya' know? Hard to change," she jokes.

I look at her. She's got a faint color in her cheeks as if she's embarrassed. I need her to see the truth.

"I don't want you to change anything about yourself, Cooper. You're perfect just the way you are."

"I think it's only fair to tell you perfection doesn't exist. Heck, even those abs you sport aren't perfect. I think the last can in your six pack isn't quite defined as the rest of them." She grins, trying to shrug off the compliment.

"I'm serious, CC. You're perfect to me... for me."

"Gray..." she whispers, and I think she's getting it. I can see the fear in her eyes, but there's something else there and that's what pushes me to take it a little farther. CC is new territory for me. Not only am I in love for the first—and last—time in my life, but she sure as fuck is not getting away. She's also new territory because she's the first woman I've ever met who is afraid to commit to me. She doesn't trust people in general. I think that comes from her past and her mom. But she's doubly afraid of me and it makes me ashamed of my past. She brings it up sometimes when we're joking and it feels like it doesn't bother her, but still, the truth of it has hit her and has settled in her mind and that can't be good. Still, this is the first time I've seen anything from her that might encourage me, so I have to start trying to break through.

"CC, you have to know you're special to me," I tell her—a fucking understatement of epic proportions.

"I..." she starts, then stops. She looks at me and slowly nods. "I know, Gray. You're special to me, too."

Fuck, that's such a simple statement, but with it, I feel better than winning any damned match or tournament has ever made me feel. It feels like fireworks are going off. I get lost in the feeling and push harder—which might be a mistake.

"I want everything with you, Cooper. Everything," I tell her, laying it bare as gently as I can. Everything in me is wanting to tell her I want to give her my last name. I want kids with her. I want to grow old together. She's the last face I want to see when I close my eyes and go into the next world. I'm pretty sure those words would scare the hell out of her.

"What if you're disappointed?" she asks.

"If there's one thing I'm one hundred percent sure of, Cooper, it's that I could never be disappointed in you. Never."

I hate seeing the fear in her eyes. I think it's probably a good thing I never met her mother. I'd probably want to kill the woman. I bring CC's face closer to mine and kiss her.

"You better get a quick nap in. We'll land soon, and I'm going to need you again."

"You cannot be serious."

"Watch and see, sweet lips, watch and see," I tell her with a wink. She watches me for a minute, then reclines her seat back to rest. I stare out the window wondering how in the hell I'm going to knock down all of CC's walls. I may have to call my family in for reinforcements. They're crazy as fuck, but they're hard to resist and CC is already drawn to them.

I'll figure it out somehow. I have to.

Chapter Fifty-Three

CC

"Claude, I didn't expect to see you here," Cammie exclaims, and it's a real struggle to keep myself from slapping her. If there was ever a woman in need of someone knocking some sense into her, it'd be Cammie.

"And yet, here I am," I say with a shrug. I hear Gray snort in the background, but I don't look at him. If I do, I'll probably start laughing and I need to at least appear like an adult here. It'd be much easier to control myself if I could just slap her once. Okay, maybe twice. Three times, tops. "Did you want something, Cammie?"

"I was looking for Grayson. I was hoping I could meet with him before the press conference this afternoon introduces him as the face of Riverton golf clubs and merchandise," she says, sounding put-out. "It's extremely important we present a united front and send this venture out with a bang," she explains, but honestly, her voice is droning on so I'm tuning her out. I pull the door to my and Gray's hotel room back to give her room to enter.

"I'm ready, Cammie. Just give me a minute to grab my jacket and tell CC bye."

"Oh, no rush, Gray. I'm just excited to get this venture underway. With your face and our quality product, our clubs will become a household name," Cammie says, and Gray turns his back on her and rolls his eyes. I grin. God, I love him. Shit.

"You sure you don't want to go with us, sweetheart?"

"Of course she doesn't, Gray. What on Earth would Claude do while we were talking to the press and deep in business? She'd be bored silly," Cammie interjects.

I stick my tongue out at her. Sadly, the gesture is hidden by Gray's chest as he blocks me. He laughs, though. His hand rests on my hips and he looks at me when he answers Cammie.

"CC is very astute when it comes to business. I can always use her in my corner. I admire her." The way he stresses the last part of that sentence is like a verbal blow that sails right over Cammie's head.

"I suppose, but honestly, that little garage that Claude runs can hardly be compared to the millions we are dealing with. I doubt CC could imagine the money this contract between you and Riverton involves."

I close my eyes and try to count backwards. I shove down the old insecurities which threaten to rise to the forefront. I'm not the innocent little girl that the Riverton's nearly destroyed—not anymore. I've been trying to play nice with Cammie and her father before I had Banger to worry about. Why do I care now? Why am I not lashing out? Habit? Do I still have the fear? Hell, maybe I just don't care enough to try and defend myself.

"Cammie, do you have any idea how you sound when you talk?" Gray says, and I freeze. I look up at him and I can see anger and frustration on his face, but it's not directed at me. It's totally focused on Cammie. *Wow...*

"What? I'm sorry, Grayson, I don't mean to hurt Claude's feelings..."

"You're not," I interject.

"You do," Gray says at the same time, and I look up at him again. "Claudia Cooper is one of the smartest, most dependable women I know. I have no doubt she would have no trouble running a Fortune 500 company if she wanted and do it amazingly."

"Yes, well... I think you might be exaggerating a little, Grayson. But maybe we should just agree to disagree and make it to our press conference," Cammie says.

"You do realize you just made me sound like a Volkswagen or something, right?" I chastise Gray, because honestly, his words blew me away. Unlike Cammie, I don't think he was trying to get laid or just defend me; I think he truly believes them—and believes in me.

He kisses my forehead and laughs. "Always busting my ass, Cooper. You own my dick now. I think you get that to me, you are the most beautiful woman I've ever laid eyes on."

"To you? So you're saying other men wouldn't do the same?"

"Jesus," he grumbles, shaking his head.

"I think I'll just meet you at the meeting. I can tell you're not in the mood to listen to anything logically."

"No, he's leaving now," I tell her, but all my focus is still on Gray.

"I am?"

"Yeah. I'm thinking of calling Apple. Their stocks fell last quarter. I'm going to pull them out of their dark tunnel and show them the light."

"I'm going to spank your ass when I get back," he grumbles, giving me a quick kiss and then walking to the door with Cammie following him like an obedient little dog.

"I'll look forward to it, Lucas."

"I'll hold you to that, Cooper," Gray says over Cammie's exaggerated huff of breath.

"Go knock 'em dead and leave me to my financial planning," I tell him. He winks and then closes the door as they leave. I just stand there watching the door with a sappy look on my face. Then, I do something every teenager does when the boy they like picks them for the prom—or what I imagined they did, because I was never that girl: I run to the bed and jump on it, squealing.

Chapter Fifty-Four

GRAY

"What are you doing?" I ask Cammie once the press conference is over. It went really well, I suppose. I'm always kind of lost at these things. Since CC, honestly, I'm getting kind of bored with it all. Golf isn't even fun anymore; it's a means to an end. When did that start? Once I get this tournament behind me, I think I may take a year off. Hell, maybe I'll buy that farm across from Blue. Would CC like to live on a farm? Would she be willing to let go of her garage? I could live in Kentucky. I wouldn't hate it, though it wouldn't be my first choice. Still, if I get CC in exchange, I could live there happily. Decisions... I need to make some decisions.

"Texting father some information he needs to know. He asked that we meet him in the south banquet room for lunch with the stockholders."

"I need to get back to CC, then I will. She's probably hungry, too..."

"Father was called away on business, Grayson. Surely you can go make an appearance and then go find CC, right? So they aren't left alone?"

I frown, wondering if Cammie is up to something, but since she'll be glued to my side, I figure it's safe.

"Fine," I tell her, and I know I sound like a sulking child, but the last thing I want to do is spend more time with Cammie Riverton. I really want to get back to CC. My phone rings and I look down at the number and grin. "I need to take this. It's my manager," I tell Cammie, already answering the phone.

"Fine, I'll meet you over by the door," she says, but I'm already turning away from her to grab the phone.

"Manager? Fuck that shit," White says. "I ain't wiping your ass, doesn't matter how much the job pays."

"Always great to hear from you, brother, and the day you have to wipe my ass better be the day they put me in the ground."

"Same goes. How the hell are you?"

"Great, fucking great."

"Still pussy-whipped over that sexy piece from Kentucky?"

"Sewn up, signed, sealed, and delivered," I tell him with a grin.

"It's nauseating how quickly you've fallen. Shit, you'll be like Green before you know it," he says. The reminder of my brother and his situation cuts like always.

"That won't happen. We all know what a piece of work he married. CC is nothing like Marissa."

"Sure as fuck hope not. You know that bitch had the nerve to ask him for money last week?"

"You're kidding? He pays a mint in child support. Hell, with what he pays her, I could retire on a beach in Greece living the good life."

"My words exactly. Well, except the Greece thing. You really need to visit the islands more, little bro."

"Whatever. Want to tell me why you're calling?"

"A friendly warning."

"Warning?"

"Yep. Mom, Petal, and Maggie have all been talking to CC pretty regular."

"I know. CC really likes them," I tell him with a grin. In my book, that's just another sign she's nothing like Marissa. Marissa couldn't stand anything about our family or, fuck, anything in Green's life, really.

"Yeah, well, they're coming to Georgia to watch your next tournament."

"Oh, fuck."

"I thought that would cheer you up."

"You sound awful fucking cheerful about it."

"I've got to say, I'm enjoying the idea of you dealing with that crew on your own. Plus, hah, I have the place to myself for the next week."

"You still mending up okay?" I ask because he fucked his shoulder up bad.

"Yeah, I'm good. Hopefully I'll get the 'all clear' in a week or so."

I look over and see Cammie looking at me like she's having a stroke, pointing to her watch. "Listen, bro, I better get going. I have another damn meeting to go to."

"You're starting to sound more corporate than easygoing pro. It's fucking sad, really."

"Later, White."

"Later, G. Good luck in Georgia."

"I don't need luck. I got this."

"Whatever," he says, hanging up. I do the same, putting my phone in my pocket and heading towards Cammie. I actually like that my family is coming. It might be interesting to see how they deal with the Rivertons. Maybe I can get Petal's little boy, River to pee on Cammie and her father. CC would enjoy that.

At the thought of my woman, I grin, even as Cammie smiles at me.

Chapter Fifty-Five

GRAY

"What, did Tarzan forget he had to have a card to make the doors work?" I laugh when there's pounding on the door. I heard it when I was in the shower and jumped out, wrapping myself in a towel and half-jogging to the door. When he pounds on the door again, I open it. "Really, Gray, give me a minute, I was taking a—" I stop when I look up to see David Riverton standing there. "What are you doing here?" I ask, frozen because he was the last person I expected.

"I can see you are just like your mother. Really, Claudia, this is an upscale hotel. You could at least wear a robe when answering the door."

"What do you want?"

"I think it's time we had a talk."

"I think we said all we had to say to each other when Banger got sick."

"Apparently not because here you are causing problems yet again."

"I don't see how. I've barely spoken to you. Now, if you'd be kind enough to leave, Gray will be home in a little while. You're welcome to return then and talk to him," I tell him, moving to close the door. I knew I wouldn't get off that easy when he raises his hand and keeps me from closing it in his face. I'd force the issue, but I'm holding onto the towel with my other hand.

"That's just it, Claudia. This isn't a home. This is a hotel. You're here not because you are a guest of the hotel, but merely because you're sleeping with a guest. You being here puts your face and your very existence too close for comfort for my business, and that can't happen. We had a deal. Do I need to remind you?"

I really don't want to have this conversation. I don't want to have my air mixing with the likes of David Riverton. Apparently, however, God isn't looking down deciding I need a freak tornado to swoop down and suck the asshole into another universe. So, I back away. If I have to talk to him, I'm at least doing it with clothes on.

"I remember every detail of our last meeting, daddy dear. I don't need a refresher course," I tell him, flippantly going to the bathroom. I jump when I hear the door slam behind me, but luckily, I'm in the bathroom and my reaction is hidden from him. I guess the *"daddy"* barb struck home. Good.

"I told you to never fucking utter those words. Your slut of a mother trapped me, thinking she could use you as leverage for money."

Oooh, he cursed! I guess I did score a direct hit.

"Well, I guess you showed her. Oh, wait. You did give her money. Tell me again, how much did you pay my mother to skip town with her mouth shut?"

"Apparently not enough to make sure she took you with her."

"Yeah, you totally overestimated good old Margaret's maternal instinct with that one," I half-joke, coming back through the room with a t-shirt and shorts on. I'm running a towel through my hair, wondering how long it will take before Riverton grows tired and leaves. I really can't handle him. Today started off so well, too.

"How sad it must be to know that no one really wants you. Even that broken down old biker mostly just put up with you. He felt sorry for you, I suppose."

And just like that, his words strike like a dagger into the pit of my stomach. David Riverton is a king at knowing exactly how to wound an opponent. It's how he got to where he is in life.

"I'm not discussing Banger with you. You don't deserve to even mention his name. If you came here to remind me that I'm the scum beneath your gardener's fingernails, I got it. I got that message a long time ago, *Daddy*. I don't need it again. You're just wasting your time."

"I came to tell you that you need to tell Gray you've changed your mind and leave him alone and return to Kentucky."

"What? Why in hell would I do that?"

"Because if you don't, I'll destroy that damn garage you came and begged me to save years ago."

"The garage is mine. I paid the last payment on it three years ago," I tell him—damn proud of that fact. "There's nothing you can do to it now."

I'm trying to sound self-assured, but I'm not. The truth is, I'm scared. Riverton has money, and with money comes power. When Banger's medical expenses were destroying us, we took out a second loan from a high rate lender. They paid off the first part of the medical bills while Banger was in remission. When the cancer came back with a vengeance and we had both loans and more medical bills piling up, I swallowed my pride and bargained with the only thing I had to keep it: the dirty truth. Riverton gave me the money in exchange for my signature on documents stating that I would never reveal the truth about my mother's sperm donor. I paid off the second loan with the money and have been working like hell to pay off the original loan ever since. I got it done and the place is completely mine, now... I hope. Something in his eyes tells me it's not going to be that easy.

"You know how I know there's none of me in you, Claudia?"

"I haven't grown horns and a pointy tail yet?"

"You didn't even bother reading the contract that you signed."

"I did," I tell him, trying to keep the panic out of my voice.

"The details are always in the fine print. Specifically, in this case, the one that says, if at any time I find you are no longer abiding by our terms set forth in the contract that I will demand the entire two hundred and fifty thousand dollars back or you will hand over the deed to the garage."

His words rob me of air. There's no way I would have signed that, right? But then again, I think back to when I was a kid who felt like she was drowning. I hated coming to Riverton and I knew that I was going to lose Banger—no matter what I did. I just wanted to make sure he was comfortable. I wanted him... not to worry.

"I... don't believe you," I lie. Oh, God. What have I done?

"But I think you do."

"It doesn't matter. I've not violated the terms of our agreement."

"But you have. You're insinuating yourself into my life and interfering with my business. You're causing problems for my daughter—my true daughter."

"I haven't! I haven't done anything to Cammie!" I growl, and I hate that I can hear desperation in my voice.

That's when Riverton plays his trump card and I should have known he had one. He brings out a manila envelope he had under his arm. He opens it up and takes out some photos he had inside, throwing them on the coffee table between us. I lean down and pick one up. It's a grainy photo obviously taken from a security camera which shows me entering an employee-only entrance at the country club back home. The others show me in the room. There's even one that shows me turning the sprinklers on. Several others are pictures of Gray and Cammie. I look at them and then back up at the monster who fertilized the egg I was unlucky enough to hitch a ride on.

"I think that picture would tell all the story I need. Don't you?"

"Get out," I tell him, my voice quiet as the implications of what this could mean settle upon me.

"I'll expect you to disappear from Grayson Lucas's life before the tournament in Georgia next week," he says calmly, gathering up the photos.

"You can't make me do that."

"I thought that would be your answer, so here's your official notice. I foreclose on your garage at the end of the month, unless it's paid in full. I hope being Lucas's whore is worth your garage, CC, because that's all you are. Men never pick women like you permanently. I had to explain that to your mother, too."

"Get the fuck out of here!" I yell, grabbing wildly and throwing something from the table at him. I shouldn't have bothered because once he has the photos, he's gone, leaving only the foreclosure papers and likely feeling secure in the knowledge that he's destroyed my world.

What do I do now?

Chapter Fifty-Six

GRAY

"You okay, Cooper?"

"Yeah. Why do you ask?"

"Sweetheart, I don't know if you realize this, but you've barely said two words."

"I'm just eating, Gray."

"Really? Because all your food still seems to be on your plate."

"Okay, fine," she sighs, pushing her plate around. "Some things came up at home today and I need to get back and try to figure them out."

"Well, that's clear as mud."

"You wouldn't understand," she says with another sigh. I study her face. She looks so lost. I want to shake her for not letting me in.

"Try me."

"The shop. It... appears there was a problem with the loan, and instead of having it paid off, there's an... an outstanding balance now."

"Let me pay it."

"Gray!"

"What? I have it, and the garage is important to you. I can pay it. Problem solved."

"No. Problem is not solved. I'll deal with it. We're going back to Kentucky tomorrow anyway."

"Can you promise me one thing?"

"Depends on what it is," she says, smiling a little.

"If you can't work it out that you will at least consider taking the money from me, it can be a loan. You can pay me back, if you insist."

"Gray, you don't even know how much it is."

"I don't really give a fuck, CC. You're important to me. Not the money. And if I win the tournament in Georgia, I can buy three garages once I put that with the money I got from signing the Riverton contract."

"You'd really do that?"

"Definitely. You don't seem to have grasped it yet, sweet lips, but this thing between us is special. I'm not going anywhere. I'm here and I'm staying here."

"Sometimes, life throws curveballs that are beyond our control, Gray."

"Good thing for you that I've become a master at learning just how to hit balls so they curve the way I want them to."

"Ouch. That was a really bad pun."

"They can't all be gold. How about you give up pretending to eat and I take you back to the hotel and ravage you."

She drops her fork in her plate and grins at me—and this one almost reaches her eyes. "I was hoping you would suggest that."

I throw some money on top of the bill the waitress left earlier, then get up and walk over to her seat, pulling it back and helping her up.

"I do aim to please," I tell her, kissing her lips gently. "It's going to be okay, Cooper. I promise. I will always be here for you."

She hooks her hand against my jaw and looks into my eyes. Then she burrows her head into my neck, placing a gentle kiss on my chest.

"I could love you, Grayson Lucas," she whispers, and it feels so close I can almost taste it.

"I'm counting on it, sweet lips. I'm counting on it," I tell her, trying to swallow down the emotion that's choking me. CC doesn't know it yet, but I've made it my goal that she falls in love with me. I'll do everything in my power to make it happen. I'm keeping her.

Forever.

Chapter Fifty-Seven

CC

"I'm sorry, CC. There's nothing I can do. The contract clearly states the terms of the loan and I'd say the pictures you described would sway a jury or a judge."

I hold my head down, the phone away from my ear. Mack is a local lawyer in town and, as lawyers go, he's about the only one I trust not to rat me out to Riverton. He is new to the area, having moved here after marrying Belinda, a local girl who's a few years older than me.

"So I'm royally fucked?" I ask, my eyes still closed.

"The only alternative is to take out a loan on the bank again. The garage would clearly be worth that."

"You forget one thing, Mack."

"What's that?"

"Riverton owns all the local banks. You don't think he's already put word out against me?"

"You really think he'd go that far?"

"I know so."

"What about an online lender? Or a national bank?" he suggests.

"I'll try it, but my personal credit rating isn't that great."

"I'm sorry my news isn't better, CC. Hell, I'm even sorrier I wasn't around to keep you from signing this ridiculous contract."

"It doesn't matter. Back then... even now, I would have signed anything if it meant making sure Banger would keep from worrying and be able to die in peace."

"He was a lucky man to have you. There's still a small chance we can go to court and win because of the outrageous contract terms and your age."

"Yeah," I answer him, but I know that's not going to happen. For one, I don't think I could handle court and having my mom's sordid past out everywhere. For another, I doubt there's anything like a fair trial around here.

"I do my banking in Lexington. Go talk to a Jim Graves there. Tell him I asked you to contact him. See what he can do."

I write the name down with little hope, then Mack and I say our goodbyes.

I've only been back in Kentucky for a couple days. I've had trouble breaking away from Gray to try and figure out what to do with the garage. If I told him, he'd buy it. That's tempting. Fuck, it is. But, I can't let him do that. This is my problem, not his, and I'm not about to ask a man I... care about... to bail me out of a mess I made. That reeks of something my mother would have done and that's not who I am—or ever will be.

I need to talk to Jackson and warn him. He deserves a heads-up. I'm just not sure I know how to tell him. Telling Mack was bad enough. It made it sink in deeper. It made it real. I'm going to lose Banger's garage. I don't care so much for myself, but the thought of his legacy being gone... of giving up my home for Riverton to tear down and put another Cash-n-Dash store or something else equally stupid kills me. I feel so stupid for signing that damn contract. I wasn't lying to Mack; back then, I would have signed a deal with Lucifer himself if it meant making sure Banger could die in peace. Too bad that's exactly who Riverton turned out to be.

"Woman, you're making us late!" Gray says, sticking his head in the door. He looks so happy and he says I'm the one who makes him that way. What happens when I fuck this up? What happens when he discovers I'm not worth sticking around for? I do my best to plaster on a smile. I can't let on to him that my whole world is crashing down around me.

"I told you I had business to do, Crayon Man."

"I know, I'm just anxious," he says, coming further inside. He walks over by my desk and sits on it, ignoring the papers that litter it. "Hey, you okay, sweet lips?" He bends down to study my face.

"Just tired," I tell him, trying to joke it off. "You're wearing me out."

"Well, I was pretty spectacular last night, if I do say so myself. What was it... three or so world-shattering orgasms?"

"Stop bragging. Nobody likes a show-off."

"That's not what you were saying last night," he grins, and even as down as I am, I have to smile a little. He's crazy. "Seriously, are you okay? All joking aside, you don't look happy or tired. You look like you... want to cry. And that's not a look I want my woman to have ever."

"Your woman? Careful, Tarzan is showing his loin cloth again."

"I'm serious, Jane... I mean CC." He winks. "Talk to me, sweetheart."

"It's just work, Gray. I told you the garage was having some financial issues. I'm just trying to wade through and figure out how to fix it."

"Let me give you the money."

"Yeah, that's not happening. I've been in business a long time and weathered some pretty rough storms. This is just a minor bump," I lie. "I'll get through it."

"My beautiful CC. Always so independent. Are you ever going to let your guard down enough to let me take care of you?" he asks, pulling our faces closer. I close my eyes and let his warmth and the feeling of having him nearby wrap around me. His words are beautiful and he'll never know how much I wish I could trust them enough to try. Though Gray is one hundred percent honest in his offer, he doesn't know me yet. Not really. It's just a matter of time when he finds out what my mother, and everyone else I've loved, had already discovered. I'm not the kind of girl worth a forever commitment. Even my own 'father' knows that. I might be Riverton's biological daughter, but what kind of monster would do this even to an illegitimate child?

"You took care of me last night. Remember?" My thoughts are bordering on self-pity and, though it's tempting, I can't go there. It's time I stiffen my back. I don't want Gray to see how low I really am.

"Oh, sweet lips, I definitely remember."

"We have thirty minutes before we're meeting your mother at the airport. If you were to hurry, I'd say you could take care of me again."

"You sure, C?" He pulls away to look at me again. "I mean, not that I wouldn't love to, but you don't actually seem in the mood for sex."

"I am," I assure him, reaching down to massage his already half-hard cock through his pants. "I'm more than sure. When you make love to me, Gray, I forget everything else around us. Everything in the world stops and it's just you and me. I really need that right now."

"CC..."

"Come on, Gray," I urge him, standing up and taking my clothes off while he sits there and watches. "Show me that nine-iron the world brags about." I grin. When I have my clothes off, I look up at him. "Besides, there's something I've always wanted to try and never have."

"Fuck," he groans as I reach over and pet the hard outline of his cock, squeezing it. "What's that, baby?" he asks, his voice muffled because he's standing up and undoing his pants.

"Being bent over my desk and fucked hard," I tease him, leaning over and sticking my ass out to tempt him even more.

"Christ. You're perfect, CC. Have I mentioned that?" His hands bite into the cheeks of my ass, pulling them apart.

A few seconds later, Gray gives me what I need, and I was right. Everything but the two of us cease to exist as he slides into me and makes the world disappear.

Chapter Fifty-Eight

GRAY

"Please tell me you did not just have sex on CC's kitchen table," I state, already knowing they did and just hoping someone can deny it so I can try and live in ignorance.

"It's a strong table, dear," Ida Sue says, buttoning up her shirt.

"Almost as good as the one back home," Jansen agrees as I hang my head down in shame. I would be completely humiliated if I didn't hear CC's muffled laugh. I look over at her and her head is hiding in the back of my arm, her body moving in mostly silent laughter. She's been so down that, just like that, I forget the fact that my mother just had sex on my girlfriend's table and I'm thankful they've cheered her up.

"Don't laugh. You'll just encourage them."

"Jansen doesn't need encouragement, dear. They make those pills now that do that."

"Mom! For Christ's sake."

"You know how I feel about you bringing the Lord in your foul language," she grumbles.

I love my mom, but her mind constantly leaves me scratching my head. If the Lord would be upset with me for using his name, I'm not sure how he's supposed to feel about my mom having sex on a kitchen table with her boyfriend.

"Lovey, damn it. You aren't supposed to tell anyone about those damn pills."

"Relax, Jansen. Gray and CC are family and there's nothing wrong with having to prime the pump. If Gray isn't already doing it, he'll probably have to soon. He's not getting any younger either."

"Mom, do you think you can reel it in before you scare CC off?"

"Dear, CC is not going anywhere. Are you CC?"

"Well, I mean..."

"A blind man could see that she loves you," she says. I hear CC's gasp and squeeze her into me encouragingly. "Please tell me you've told that girl how you feel about her," Ida Sue scolds.

"I haven't wanted to scare her," I try to explain.

"Horse shit. I ought to set your ears on fire, son. A woman likes to know how a man feels about her. She needs to know she can depend on you. That she matters."

"She matters, Mom."

"I know that, son, but it's not me you're knocking boots with. You need to tell her," she says, crossing her arms.

"I think I'd better go. I'm going to be late. You sure..." CC starts, her body tense.

I might want to strangle my mother right now, but the door is open and not saying anything will give her the wrong idea. I turn her to me, holding her neck gently, letting my thumb sweep across her chin.

"You matter, CC."

"Gray, come on. Your Mom means well, but you don't have to say..."

"I love you, Claudia Cooper. I've loved you forever."

Her face goes white, and she trembles a little in my arms.

"Gray..."

"I love you, sweet lips."

"About damn time," Ida Sue says, slapping me on the back and jarring my attention from CC, but not before I can use my thumb to gently drag away a couple of the small tears that have fallen from her eyes. "Now, I want to see this garage I've been hearing so much about."

"Ida Sue, are you sure? It's liable to be pretty boring," CC tells her while trying to clear her throat and button down the emotions that are showing on her face.

"Nonsense. I get to spend the day with my new daughter. How can that be boring?" Ida Sue counters. CC's eyes jerk to mine and I just smile to try and calm her as best as I can. Ida Sue is a tornado; it's best she learns that now.

"Well... if you're sure," CC says, sounding a little lost.

"Definitely."

"We should head out then. I have a phone conference I can't miss this morning. Gray, I..."

I kiss her before she can say something I might not want to hear. It's a brief kiss and nothing like I would give her if my mother and Jansen weren't around.

"Jansen and I will pick you up around three this afternoon. We're going to look at the scenery and maybe go out on the course for a bit. I need to keep my stroke in perfect form before the big tournament."

CC hugs me tight, her lips get close to my ears. "I can confirm that your stroke is more than perfect, Crayon Man."

I kiss her gently on her forehead with a laugh. "Always busting my ass. See you soon."

"See you soon."

I stand beside Jansen as CC and Mom head out. The door has been closed for ten minutes before I finally shake off the feeling of contentment that thrums through my veins and I only do it then because Jansen demands my attention.

"Let's get a move on, son."

I nod agreement, but I'd rather follow my woman to that garage and spend the day with her.

Chapter Fifty-Nine

CC

I stare at the phone as the last amount of hope I had fades. Mack's bank wouldn't help at all. I kind of expected it, but I was still... dreaming. I was dreaming. There's going to be no magic way out of this and there's no one to blame but me. Would Banger be as disappointed in me as I am in myself?

"What the hell are you doing here?" I hear growling outside my office. At first I'm afraid Ida Sue has done something, but that's Jackson yelling. With a deep breath, I go outside, wondering what my next catastrophe is. "I asked what the fuck you were doing here?"

"Do you have a problem with this man, Claudia dear?" Ida Sue asks. I don't turn to look at her, though. I'm busy staring into the eyes of David Riverton. He's here, at my garage. He's with three other men, all dressed in suits, though the other three don't look nearly as expensive.

"What are you doing here, Mr. Riverton?" I ask, doing my best to keep my voice civil, but not entirely successful.

"I've brought by the company engineers."

"And why the fuck would you do that?" Jackson growls.

"Because they want to get some early measurements in."

"Why would they need measurements?" I ask, fear curling tight in my stomach.

"Oh. I forgot to tell you the plans I have for this place, didn't I?"

"You can take your plans and stick them up your ass where the sun doesn't shine. That's what you can do with your plans. Claude isn't about to sell this place to the likes of you," Jackson yells, and that sick feeling in my stomach only gets worse. I know the color is gone from my face.

"Oh my, it seems you're keeping secrets from your employees, Claudia. I take it he doesn't know. I completely understand. Though, you might want to explain it to him soon. That way, instead of showing up here to a job he doesn't have anymore, he can go straight to the unemployment office. Honestly, he might want to go there sooner. However, I suppose I will be hiring a few when I take over."

"You're going to run a garage? I have trouble seeing that," I tell him, ignoring the way Jackson is staring at me.

"A garage? Good heavens, no! I'm going to be demolishing the garage. I'm going to be turning this place into a landfill station."

"You're what?"

"It seemed apt that it becomes a place for garbage, since that's exactly what built it to begin with." His verbal blow is delivered hard, striking me and momentarily robbing me of breath. He's never been a father to me. The fact that he's putting me through all this is proof enough of that. Still, it's hard to hear the man who fathered you call you garbage.

"I think you'd better leave," Ida Sue says, coming to my side and wrapping her arm around my shoulders as if to protect me. She can't really, not from the cold hate that lies between me and David Riverton, but it's good she's here. Right now, I'm not sure I could keep standing if she wasn't giving me her support. I feel Jackson move in on my other side. He has to know I've fucked up, but he's still here. I try and hold on to that.

"Oh. Gray's mother, right? Ida Joe, Right? Perhaps you can see now just what type of woman your son has gotten himself involved with."

"I can, and I completely approve. His choice in business partners, however, I'll definitely need to talk with him about."

"I have heard that your past is rather colorful. I guess your reaction shouldn't surprise me," Riverton replies. "Bad blood always shows. Maybe I need to find a new face of Riverton Metals before your offspring can tarnish it."

"Why, you son of a bitch! You want to lock horns with me? Feel free. But you better be ready for what you're inviting. I can't–"

"Leave," I order him, interrupting Ida Sue.

"I don't think I want to right now," he retorts. "I'm finding this is kind of fun."

"Leave or I'll have you arrested for trespassing."

"Fuck, yeah," Jackson grumbles.

"This place is mine. The paperwork is a mere formality."

"You don't have possession of it yet, and if you don't leave, I'll call Sheriff Tykes and press charges for trespassing," I tell him, proud that my voice is firm. For some reason, I'm feeling stronger. I'm intent on Riverton, and for that reason, I don't even notice that Ida Sue isn't beside me anymore. And because I'm not watching her, I'm completely taken by surprise when she blasts Riverton with the water hose that's hooked up.

"Ida Sue!" I yell, astonished and laughing despite being horrified. Riverton doesn't need more reason to destroy me.

"I'm just hosing down the place, sweetie. The stench of the garbage was starting to make me sick."

Riverton is yelling out that I'll be sorry, but when Ida Sue aims the hose full-force right at his face, he shuts up and takes off running with his buddies. Ida Sue lets up on the trigger of the water hose nozzle. No one talks for a few minutes. I think Jackson might be too mad, I'm afraid. That leaves Ida Sue. My eyes go to her and I wish I could read her better.

"I think it's time we talked, Claudia," she says.

"I do, too," Jackson says, and the hurt in his voice almost undoes me.

"Ida Sue, I probably should talk to Jackson alone. I owe it..."

"Nonsense. We're family now. Now, I don't know what's going on and I'm pretty sure my son doesn't know either. If he did and he's still doing business with that snake in the grass, then I'm going to rip him a new asshole."

"He doesn't know," I confess.

"I can only assume you have a reason for that, dear. But you, I, and Jackson here are going to talk, and for now, we'll keep it between the three of us. We're going to have to figure things out soon, however, because that sad waste of ball sweat will be back and I'd lay odds he'll only get meaner," she says. I look over at Jackson and he's nodding his head in agreement. I take a breath and agree.

"Okay. Let's go talk in my office, though. I think people on the street have seen enough for one day."

As the three of us walk back into the garage, nervousness floods through me. I know they're right. I do need to talk about this. I need to find a way to tell not only them, but Gray too. I just don't know if I can handle feeling everyone's disappointment on top of everything else.

Especially Gray's.

Chapter Sixty

GRAY

"The trick is the follow-through. See, if you choke your hold on the driver, you're not allowing the force to hit the ball and you're just not going to get a long drive," I tell CC, adjusting her hands on the club and pulling her back into my body as close as I can.

"Is that a golf ball in your pocket back there, Crayon Man?"

"Ouch. Golf ball? Couldn't you at least call it a putter or something? I mean, I'm just asking for a little respect here."

"I didn't realize you were so insecure," she says, wiggling her ass against my dick. It doesn't matter that I'm wearing slacks or that she has a skirt and panties on; when I get close to her and she rubs against me like that, I am instantly hard as a rock.

"Quit trying to make me spank your ass, Cooper. Now pay attention to your lesson."

"Not that I'm not loving my lesson... and other things," she says, pushing her ass against me, "but shouldn't you be resting up for day two? I mean, you're a few strokes behind the leaders. I'm not sure what all that means, but I don't want to be the reason you're too tired..."

"Do I feel too tired to you, Cooper?"

"You never feel too tired, but despite your other super hero attributes, you're only human, Gray Lucas. Maybe you should sleep."

"You could wear me out and then maybe I'll nap."

"We could go back to the hotel," she suggests, turning in my arms to look at me. She's wearing a cute little outfit complete with a short skirt, and I've been dying to fuck her since I first saw her in it. She's been better the last couple of days. Ever since Ida Sue came in, actually. Those two have become thick as thieves and whatever Ida Sue has done, she's somehow worked magic and CC seems less stressed about work. She still won't tell me what's going on, but she says she has it handled, and I guess that's all I need to know. I offered to help; that's all I can do.

"What if I told you I'm not sure I can make it back to the hotel?"

Her eyes dilate and she looks around the course nervously. There are a few people out today, but not many. I don't know where Riverton or Cammie have gone the last couple of days, but it's been nice not having them around. I'm regretting ever listening to Seth about getting Riverton's sponsorship. It might have been harder to get where I am now, but I would have done it. I've actually been talking to my lawyer to see if he could get me out of the contracts with Riverton. I don't know the full story with Cammie, but I know enough to know she and her father don't respect my woman, and that is not acceptable. Not now... not ever. My need to advance caused me to overlook that for a little bit. That will not happen again. There's nothing more important than CC to me, and that includes this tournament or any future ones. Without CC, I don't care if I ever golf again.

"Gray, it's broad daylight and the tournament... it's crowded," she whispers worriedly.

"It was earlier. Now everyone has gone home. C'mon, Cooper. Live dangerously."

"I'm beginning to hate it when you say that to me. It never ends well."

"This time, it will. I'll make sure you get a happy ending."

She rolls her eyes at me and I can't help laughing. But she reaches out her hand, which is a yes, and that's all that counts. I take her hand in mine and begin leading her to the edge of the woods.

Time to show my woman how much fun a golf course can really be.

Chapter Sixty-One

CC

I can't believe I'm doing this. I've been through a lot this last week, so maybe I've finally cracked under the pressure. Maybe it's the fact that Gray makes me feel like a teen again. Back when sex was new, emotions were honest and raw, and life held more promise. Back before reality slowly chipped away at my dreams.

It's been a rough week. Ever since the run-in with Riverton, I've been scrambling trying to figure things out. Ida Sue has taken control, though. She told me she had some connections in Texas with a bank and getting the loan wouldn't be a problem. My lawyer told me that as long as I don't give Riverton further reasons to foreclose, I have until the end of the month, according to the notice he gave me in the hotel. That gives me almost three weeks, and Ida Sue assures me it will be done way before then. I owe her so much. There's no way I would have gotten a bank in Texas to save me if it hadn't been for her.

So in the meantime, I'm staying away from Cammie and her father—from everyone here at the tournament, really. I spend my time with Ida Sue and Gray's crazy family, and Ida Sue is helping me to find ways to avoid business dinners and networking luncheons. The last press conference, I declared a migraine, but it's getting harder and harder to make sure Gray doesn't know something is going on—a fact Ida Sue is not totally happy with. According to her, she doesn't want her "little boy" doing business with people like that. He's too "innocent" to know how people work. I have to laugh. I know they say a mother's love is blind, but there's nothing little or innocent about Grayson Lucas.

Case and point, he leads me to the edge of the woods where there's a hole of sand. He helps me step down into it with this big grin on his face.

"Time to strip," he says.

"Um... I don't think so," I tell him, looking around. "I'm not getting butt-ass naked in a sand dune on a public course. There were hundreds of people here today, Crayon Man."

"They're gone now."

"Not all of them." My eyes go wide as he starts to strip. "Gray!"

"We're in no-man's zone. It's a bunker, by the way, not a dune. I really need to teach you more about golf."

"Whatever. You aren't getting me to lay down here and have sex with you."

"You aren't going to throw caution to the wind? C'mon, CC. Live—"

I put my hand over his mouth, not letting him finish. "I told you to quit saying that. It never turns out well. Besides, it's easy for you to say that. It won't be you who has sand crawling up their ass."

"I got a plan for that."

"You do?"

He nods, laying his pants and shirt down for a makeshift mattress. Then he looks up with a sly look on his face. "Your chariot awaits, my mistress."

"My chariot?"

"You got it, babe, because I'm about to take you on the ride of your life."

"You really are ridiculous. You know that?"

"But I make you smile," he says, and this time he's completely serious. He's looking at me and I get the feeling he sees deeper than anyone has ever bothered to before. "I make you laugh."

"You do," I tell him. Then, something spurs me on, and before I can stop myself, I'm admitting to something I normally wouldn't. "You make me happy."

His eyes close for a second, and then he's holding the side of my neck, his lips close to mine.

"That's all I want in the world, Cooper. That's all," he whispers before taking my mouth in a sweet kiss. It's different from any we've really shared before. It's filled with emotion.

When we break apart, I lift my shirt over my head. Suddenly where we're at is not half as important as being with him.

Chapter Sixty-Two

GRAY

I make her happy.

It's not admitting she loves me, but it still makes me feel as if I'm on top of the world. I help her undress, making sure we're still alone. There's a reason I've led her out here away from everyone and everything. I want CC to experience letting go and being free, but I don't especially want others to see her. That's all mine. She's all mine.

I help her lie down on my clothes and then lie beside her. I move my hand down her neck and over her breasts. Her nipples are already hard from a mixture of excitement and the cool breeze in the air. I spend some time teasing them more, loving the way they pebble tighter, straining towards me and reacting to my every touch.

"I love your breasts," I whisper right before I take a nipple in my mouth, using my tongue to toy with it.

Her body stretches up towards me, her hands pushing me into her. I can feel her nails score my back as her legs shift, opening for me. My CC is always so responsive, so ready for anything I'll give her.

"Gray, stop taking your time," she urges.

I have every intention of dragging out her torture, making her need me until she can't think of anything else, but she does something unexpected: She leans up and places a gentle kiss on my shoulder. It's sweet, loving... and completely CC. Then I feel her teeth scrape the skin. My cock jerks, wondering just what she's going to do next. Then she bites into the skin there, sending a sharp sensation that borders on pain but is something else. She does this while at the same time reaching between us to grab my cock, squeezing him and leaving me with no illusion to what she really wants.

"Are you hungry, baby?" I ask her, my hand already moving between her legs to see if she's ready. I move my fingers over her clit. She's already soaked for me, but I want her to the point that when I slide in, she explodes. She whimpers when I thrust a finger in, using my thumb to press down on that throbbing little button while I stretch her. I add a second finger, thrusting into her and stretching her before repeating the movements. My lips find hers again and I swallow her gasp as my fingers plunge inside of her hard and fast. Her cream gathers around them, allowing me to slide in and out of her with ease.

"I'm going to come, Gray," she whispers. I don't have words to explain what it feels like when she says my name like that. My balls literally ache with the need to empty inside of her and make sure I've claimed every slick inch of her.

I regretfully remove my fingers, then wrap my arms around her to hug her close.

"Gray?" she questions, confused, her voice thick and filled with need.

"Shh, sweet lips. I'm just moving so I'm on the bottom and you control this ride," I assure her. It just seems wrong to fuck her hard when she's against the hard ground.

She moans as we roll, but settles on top quickly. Her legs tighten around me as she seats herself atop me. She's a fucking goddess. The red hair framing her face and cascading down her bare shoulders shines bright as the sun seems to pick up every different shade she has. Her breasts are thrusting out, the nipples so hard it looks painful. Her curves and shape hypnotize me, especially as she reaches her hand between us, encircles my cock, and holds it at her entrance.

"I really love the way you think," she tells me.

"Is that so?"

"Mmm... hmm," she breathes, then lowers down on me so as to take my dick inside achingly slow. "And I really like being on top," she adds.

By this point, I'm too far gone to respond. It comes out as an unintelligible grunt because the woman of my dreams is sliding up and down on my dick and I can do nothing but feel. She puts her hands on each of my shoulders and begins riding me hard, pushing up and down and driving us both fast towards the point of no return. I can't look away from her, watching as pleasure shoots through her body and begins to overtake her. My body is so hot, it feels as if it's on fire. I know I'm not going to be able to hold out much longer. My hands knead her hips as I encourage her to ride harder. She puts a twist in her movements that is nearly my undoing. I know I'm holding her so tight that I'll probably bruise her. I thrust up, wanting to get as deep into her as I can.

And then... it stops.

"CC? Honey, you have me on the edge here. You need to move," I grunt, a second away from taking control away from her. She doesn't respond and her body is completely stiff. No more, warmer, soft, and pliant CC, and damn if that doesn't suck. "CC?" I growl like a wounded animal because I'm way too far into this now for her to be backing out. I will if she insists, but I'm not going to like it one bit.

"Gray! Hush!" she whispers fanatically and so quietly that even as close as we are, I have to strain to hear her.

Immediately, concern fills me. I hold her close, trying to look around us to see what's wrong. From where I'm at lying down, I can see next to nothing. I can't see one thing that would have her in such a panic—and there is panic and fear in her voice. I don't like that at all.

"What's going on?" I ask, holding her and trying to sit up at the same time, but she's pushing me down and sitting so stiffly, it's making it impossible.

"Hush! We're not alone!"

Shit. One of the other golfers must have ventured out here. I try to pull her down to reassure her that if we hide in the bunker, they will never know we're here. I pull her head down on my chest. The shift in her causes my dick to move into her even farther and I groan. Fuck... there's only so much a man can take.

"Hold still, baby, or I'm going to fuck you regardless. I don't care if there is another person around. Just be quiet like this and don't move. He'll take his turn and move on to the next spot on the course. Then, we can finish."

"What are you talking about, you idiot?" she hisses in my ear.

"The person you said was here. The golfer. He can't see us if we just..."

"It's not another golfer, you freak!"

"What? Then what the fuck are you going on about?" I ask her, frustrated and horny. Shit. I'm really, really horny.

"There's a skunk!"

"A what?"

"A skunk! He's about ten yards away from your head and if you don't shut up, he's going to... Oh, fuck."

"What?"

"Gray, he's coming over here. What do we do?"

Shit. Fuck. Damn.

Chapter Sixty-Three

CC

Panic has seized me. I feel it through every inch of my body. My heart is almost pounding out of my chest as I watch the little black and white terror stare at me. I mean we lock eyes. I always thought skunks looked so pretty. Flowers was my favorite character on Bambi. But watching as he stares at me, this animal doesn't look cute. He looks mean, hateful, and mocking—almost as if he knows exactly what he interrupted and what he's doing.

"Gray answer me!" I whisper again as fear threatens to consume me because the little shit is walking towards us. Strutting, even!

"Just hold still. If we don't scare it, it won't do anything. It will grow bored and leave."

Really? That's his advice? Okay, he grew up in Texas. Do they even have skunks out there? Because we do in Kentucky, and I've never known that advice to work. Of course, it's usually hunters that I've known who've been sprayed, so there's a chance he could be right.

As the skunk gets closer and closer, however, I start to experience serious doubts. "He's getting closer," I whisper in panic.

"Hang tight, Cooper," Gray whispers next to my ear, holding me close. I do my best. My body is so still, it feels like I'm balancing on a tightrope. I'm afraid to move, afraid to breathe... until I feel Gray's dick move inside of me. Good Lord!

"You cannot still be horny," I whisper into his ear, biting it to get my point across.

"I'm inside of you, Cooper. You can't expect me not to be horny."

"There's a rabid animal circling us!"

"He'll move on if you'll shut your sweet ass up," Gray counters, which pisses me off.

Now I think it's safe to say that I do not react well when my emotions are running high. I don't plan. I don't exercise caution. So his pissing me off, combined with being naked, feeling helpless, and having an animal circling us—not to mention all the stuff swirling in my mind about Riverton—pushes me so close to the edge that I feel the line at my feet, a line that I'm going to cross. I know it. I try to gain control one last time, and that's when I feel it. It's a feathery brush around my calf, so soft and light that it kind of tickles. Then I feel something wet and cold. My head moves carefully away from Gray as I look over my shoulder. There, I see a furry black face moving against my leg, nothing but a ball of fur, but I see the long white streak down its back and watch as its tail moves from a soft sway. It ever so intricately raises and I watch it go centimeter by centimeter. I push against Gray's shoulders.

"Don't do it, Cooper," Gray growls because he can feel my panic. He's holding tight to me. If he wasn't, I'd be gone. I'm afraid to speak, so I look in his eyes. I'm busy sending him looks that would kill a lesser man. He still doesn't let go. The idiot is still convinced his plan is going to work.

That's when the cold, harsh smell of reality strikes us both—literally. The spray hits us and the smell blooms like we just walked into a hog pen in the mid-august. It's so strong, it literally robs my air, but I don't have time to worry about breathing. I jump up the minute Gray's hold loosens. It doesn't matter that I'm buck-ass naked. Nothing matters except getting away from that damn skunk. I can hear Gray beside me, but I don't look at him; I'm running as hard and as fast as I can.

And I only have two thoughts on my mind: I will never have sex outside again, and I will kill Grayson Lucas if he ever taunts me with not living dangerously again.

Chapter Sixty-Four

CC

"Whoa! Where do you think you're going like that??" the doorman yells, grabbing me around the waist. I was so intent on getting inside that I didn't even see him coming to block the entrance. "Good Lord! What is that smell?" he bellows. I try to pull away from him, but his grip is tight. I hear Gray come up beside us.

"Get your hands off my woman!" he growls like the caveman he is.

My head is swimming, my breath is ragged, and my heart is still beating out of my chest. I'm so hyped up on adrenaline that it doesn't even hit me that I'm still completely naked—not until the exact moment I feel the doorman's hand grope my ass. I push away from him immediately, but I needn't have bothered because Gray is all but tearing me away from the man. I wince at his hold, knowing there will be a bruise there tomorrow.

"What the fuck do you think you're doing?" Gray yells, and I can feel eyes on us. Gray moves me behind his back.

"Gray," I whisper, hoping to get his attention before this gets worse. When I look over his shoulder and see the small crowd gathering, I realize it can get a lot worse. There's at least fifty people standing around watching us, and I'd lay odds that all fifty have seen as much of me as Gray has. I burrow against his back, feeling embarrassment and shame wash through me.

"Mr. Lucas? What are you doing here? Do you know that young lady? Why are you both naked?" another man asks from beside us. I look up enough to realize that he must be the manager. Great.

Gray can't take the time to acknowledge the man, though, because he's taking a swing at the doorman. Which, by the way, makes it very hard to hide behind him. I've wrapped my arms around myself as best as I can. Someone is handing me a black suit coat and I reach out to get it. When I see the man holding it looking at my body, it feels wrong to take his coat. I start to anyway, but Gray is there in front of me and he's holding the black suit jacket the doorman was wearing. He wraps it around me.

"Get the fuck away from my woman," Gray growls towards the other men and several others who have joined the small crowd and gather too close for comfort. I feel like I'm hyperventilating. The world is starting to spin, and if I pass out, I figure that will be the ultimate embarrassment. I manage to hold on enough to watch Gray take a tablecloth from someone. He wraps it around himself. The fabric strains to meet at his hips and doesn't quite make it, but at least he's mostly covered. He's exchanging words with the manager and is demanding the doorman be fired. I really can't listen to any more, and if one more person in the background keeps asking what that horrible smell is, I might go off.

That's when I realize I'm crying. I feel the tears sliding down my face and it makes me mad. I'm not a crier. I don't cry hardly ever. And the fact that I'm doing so now in front of all these people who have seen me naked—and in front of an irate Gray who is still yelling about the doorman copping a feel of my ass—pisses me off. I can't control it. The more I try, the faster the tears come. So before I start sobbing in front of the vultures, I take off toward the elevators.

Not nearly fast enough, however.

"Claudia, can we talk to you?"

I turn when I hear my name and freeze when I see a reporter there with a photographer behind her, his camera zoomed in on me. Then I take off running because, yeah, the sobs have started.

What did we do?

Chapter Sixty-Five

GRAY

"Ow! Damn it, Mom, that shit stinks worse than the skunk."

"It definitely does not, trust me on that one, son. You smell like old Mr. Simpson's outhouse. If you're going to pick wildflowers with your woman, you should at least wait until you're home. There, at least I have my own tomato juice. This store crap is hardly making a dent in it."

"I didn't exactly plan on getting sprayed by a skunk, Mom."

"Apparently not. Why on Earth you felt the need to do something this asinine is beyond me. I mean, you have a king size bed and a kitchen table here. Not to mention that big shower, or heck, even that chair in the sitting room!" she mutters, pouring another can of tomato juice into the tub.

It's a good thing I'm not a modest person because having my mom pour juice over my naked ass would definitely be on my list of things that would kill me. I hang my head down as she pours another can over it. Shit. I feel like the biggest asshole on the face of the Earth.

"How's CC?" I ask, afraid to know the answer, but scared not to. I haven't gotten to speak one word to her since we went running back to the hotel.

There was chaos downstairs when the doorman grabbed CC.

My fist found its way to his face, and then a reporter showed up trying to get a picture of me and CC. It was all bad. It probably didn't help that I ripped the camera way from the photographer and threw it on the ground so it busted into a million pieces, inadvertently dropping the damn tablecloth I had covering me.

I followed CC up to our room, but she didn't talk; she was too busy crying. I wanted to console her, but when got to our room, it finally hit me that without my clothes, my wallet, or anything else—we were stuck... which required me knocking on the door of my mom's room. Which brings me to getting drowned in store-bought tomato juice and vinegar by Mom in my hotel room after she already did the same to CC in hers... and not getting two minutes alone to check on my woman. I'm mad, worried, and stressed the fuck out. I've already put a call in to Seth about the press, but as much as I don't want to admit it, there's a very real possibility that pictures of me and CC in our birthday suits will be all over the papers in the morning. CC has to be so pissed off at me, and I can't blame her.

"How do you expect the girl to be after running across a busy golf course butt-ass naked, getting groped by a doorman, and then having her future mother-in-law washing her from head to toe and seeing every nook and crevice the good Lord saw fit to give her?"

"Can I see her?"

"After you smell better, maybe. Now hold still or this scrub brush will take off your hide along with the smell."

"Yes, ma'am," I grumble unhappily, and for my tone, I get the brush slapped upside my head. Fuck. Will this day ever end? Better yet, will CC be back in my arms when it does? This is all my fault and I'm feeling like shit for getting her into it.

Chapter Sixty-Six

CC

"You okay, sweetheart?" Gray asks again.

I've lost count, but we're surely in double digits by now.

It's the day after the entire mess. The tournament has been postponed because of a rainstorm, so we're just trying to recover. We're snuggled on the couch watching TV and wearing the hotel robes. Finally clean... and finally Ida-Sue-and-crazy-Lucas-family free. If it wasn't for smelling like tomato juice and vinegar, I would pretend it was all a bad memory.

I'm trying to act normal, but there's this fear that keeps swamping me. There were a lot of people around when we made it back to the hotel. A lot. Gray said he had it handled, but fuck, I don't know how many people saw me naked. I don't know what kind of chaos played after I ran away crying. It took Ida Sue an hour to calm me down, but we both know that if this gets out, Riverton will use that against me, which means there's no way I'll be able to get the loan from the bank unless Ida Sue performs a miracle. Every time the phone rings, I jump, worried it's Riverton and praying it's Ida Sue instead with word from the bank. I don't care what the terms are; right now, I'd sign away my life if it means keeping the garage from that asshole. I feel so bad. There's just no words. Jackson has been trying to get a loan, but his credit pretty much sucks after his divorce.

"I wish you would quit asking me that," I tell Gray, trying not to be frustrated with him. It's not fair that I'm blaming him, though I am. It's not his fault I'm in the mess that I'm in, but it is his fault we literally got caught with our pants down.

"I'm worried about you, Cooper."

"I'm about as good as someone can be when they've mooned half of Georgia and then got groped by some perverted doorman."

"Fucking bastard. I should have hit him harder."

"Let's try to just not talk about it, please?"

"I'm sorry, baby," he says. He sounds so sad. I feel like a bitch for being upset.

"I know," I tell him, then wince. I made the decision to make love with him. It's not his fault completely and yet I realize I am holding a grudge. I'm blaming him.

"C'mon, CC. Talk to me. What's upsetting you the most?"

"You need more besides what we just talked about?"

"I can't help feeling like there's something more. You need to talk to me."

He's right. I know he is. I take a deep breath. Is this where I push him away? Is this where I lose him?

"There's things you don't know," I tell him.

He pulls up, turning so he can face me, and I see the worry and maybe even hurt in his face. Guilt swamps me and I try to push it behind me so I can concentrate on what I need to tell him.

"Talk to me, CC."

"Gray, when Banger got sick, things just got... really bad. It was just me and him. There wasn't anyone else to depend on."

"I'm sorry, honey. I'm sorry I wasn't here to help you."

My next words stop, and I feel like I'm choking on them. He's completely serious. I want to believe him, and I think most of me does. There's still this small voice in my head telling me not to believe him—not to trust him. I have this war going on inside of me. Will he let me down like others have? Will he leave me? Am I being unfair? Why do I insist on making Gray pay for the sins of others?

"Okay, fine!" I tell him, more upset with myself than him and deciding just to lay it out for him. "Gray, I'm in trouble. I made a huge mistake..." I start, when a knock at the door stops me.

Both of us look at the door and Gray huffs in frustration.

"Stay right here and don't move." I don't respond, my eyes still glued to the door. I have a bad feeling. "Do you hear me, CC?" he prompts, and I tear my eyes from the door to look at him.

"Okay," I say weakly, sitting up.

"I love my family, but I swear they have the most horrible timing," Gray mutters, walking to the door.

I just keep staring at the door like a deer caught in the headlights of an oncoming car. He might think it is family, but something inside of me tells me different, and I know once that door opens, my world is never going to be the same.

Chapter Sixty-Seven

GRAY

Son of a bitch, I can't believe I was just about to get CC to talk and my family interrupts me. I'm tempted to just ignore the knock, but I know CC won't let me by with that. My only option is to get rid of them quickly and hope that she doesn't backpedal. CC's been better the last few days, but I know something has been bothering her since she left Florida and I had to follow her to Kentucky. I can't let her weasel out of telling me. I need to know. More than that, I'm tired of dancing around how I feel about her. We've been together long enough; she should know that I'm here for the long haul. I should be able to tell my woman I love her without worrying it will make her run for the hills.

"Mom, I appreciate you being worried about—Oh, Riverton. What are you doing here?" I ask once I open the door and discover it's him there.

"I'll tell you what the fuck I'm doing here. Would you like to explain to me why the spokesman for my new line of golf merchandise was caught buck-naked running across the golf course during the most important match of the season?" he growls.

He probably has good reason for being upset. He has a lot of money tied up in this new venture. I sigh and hold my head down, knowing that this isn't going to be over soon. I'm about to shut the door after him when his daughter walks in.

Just what I needed to make today an extra special shit pile.

"Listen, I know you're upset and you have every reason to be, but it's not as bad as you're letting on. I already have my men on it to stop the media attention. We'll contain this, and..."

"Contain this? You and that woman are already plastered across every tabloid rag out there," he growls, shoving a couple folded newspapers into my gut. I put them on the table, grabbing the top one and opening it up. Fuck me running, it's worse than I imagined. It's a picture of me and CC running across the golf course in nothing but our birthday suits. The butts have been blurred out, but it clearly shows that we're naked. The headline reads: "Golf's bad boy caught once again with his pants down."

"Fuck!" I growl.

"They get worse. Look at the next one," Cammie says just as CC comes to my side looking broken. She leans in and reads the picture. She gives a soft cry that rips through me. Her hand covers her mouth when she sees the picture.

I'm almost afraid to read the next one, but I do. I have to because CC is already reaching for it. That's when I discover that Cammie has a knack for understating. The headline on the inside is not only worse; it rocks my entire world: "Golf pro Grayson Lucas caught cheating on fiancé with her father's secret love child."

"What the fuck? We'll sue the bastards. By the time I get done with them, they won't own a paper to print their vicious lies in anymore," I growl. "CC, you have to believe me, I will handle this," I tell her, holding her shoulders and forcing her to look at me. When her face slowly lifts, I see those big tears in them I've come to hate. Her face has gone white. Fuck! I've got to find a way to fix this.

"Gray," she whispers, but I just pull her close. I need to deal with Riverton and get them away from CC. She has too much to deal with; she doesn't need them here, too.

"Why in the hell do they even think they can get away with printing this garbage? I mean, calling Cammie my fiancé? And who the fuck knows what was in their heads when they said that shit about you and CC. David, you have to admit this is overboard. You can help me take them down. We'll file suit today."

"It's true," CC whispers.

"Of course it's not, baby. Don't you worry about... What did you say?"

"I said it's true, Gray."

"What are you talking about?" I ask, confused. But when I look around the room, there are three sets of eyes on me. Three sets that don't look the bit lost.

Three sets of eyes that look eerily alike.

"My mother... well, I've told you enough that you know she's not the best person in the world."

"Yeah, but..."

"She had an affair with... this man," she tells me, indicating Riverton. "He had money and power and she thought that she could trap him into marriage by getting pregnant with me. The plan backfired because even as fucked up as Margaret was, she had no idea just how cold the bastard she was sleeping with was." Her voice is still a whisper, but there's a coldness in it. When I look up, I see she's staring straight at Riverton.

"Jesus," I mutter, not sure how I feel about this shit or the fact that she kept it from me. I mean, why? Why wouldn't she tell me? I went into business with this asshole and that alone makes me sick. I don't want to work with anyone who can't even acknowledge his own daughter. "Why didn't you tell me?" I ask her, not wanting to have this out with Riverton and his daughter around, but unable to keep myself from asking.

"I wanted to. It's just... I was..."

"She was using you, Gray. She wanted into the world my father and I have because she's jealous. Jealous of me. Jealous of the fact that she's just too far out of your league," Cammie chimes up in her annoying voice. There has to be a mistake somewhere, because this woman cannot be kin to CC.

"I was not! I..." CC starts, but I interrupt her.

"You need to shut it, Cammie. CC has been through enough. She doesn't need you trying to land digs at her expense," I tell her, defending my woman even if I don't understand her right now.

"Gray, I really was going to tell you. I started to before they got here, I promise."

"It's not important right now. What's important is we need to figure out a way to do damage control here," I tell her. I sound short with her and I regret that. I'm not really upset with her over the secret, just the thought that she kept it from me. I'll think about it later. It was her secret she didn't have to tell me, no matter how much that upsets me. Still, my main concern right now has to be how to get these pictures taken down.

"It's much too fucking late for that," Riverton says.

"No. We just need..."

"You don't get it, Lucas, so I'll spell it out for you. You've been suspended from this tournament."

"What? They can't do that!"

"They can. You signed a contract with a morality clause. This is clearly in violation of those terms. You're out. The sponsors have given you and your entourage until the end of the day to leave the club."

CC's startled gasp tries to grab my attention, but I stay focused on Riverton.

"I understand the temptation to lie with pigs, son," he goes on. "After all, I did it myself, but you can't allow them to drag you down into their mire."

I blink. For a second, I think I must have imagined what he said. Surely the asshole wouldn't say that shit in front of CC—a woman who is apparently his own daughter.

"We can still spin this, Grayson. I'll go out with you and we can present a united front. We'll tell them that we were separated at the time..." Cammie chatters.

I'm barely listening to her, still going over what Riverton says, and I can't control myself. I slam my fist into his nose, and even when blood is spurting out and he's groaning in pain, I don't feel better.

"You fucking loser! How dare you talk about CC like that! She's worth ten of you and your crazy-ass daughter!" I growl, hitting him again just because I have more frustration and I can't hit Cammie. I do turn to her, though. "And you! Are you crazy? 'Separated?' We were never together! Are you the reason the press thinks we're an item?"

"I'll sue you for this, Lucas. You won't have a dime to your name when I'm through with you!" Riverton mutters through his blood-soaked hand which holds his obviously broken nose. "I'll sue you right before I foreclose on your whore's garage and burn it to the ground!" he spits. Before I can respond, the door opens with enough force that it slams against the wall.

"Like hell you will! You'll tuck your head between your tail and leave my son and CC alone or you'll regret it," Ida Sue says while standing at the door. CC's trying to pull away, but I don't let her. I hold her close and together we turn to look at Ida Sue. I know my mother well, and there's a fury behind her words, but that face is what I'm concentrating on. She's got something big up her sleeve and I'm suddenly very anxious to see what it is. Hopefully she's getting ready to hand Riverton his ass because if she doesn't, I sure as hell will—one way or another.

Chapter Sixty-Eight

CC

I feel like I've been standing in the eye of a hurricane, every horrible thing I can imagine battering me over and over. Now with Ida Sue standing there looking like she's about ready to commit murder, I'm afraid to move and I feel out of control. I've not been like this since Banger got so horribly sick. I'm not myself. If I was, I would have throat-punched Cammie. Instead, I'm left staring at Ida Sue, wondering what could possibly happen next.

"What the hell are you doing here?" Riverton growls, probably remembering being on the wrong side of Ida Sue in Kentucky.

"When I saw the paper this morning, I just had a feeling you'd be like the snake you are and come here slithering on your damn belly and bothering my kids."

I could almost smile at her. The only thing to make it more complete is if she had a shotgun in her hand. But my stomach feels like someone just kicked it: Her kids?

"Is Ida Sue... claiming me?"

"She did that weeks ago, Cooper," Gray whispers, squeezing me tight. I hadn't even realized I said the words out loud. "How did you miss that?" he asks.

"We're all claiming you."

That comes from Gray's family, who comes in and stand behind

Ida Sue. They say it in unison. There's White, Cyan, Petal, Maggie, Jansen, and Green. What they are saying is so huge, I'm momentarily stunned.

How did I miss this? A warmth fills me that I can't explain, mostly because it's like nothing I have really felt before. But standing there among two people I hate more than anything in the world, I'm happy. I'm good because I'm standing with... a family. My family. Gray and his crazy bunch are my family.

"I'm not changing my name to Chrysanthemum," I tell Ida Sue, and I have a few tears in my eyes, but I'm okay with these because even though I'm about to lose Banger's garage—and my naked ass is plastered all over the world—at least I belong somewhere.

"Of course you're not, dear, though speaking of Mums, I could always use some grandkids. Just make sure you don't name him Skunk. That would never work."

"Yes, ma'am," I tell her, shaking my head.

"Though Sandy would work. We don't have one of those in the family yet," she says.

"What the hell are you all doing here? It's like The Beverly Hillbillies visiting..."

Riverton doesn't get to finish because Gray turns around and, as quick as lightning, punches him hard in the already-busted-up-and-bleeding nose. Riverton falls backwards and this time he's down for the count.

"What have you done? Daddy! Daddy, can you hear me?" Cammie cries. She steadies Riverton's head and helps him sit up.

"I'll sue all of you assholes. I'll bury you so deep, you'll never see daylight!"

"I don't think so," Ida Sue says, walking over to him. "My daddy always told me if you had a snake in the henhouse, you should follow it back to its hole and make sure you cut its head off. I never much paid attention to that until I had kids. Then I discovered that I was a lot like a mama bear over her cubs. You ever seen a mama bear if she thinks someone is trying to mess with her baby, Mr. Riverton?"

"You're crazy," he growls, holding his face and standing up. It takes him three times to stand up, but he finally gets on his feet.

"I am crazy. You really should have factored that in. You mess with my kids and I'm going to fuck you up."

"Lovey," Jansen growls.

"It's okay, Jan. The good Lord understands sometimes there's only certain words you can use."

"I meant, get it over with before Gray murders the bastard and we have bigger problems on our hands," Jansen says, and that's when I notice that Gray is tensed up beside me and looking at Riverton like he really is planning on killing him.

"Gray, sweetheart," I tell him, pulling his attention back to me.

He gives me a smile, but it's a strained one.

"I'm okay, Cooper. You and I are going to have a talk later, though." I grimace at his words because I can only imagine what that's going to be like.

"Fine," Ida Sue says, reaching in the back pocket of her jeans to pull out a paper.

"What's this?" Riverton says, looking at the paper as if it might bite him.

"A signed and notarized statement showing that CC's loan is paid in full."

"No fucking way. I wouldn't accept payment."

"Ida Sue," I cry, completely blown away. She said she was working with the bank. How did she get the loan without me signing papers? She couldn't have! Unless...

I look around for a place to sit down before I fall. I finally give up and just sit on the wooden coffee table. "Ida Sue, why?" I cry again, feeling horrible.

"Because you're family, and family takes care of one another."

"I guess I should have known you'd have your boyfriend pay your way out of trouble. Like mother like daughter, I guess." Riverton sneers at me.

"I wouldn't... I didn't," I cry, looking from him to Ida Sue and back up at Gray, afraid he would think I took his mother for a ride.

"You didn't, sweet cheeks, but I did," Ida Sue says. If I wasn't knee-deep in fear and this sick feeling at having Gray's mom shell out two hundred and fifty thousand dollars, I'd have to wonder about that nickname. Gray obviously takes after his mom. That could mean trouble for me, if he doesn't kick me to the curb once he realizes how much money his mom is out.

"Whatever. I'll use all the money I have to bury every damn one of you," Riverton growls.

"That might be difficult," Ida Sue says, and Jansen comes beside her and hands her an envelope. "Consider yourself served, Mr. Riverton," she says, handing it to him. "Of course I don't trust you to say you didn't get it, even with all these witnesses, so the sheriff's office will be hand-delivering one to your corporate offices this afternoon."

"What are you talking about, you old bat?" Riverton snarls, tearing open the envelope. Gray makes a move to hit him again and Jansen pushes him away.

"He's not worth it, son," Jansen says after pushing him back a few feet. Gray doesn't look happy, but he steps back. "Besides, it's my woman he's going on about," he adds, and then he grabs the back of Riverton's collar and uses it to slam him head first into the wall. "You need to learn how to talk to a woman, son," he says as Riverton falls to the ground, completely out.

Cammie is crying, and she looks down at her father and then back at all of us. "What's in those papers?" she asks, apparently more concerned with that than her father. Of course David Riverton doesn't exactly inspire family loyalty.

"Those would explain that I am now fifty-one percent owner of all stock concerning Riverton Industrial. They'll also notify you and your daddy that there will be a stockholder meeting next week to talk about a change of leadership."

"What? You can't do that."

"It's already done. I've been talking it over with Cyan and he feels like he might enjoy restructuring the company."

"Mom? How did you do all this?" Gray asks.

"You know those oil wells that Blue let them drill on that pasture along the Northside, just to alienate our neighbor?"

"Yeah?"

"He's been giving me the money, and I've let Cyan handle investing it. Turns out, I can buy and sell Riverton."

"There's no way!" Cammie says, stomping her foot.

"But I did, Cammie darlin'. Who knew you and your father could be bought so cheaply?"

"Me. I definitely knew that," Maggie says.

"Boys, drag this piece of trash outside," Jansen orders, and White and Cyan jump to do his bidding.

"But if you do this? What will we do? What will happen to me? Grayson! You can't let them do this! What will I do?" Cammie cries as Maggie all but pushes her out the door.

"Try getting a job," Maggie suggests, then closes the door once her brothers come back in.

"Now that's what I call a family meeting," Ida Sue says. "Now how do we take on the stuffed shirts over the tournament? Because come hell or high water, my boy will be knocking balls into holes tomorrow morning and doing it better than any man out there."

Everyone starts laughing and all I can do is look up at Gray. He's laughing too, and he seems okay, but he's tense. I see it in everything he does.

Does he think I took advantage of his mom? How will I ever get the money to pay her back?

Chapter Sixty-Nine

GRAY

I close the door behind my crazy family and just stand there holding my hand against it for a few minutes, trying to get my emotions in check. It's been a fucked up day, the least of it being the fact that my woman's naked body was plastered in every gossip rag coming and going. Seth is working on that as we speak, but that will never go completely away—and that's my fault. I failed her. Apparently I've been failing her a lot and didn't even know. I don't know how I feel about the fact that my mother knew CC was in trouble and I didn't. Did CC feel she couldn't come to me?

"Gray?" CC asks, wringing her hands from across the room. I don't have to see her to know that's what she's doing; I know by the tone of her voice.

My eyes close and I try once again to rein in the fact that I'm hurt. That's not truly what's important right now.

"You didn't tell me," I say before I can stop myself. I turn around to look at her and I see the embarrassment on her face.

"I know."

"My mother knew that you were in trouble and I didn't."

"That was by accident. She was at the garage when Riverton showed up..."

"He came to the garage?"

"He was just poking at me, wanting me to know he had me in a corner," she explains, not quite meeting my eyes.

"He harassed you? The fucker came to your business and harassed you and you didn't feel like that was something you needed to tell me? You let me conduct business with these people, CC!" I growl loudly, anger filling me at the idea of CC standing up against that twisted fuck by herself. What would it feel like to have the man who is responsible for your birth treat you like garbage?

"Now wait a minute. You went into business with them way before I even came into the picture. I don't have anything to do with that."

"I wouldn't have gone into business with them if I had even an inkling of an idea that he was this twisted. If you had told me he was your father..."

"He's not my father! He may have been a sperm donor, but under no circumstance has he ever been my father. I've only had one of those and he died."

I swallow down the anger and frustration when I see the pain on her face. Right now, CC reminds me of a little girl, lost and... unloved. Except she is; she's loved more than she could ever imagine.

"Okay. You're right. You're completely right. It's just... damn it, CC. You should have told me what was going on."

"Why?"

"Why?" I repeat in disbelief.

"Yeah, why? It's my garage, my horrible past that was circling. Whatever happened, it didn't affect you. It was my problem and my business. That's it."

"That's it? What affects you affects me! *You're my woman.* You're a part of my life. I thought we were building something here? I thought we were in a relationship. Instead, I find out that you're going through all this shit and that my mother is the one who paid Riverton off and got rid of it."

"I know you're upset about the money. I mean, two hundred and fifty thousand is a lot of money. But you have to know I will find a way to pay her back. It may take me some time, but I will. I had no idea that she was going to—"

"Will you stop?! Do you honestly think I give a fuck about the money? I'll give mom the money back tomorrow—if she'll take it."

"Gray! It's two hundred and fifty thousand dollars!"

"So?"

"It's a lot of money!"

"CC, how much money do you think I'll make if I win tomorrow?"

"You don't even know for sure if you'll be able to compete."

"I will. But it doesn't matter. I can pay the loan back without even winning. Still, if I win, I'll make over a million dollars."

"Over a million?"

"Yes."

"I... think I need to sit down," she says, falling back on the coffee table.

"Are you okay?"

"You get a million dollars for hitting little balls all day?"

"It's a little more complicated than that, Cooper."

"If you guys make that kind of money—why do you wear such weird clothes?"

"Will you stop fixating on golf clothes? *Jesus!* We have things to discuss here."

"We don't. Not really. Your money is not mine. I'm going to pay your mom back."

"Jesus Christ, Cooper. Will you quit talking about the money? It's not important!"

"Spoken like a man who makes a million dollars for getting ducks all day."

"Ducks?"

"You know, when you don't make a hole-in-one, but you manage to get the ball in before the hole number, or something..."

"Are you talking about a birdie?"

"Whatever. They both have wings and beaks."

"You are completely insane, Cooper."

"I'm starting to feel that way..."

"You should have told me you were in trouble."

"Why?"

"*Because I love you!* Damn woman, it shouldn't be this hard, Cooper."

"You love me?"

"Of course I do! What did you think we were doing here?"

"I... I wasn't sure."

"CC, I love you. I want you in my life. Not just for a week here and there, or a month. I don't want quick sex with you. I want to grow old with you. I want kids with you. Fuck, I want to spend every fucking day of my life with you by my side. I'm not doing this until I grow tired of fucking you, CC. I'm here because I know in my heart that I will never get tired of you. I will never be happy unless you are with me."

"Gray..."

"Please tell me I'm not alone in this, CC."

"Gray," she says, walking towards me with tears in her eyes. She pulls me near, going up on the tips of her toes so that our faces are close. "Gray," she whispers again, her voice thick with emotion.

"What, CC? What?"

"I..."

"CC?"

"I love you. I just really love you," she whispers, then brings her lips to mine.

Chapter Seventy

GRAY

"You love me?" I ask her when we break away from each other. My heart feels tight. I wasn't sure how this talk would go. In the back part of my mind, I really thought she was going to break up with me. The fact that she told me she loves me seems completely unreal.

"I do. I love you with all of my heart."

"If I knew this would be your reaction, Cooper, I would have cornered you a long time ago."

"I'm not sure I would have been ready until right now."

"You're ready now? For everything? To go all the way?"

"Are we talking about sex here? 'Cause we kind of already..."

"Not sex, you nympho, though we will be doing that. I'm talking marriage, kids, happily ever-after."

"I haven't had many role models for parents, Gray. I might not make a good mother."

"You have Ida Sue and Banger."

"If Banger heard you refer to him as a good mother, he'd come back and gut you."

"Quit busting my balls, CC. You get what I'm saying. Tell me you're willing to go on this crazy ride with me."

"What if I mess it up?"

"What if I do? There's no guarantees except that we promise each other no matter what that we stick together," I tell her, locking our hands together and threading my fingers through hers. I bring our joined hands up and kiss them. "Together, CC."

She stares at our hands and then at me. "I'm ready," she whispers.

The weight of those soft-spoken words curls inside of me and rips through my heart, pulling it apart and then stitching it back together in a way that I know this woman will always be here. I let go of her hand and then, without words, I pick her up in my arms and carry her into the bedroom. The next few moments are filled with nothing but heavy breathing and a blur of clothes being pulled off, ending only when both of us are naked and lying on the bed next to each other on our sides.

I bring my hand down her shoulder and arm lightly, just enjoying the feel of her soft, warm skin. I let my hand rest on her hip as I look at her.

"You're so fucking beautiful, Cooper. So beautiful you make me ache."

"Let's see if I can cure that," she whispers, kissing me on my chest.

"I like the sound of that," I tell her, rolling over on my back when she pushes against me. She climbs on top, her body feeling like heaven this close. She slides between my legs and drapes herself over me, letting her lips kiss down my stomach. I let my fingers play in her hair, not urging or rushing her. No, I'm just enjoying CC and anything and everything she wants to give me.

She doesn't seem to be in a rush either. Leisurely kissing me, whispering, "I love you," after each kiss. I could do this and nothing more than this and die happy. It might sound girly to admit it, but she makes me feel cherished.

She shifts on top of me so that her legs come down on the mattress on either side of my body. I look up at her—a goddess, her breasts tilting out, her soft feminine curves almost glowing in the soft light, and her hair lying lazily against her creamy white skin. My dick jerks, thrusting out against her. It can't go far since she's almost sitting on it. The tip has somehow made it under her enough that it's resting against the inside of her thigh and there's a slick wetness against him. I couldn't tell you if it's from her excitement or my own. I figure it's a mixture of both, and I fucking love that idea. I shove down the urge to roll her over and bury my head there, drinking down any of her juices I find. This isn't about me. I'll get that later. This is CC's show, and I can't wait to see what she does next.

I don't have long to wait because she slides down and then grabs my cock, positioning it lying down underneath her. Then, she settles on top of the lucky bastard. My dick is instantly enveloped in her sweet cream as it pushes between the lips of her pussy. CC moans above me and I look up to watch her. She's got her hands on her breasts, holding them and gently teasing her nipples. My hands lock on her knees to stop from giving into the temptation to turn her over and fuck her hard. I want to give this to her. I want her to take what she wants. It's beautiful to watch.

She begins sliding up and down on my cock, painting him with her desire and riding him.

"God, Gray, that feels so good. I could come just like this," she whispers above me, her head thrown back, her eyes closed, and her hips moving as she takes her pleasure.

"Do it, baby. Take anything you want," I urge her. She pulls her head back up to look at me, her eyes glowing with need, desire... and love. It's always been there. Why didn't I notice it before this moment?

"There's something I've always been meaning to try," she says, and fuck if that isn't something a man loves to hear from a woman. I want to make every one of her thoughts and fantasies come to life.

"What's that?" I ask her.

She studies my face, her tongue coming out to lick along the bottom of her lip. Her top teeth bite into the flesh and she pulls on her lip. It's fucking sexy, and my dick tries once again to push into her without success. She has the bastard pinned, but it's a position I could die a happy man in. CC surprises me next. She lifts up off of me and this time it's me that has to bite back a cry of disappointment. It doesn't take me long to figure out what she has in mind though when she turns herself around. I kiss up her back as she settles back down.

"I don't know how to break it to you, darling, but we've done this position before," I tell her, my voice hoarse as I feel her hand wrap around my dick.

"You've taken me from behind, Gray. But I don't think we've done this before," she says, and then she's backing up. I lie down as she moves so her pussy is over my face. The sweet aroma of her hits me and I feel pre-cum slide down my cock. Fuck, this won't last long, and I know it was her show, but there's only so much a man can handle. I grab her hips and bring her down on my face, hard. I smother myself in her cream that slowly drips from her sweet cunt and covers the sides of her thighs. I drag my tongue through her depths, thrusting up into her, burrowing and wanting more. I growl into her cunt when I feel her tongue sliding against my balls. When she sucks one in her mouth, teasing it with her tongue, I nearly lose it.

I move my hands to grab her ass, biting into the cheeks and pushing her even harder into my face. My fingers push into her skin and move until they find that sweet little entrance. I slip a finger just inside the ring of her ass while bringing my other hand around to thrust a couple fingers in that sweet pussy I've been eating. When I turn my attention to her clit and tongue it, her entire body shudders, she squeezes my fingers tight, and her cry gets muffled as she moves from my balls to my cock and swallows him down that hot, slick throat of hers. Her hand stays tight around the base of my cock as she tunnels up and down on my cock, fucking her mouth with it. I know I'm going to blow. I can already feel the heated electric spark spread down my back, but I want her to come first.

I push my finger deeper into that tight, virgin ass. Then I bite her clit before sucking on it hard and lashing my tongue repeatedly over it. The swollen nub is pulsing so hard, I can feel it, even with all of the sensations I'm experiencing. I curve my finger inside of her, scraping against the warm, hot, sugary sweet wall and that's all it takes. She cries out, though the sound is garbled because she's choking on my cock, deep-throating me. I explode into her mouth, feeling jet after jet of my cum release. When her orgasm starts, I don't stop eating her. I lick it all up and keep going until she gives into me again.

When it's done, we're both breathing hard. I feel her place a small kiss against my still semi-erect cock, and then burrow her head against my balls and let out a shaky breath.

"I love you, Gray," she whispers, already half asleep.

I kiss the inside of her thigh. "I love you, too," I tell her. I wait for her to say more, but the next thing I hear is a cute little snore. She fell asleep lying on my balls with her hand wrapped around my dick. I smile and kiss her thigh again and she whimpers.

I'll let her rest and then wake her up with eating her out again. That sounds like a damn good plan. I'm brilliant, really. I'll make sure she appreciates that fact later.

Chapter Seventy-One

GRAY

"Gray, how does it feel to have won golf's biggest tournament and to now have your name in the record books with some of the greats of the sport?" the blonde reporter I know as Jenn asks.

I look over at my crazy family and CC standing behind the ribbon. "It feels like I'm on top of the world. I have so much respect for the guys who wore this blazer before me. Just to be mentioned among them is a great honor."

"Gray, that was the most convincing win this tournament has seen in ages and you looked so relaxed out there. Do you think that gave you a leg up on your peers?"

"Jenn, to be honest, I was relaxed. Going into this tournament, I already had everything a man could ask for. I had my health, my family, and the love of my life. This tournament, as important as it was, is just icing on the cake for me. I really am a blessed man."

"You mean it doesn't have anything to do with your attire? That's quite a statement you're making out there. I can honestly say, I don't think I've seen anything like those pants before."

I look down at the pants I'm wearing. They have this horrible combination of pink, turquoise, and bright yellow diamonds interlocking on them. CC gave them to me this morning as a good luck gift. She honestly didn't think I would wear them. I figure I'll make sure she shows me her appreciation tonight.

"These? You like these, Jenn?" I joke, motioning CC over to me. She's all smiles as she runs to my side. I pull her in close.

"They're definitely making a bold statement," she says, trying to be nice.

"These were a gift from someone I love. I couldn't not wear them in the most important tournament of my career."

"I see. Well, before I let you go to your victory party, can you tell your fans out there what's next for golf's most notorious bad boy?"

I look down at CC, and I can't resist kissing her. When I look back up at Jenn, it feels as if my heart might burst it's so full.

"That's easy, Jenn. I'm getting married," I tell her, and after kissing CC again, we walk back towards my family.

EPILOGUE

Ida Sue

"You okay in here?" I ask CC, knowing she's not. The poor thing looks like she's about to faint. She looks beautiful. It is a simple, strapless, white silk dress that hugs her, yet somehow makes her look innocent at the same time.

"I'm a nervous wreck, Ida Sue," she whispers and her eyes are glowing with tears.

"Now, now, none of that. You're beautiful and Gray is one lucky son of a gun," I tell her, but that seems like something I shouldn't have said, because the tears slip from her eyes. I reach over and grab a napkin and dry them up.

"C! Stop that crying. This is a happy day! My best friend is getting married to a three-peater and is going to live the dream. Today, we celebrate!" CC's best friend Mir says from beside us. Mir is a pretty girl, despite that name. It doesn't even stand for mermaid, which is kind of sad, and if my old body was still able, I'd have another girl just to name her that. She has this pretty pale skin, and blue eyes that remind me of my girl Petal's. She's much too skinny, though. A good, stiff wind would blow her over.

"What's a three-peater?" I ask out of curiosity.

"Don't ask, please?" begs CC. I look to Mir, who grins from ear to ear.

"What? I think Gray's Momma would like to know how special her son is," Mir says with a saucy grin. I think I like this one; she has a little fire. She definitely needs to fatten up, though. One of my boys would clearly break her in half. Maybe Green. He needs a good woman. Lord knows the sour one he got a hold of has done nothing but poison him. I'm going to have to keep my eye on this one.

"I think I would," I tell them just as someone knocks on the door.

"I'm supposed to escort my best girl down the aisle," Jansen says, coming in. Damn, that man cleans up good. He may have some miles on him, but he's the best damn ride I've ever had. In fact, I may have to ride him now.

I lean in and kiss CC's cheek, handing her the note I fixed for her earlier.

"You look beautiful. I've never been more proud of my son. He did great."

"Ida Sue... I don't know how to... you've done so much for me," she whispers.

"That's what family does, sweet cheeks. And you're family. You're my daughter."

"Ida..."

"My beautiful, amazing daughter. If your name was Chrysanthemum, you'd be perfect." She laughs, just like I intended for her to.

"I'm not changing my name," she insists. "Well, I guess after today, I will be a Lucas." She blushes.

"Dang straight! The sooner, the better. So let's get this show on the road," Jansen says. "Besides, Ida Sue made chicken salad for the reception. I want my hands on that."

"That's how you got such a fine catch, Ida Sue?" asks Mir. "I always heard the way to a man's heart was his stomach."

"Honey, that's just horseradish. The way to lock in your man is definitely wrangling him by the milk snake."

"Milk snake?" Mir asks, already laughing along with CC.

"Good Lord, woman," Jansen says, and I wink at my new daughter. "Let's go before you say something else I'll have to spank you for."

"Okay, sweetheart. See you outside, girls," I tell them just as there's another knock on the door. Jackson comes in looking hot as the Arizona heat in the dead of summer. "Jackson dear, you clean up real nice. If I was a little younger, Jansen might have reason to be worried."

"Ms. Ida," Jackson says with that sexy little grin of his. "I say we give him reason to worry now."

"On that note, we're out of here," Jansen grumbles just as I reach up to kiss Jackson's cheek.

"I wouldn't mind taking a ride on the J train," Mir says.

Definitely going to have to keep an eye on that girl.

I take Jansen's hand and we walk out of the room together. When we get to the front door of my ranch house, Jansen looks at me with a grin. "I know today is all about the bride, but I have to tell you Lovey, there's never been a more beautiful woman than you are right now."

I move into him, letting him hold me close. "Much more of that sweet talking and I'm going to have to take a ride on the J train before the I do's."

"The shindig is set up at the end of the yard. We do pass the little one's playhouse on the way."

"I do love a man who thinks on his feet."

"And here I thought you liked it best when I was off my feet," he says, sneaking me out and towards the small playhouse.

A new daughter, a happy son, and a ride on the Jansen train.

Life is damn good.

EPILOGUE

CC

I watch as Mir takes off to walk down the aisle. She's marching in the middle of all of Gray's brothers—a fact that made her very happy. That leaves me and Jackson alone in the small bedroom.

"You about ready to get this show on the road, Claude?" Jackson asks and I turn to look at him.

"Can you give me just a minute? I need to get my nerves together," I tell him, my heart beating hard in my chest.

"Banger would be so proud of you, y'know," he says, nodding.

"I know," I tell him, and I finally do.

"Okay, I'll be right outside the door."

I watch as he walks out and then I turn to the letter that Ida Sue handed me. My hands shake as I open it up, almost afraid to read it. I'm so happy. I have everything I could have dreamed of and I'm about to marry the man I love more than life itself. With all that good, will this be the bad that I've always had in the past?

Dear CC,

I wanted to take a quiet moment to welcome you into the family. Us girls get overemotional and the last thing you need on your wedding day is more tears. I know your new family is crazy. Some are a little mixed-up, but through it all, we stick together and weather any storm, because that's what family does. They stand up to the world and say fuck you. It doesn't matter what it throws at us; what matters is that we have each other's backs —always.

So as you walk down that aisle today, know that you, my darling daughter, are not only gaining a very handsome husband. You are gaining a family and you will never be alone again. Although I suppose I should warn you, that part isn't quite as great at times as it might sound.

Finally, I know that you gave your garage to Jackson, even after you and Gray insisted I take the money back for it. So, I did the only thing a mother could do when faced with two stubborn children: I bought you a new garage closer to home. Because this is your home now, darling girl. I know this garage won't be the same as your father's, but that one will live on through Jackson, who as much as I can gather, loved the man too. This garage will be all yours, and full of your father's memories because that's where we carry the ones we love: in our hearts. They never leave us because pieces of them are sewn into who we are. We take them with us. We teach our children about them. We celebrate them. Love never dies, my girl—it just grows.

Now don't you dare try to pay me back. If you do, I'll have to skin your hide. I wouldn't mind if you had me a grandkid or two, though. Children keep you young, so I figure if I have about a hundred of those little boogers running around, I'll be good.

Love,

Mom

I fold the note up with shaking hands, leaving it on the dresser. I stand up and use Jansen's handkerchief to dry my eyes. I pick up my flowers, securing the handkerchief inside. My heart was full before, but now I'm just completely overflowing with love and happiness. I stand at the door knowing that whatever comes, I'm going to be fine. I do a mental list in my head. My hand goes to the small locket at my neck which belonged to Banger's mom. Something old, check. I touch the pearl clip in my hair that was a gift from Gray's sisters. Something new, check. Next, I move my foot around to make sure the penny inside hasn't fallen out that Maggie's little boy Terry let me borrow. Something borrowed and a penny for good luck. My hand automatically goes to my thigh where the blue lace garter is. Something blue. I'm being silly, but I just want to make sure everything is there.

As I walk out and take Jackson's hand, we head down towards the wedding. I see Ida Sue and Jansen come out of the playhouse. Ida Sue is trying to fix her hair and her obviously rumpled dress, and Jansen is grinning from ear to ear. We hear the oh-my-gods from the crowd, the loudest coming from all of Gray's brothers. Finally, I see Gray. My husband-to-be. The man I love with my entire being. The man who made me believe I was valuable, who makes me feel valuable. Who loves me. Never have I been more secure... or happier.

I'm reminded of Ida Sue's words, and she's right. Bring it on world. I'm not alone.

Crazy mother-in-law with a heart of gold, a loud, loving family to drive me nuts, and the sexiest man alive to love me the rest of my days.

Life is damn good.

EPILOGUE

Gray

"Have I told you how beautiful you are today, Cooper?" I ask my wife as we're dancing. The wedding was perfect... Hell, life is perfect right now.

"You're going to have to quit calling me that now, Crayon Man. I'm a Lucas now."

"Fuck, yeah," I whisper into her neck, kissing her there and taking her scent into my lungs. "You look beautiful, Claudia Lucas."

"Right back at you, Grayson Lucas," she whispers, snuggling against me.

"I can't believe our mother had sex in the playhouse my son uses. We're tearing that down," Maggie grumbles from beside us.

"I think it's hot. We should try it," her date says, and I've heard about all of that conversation I care to hear. I steer my wife away from them. Too bad I apparently pick my brother and his best friend to dance next to.

"I can't believe you caught the bouquet, Kayla. Why did you even try?"

"Maybe I want to get married, White."

"Weddings are for idiots. Why tie yourself to one person when there's a whole world out there?"

"My brother is stupid," I tell CC when I pull her away from the idiot and whatever garbage he keeps mouthing off with. "He's in for a very rude awakening someday," I tell her.

"I hope she gives him hell," CC agrees with a laugh.

"Me too, but enough about them. How about we blow this popsicle stand and go get the honeymoon started?"

"I'm not sure I can wait that long," she says with a grin.

"Is that a fact?"

"Mmm-hmm... Though, I did hear there was a playhouse around here somewhere," she says.

"Claudia Lucas, I do believe my crazy family is rubbing off on you."

"God, I hope so," she says with a laugh, and I take her hand and lead her away from the crowd. She pulls me toward the small house and I crouch down and go through the door after her.

Crazy family, and the woman of my dreams wearing my ring.

Life is so fucking good, there are no words.

OTHER WORKS BY JORDAN MARIE

Doing Bad Things

Going Down Hard
In Too Deep
Taking It Slow

Lucas Brothers Series
Perfect Stroke
Raging Heart On
Happy Trail
Cocked & Loaded

Savage Brothers MC
Breaking Dragon
Saving Dancer
Loving Nicole
Claiming Crusher
Trusting Bull
Needing Carrie

Savage Brothers MC—Tennessee Chapter

Devil
Diesel
Rory

Devil's Blaze MC
Captured
Craved
Burned
Released
Shafted
Beast
Beauty

Filthy Florida Alphas

Unlawful Seizure
Unjustified Demands
Unwritten Rules

AUTHOR LINKS:

Newsletter Subscription
Facebook
Twitter
Webpage
Bookbub
Instagram
Text Alerts US Only
Text JORDAN to 797979
Standard Messaging Rates May Apply

35079532R00166

Made in the USA
San Bernardino, CA
07 May 2019